THE ONE-MAN IRIS DAVIS FAN CLUB

DAN L. WALKER

Library of Congress Control Number: 2023912650
ISBN: 979-8-218-95882-4

Editor: Joeth Zucco
Copy editing: Joeth Zucco, Melissa Alger
Cover design: Meghan Mullally
Book layout: Nanette Stevenson

Front cover photos: shutterstock.com

Printed in the United States of America

PEN & PRIMER
PO BOX 112, SEWARD, AK 99664
DLWALKER@GCI.NET

To my sisters, AMY and PEGGY,

who taught me early on that women are

without a doubt the equal of men.

ACKNOWLEDGEMENTS

When the publisher of the previous novels in this series decided to stop publishing young adult and historical novels, I was faced with finding a home for this third and final Sam Barger story. Thankfully, I have the great support of a team of people to help me independently publish a quality book. Kaylene Johnson has been a great mentor for navigating the publishing jungle, and Nanette Stevenson took my dream and built a nice book after editor Joeth Zucco cleaned up the mess of my manuscript. Meghan Mullally designed a snappy cover. Melissa Alger, and my wife, Madelyn, helped me see the things I couldn't. Finally, the encouragement and anticipation of my reader friends, who wanted to read more of my work, have kept me moving forward toward publication.

ONE

If you paid any attention at all in biology class, you know how I got Iris pregnant, so all that's left to tell you is where, when, and what came after because that's the real story. The year was 1969, and we had Tricky Dick in the White House, peace talks in Paris, and war in Vietnam. After 1967's summer of love and 1968's summer of protest, it seemed like anything could happen this summer, and we wouldn't be surprised.

One Saturday in May, we seniors were eager for graduation and anticipating summer when several carloads of us drove out to the top of O'Malley Road to drink beer, smoke pot, and watch the sunset, which wouldn't happen until midnight or later. It started with a big bonfire and some dancing, but before long, anybody who hadn't coupled up in one of the cars was sitting around what was left of the bonfire and passing around a joint. I saw Iris at the campfire, so I sat down beside her and listened to the banter while Creedence Clearwater Revival's "Born on the Bayou" twanged out through someone's car stereo. Iris said hi and gave me a hug, then returned to her argument with some hippie wannabe about ethical issues in the student draft deferment.

I had worked the previous night cleaning the grease traps at Polar Pizza, so Iris's political sparring made my head hurt. I left the fire and climbed in the back of Bob Crawford's Vista Cruiser station wagon to take a nap. I'd only had a couple of Black Labels, but when you've been up for almost twenty-four hours scrubbing ovens and scraping grease out of stove vents, even two beers will put you right to sleep.

I hadn't been asleep long when a side door opened and Iris climbed in, slapping my foot out of the way. "Nice boots, Barger."

"Hey, Freckles," I lifted my foot to show my brown cowboy boots. "Yeah, got these from Joe. After he broke them in, he decided they were too big. Good fit for me."

"Giddyap, cowboy!" she said. "I wish I had a brother to steal boots from." We shared a laugh. It was as if the calendar flipped back to last year when we were together. Her embroidered jean jacket and bell-bottom jeans made Iris look like the kind of girl that would write dreamy poetry and play folk guitar, but she was more about politics than poetry and more apt to pick up a protest poster than a guitar. She slipped out of her jacket and lay down beside me. Having her this close brought the old feelings rushing back, feelings I thought I'd left behind. I rolled on my side and looked at her eyes twinkling up at me. She smelled of incense and the pot she had been smoking.

"How you been, Barger? It's not like you to go take a nap in the middle of a party."

"I worked all last night doing a deep clean at the pizza parlor, then a full shift today."

She pushed her hair behind her ear and studied my face. "What about summer? You staying at the Polar Pizza?"

"Nope. Going fishing. Going to be setnetting on Cook Inlet. Finally."

She leaned toward me and slapped my shoulder. "Good for you!"

"You remember? It's what I always wanted. Since we left the bluff a long time ago. I just want to be a fisherman. You know, like Dad."

She smiled. "Sam Barger. Always chasing his big ideas, betting on tomorrow."

Somehow that statement moved me, and I leaned over and kissed her. It was a clumsy kiss that bumped her lips against my teeth, and she rolled away and put her hand to her mouth. "Goddam, Sam!"

"I'm sorry," I said, half laughing and putting my hands up defensively ready for her to smack me.

"It's OK. Come here, silly." And she kissed me then, soft and long. I kissed back, carefully this time. Pretty quickly we were swapping spit and letting our hands roam around each other's bodies. She wasn't wearing a bra and soon my hand was under her shirt feeling a nipple against my palm.

It had been over a year since we even hung out together, and even longer since we made out. We had a thing going for a while last summer, but that ended when I got in a fistfight, and Iris called me an immature, violent asshole, or words to that effect. We didn't break up, she dumped me like a hot rock. I thought it was just a spat, but she was done with me and made it clear we could only be friends. I didn't feel like being just friends, so we didn't see much of each other. Then here we were almost a year later, all hands, tongues, and eagerness. And, yup, we went all the way.

When it was over we were lying on our backs in the station wagon with windows steamed up, and me thinking, "What the hell was that?" I could hear Iris breathing, but she didn't say anything, just pulled her shirt down so it covered her crotch, then squeezed my hand. This was foreign territory, and I suddenly went from hot-to-trot to nervous-and-shy. I probably said something truly romantic like, "Wow!"

Iris said, "Got some tissue or something?"

I fumbled around for a tissue but had to just give her my handkerchief. "It's clean." I looked away self-consciously while she cleaned herself and pulled on her jeans. The Creedence tape started over again, and I recognized the song, "Proud Mary," wailing in the dusky twilight. I realized too late that the night hadn't gotten dark enough to give us much privacy, and anyone walking by the station wagon would have gotten quite a show.

Iris reached up to the little skylight in the roof of the station wagon and wrote SAM in the condensation on the glass. I smiled, but she took a deep breath and said, "Oh shit."

"Oh no." I sat up. "What's wrong?"

Iris turned, pushed me back down, then rolled over on top of me. "This!" She said, then kissed me. "This is all wrong." She sat with her hands on my chest. "You're wrong, Sam Barger, all wrong. When I woke up this morning, you were nowhere on my radar, and now—" She laid her head on my chest.

"You are always on my radar," I said, stroking her hair and wondering how long I could hold on to the perfection of that moment.

"Wow, great comeback, Barger. You've been taking classes?" Her hand stroked my cheek, then she leaned on one elbow and looked into my eyes the way she used to when she wanted to make a point. "Are you saying that ever since last summer you have been thinking about me? Even though I dumped you, even though I didn't call when you went through all that with your brother? Wow, Sam, you are something. You are one intense guy."

"I'm intense? Look in the dictionary under 'intense.' They used your picture."

That got her. She sat up, and I felt her muscles tighten as if any moment she'd pop the latch on the car door and make a run for it. "Maybe a little. This was intense. That's for sure." But she didn't run. She just brushed her hair with her fingers, twining the strands that fell beside her cheek. "These your wheels now?" She asked, looking around at the station wagon.

"No, I still got the pickup like before. But David Nelson is in it with some girl, so I sacked out here for a while. You want a ride home?"

"Yeah, I think so, but I shouldn't. I should run like a scared rabbit." She squeezed my leg when she said it, and we didn't talk for several minutes, and I might have dozed off some. Then she kissed my neck, "You better get some rubbers, Barger, if you want to get lucky again." I'm glad she couldn't see me blush, but she might have felt me shudder.

You probably wonder why I didn't stop and think about protection or why she didn't. I wonder that too. We shoulda, coulda, woulda, but we didn't. In fact, I wonder what created the magic that happened that spring night that made all my fantasies come true. It's not like I was too drunk or she was too stoned to hit the brakes. We were like a Zippo lighter meeting yesterday's newspaper, and we started a wildfire that would scorch a lot of people before it was done. And that's the real story I'm telling.

TWO

Two weeks later, I drove down the Seward Highway in my old pickup truck, crossed the Ninilchik River bridge, and turned on to the gravel road that followed the river toward the beach. The old Russian village was a huddle of ancient log cabins and wooden boats with a small Russian church standing watch above it on the bluff. The village sat on a horseshoe peninsula formed by the bend of the river, and I followed that bend and then paralleled the beach past the cannery to the boat basin at the river mouth.

Art Mitkof was leaning against his 4x4 Scout waiting for me. He greeted me with a man's handshake and a nod. "You got your gear?" he asked, pointing a chin at the string of boats tied up gunnel to gunnel below where we stood on the breakwater. "Peterson's here and ready to go." Art was a small, wiry man with black hair and a pencil-thin mustache. He was part of an old family of Alaska Native and Russian stock. He was Dad's friend and felt his duty to a dead friend's kid. He had lined me up with this fishing job, opening the door for me to follow my dreams.

"All set," I said, gesturing at Dad's worn and patched oilskins I'd retrieved at our cabin on the bluff. They lay stiff and mildewed on the seat beside me. I grabbed them and my duffle bag, then followed Mitkof down the ramp to the boats. The wooden skiffs and drift boats moored in the narrow basin were pointing their bows downstream as flood tide pushed the salt water up into the mouth of the shallow river. In a couple of hours when the tide began to ebb, the boats would turn with it and eventually sit on dry ground when the water drained from the boat basin. By then any boats planning to leave the river had to wait for the next tide.

"I'm surprised your mother let you go fishing," Mitkof said. "I know she didn't think much of your old man going out on the water."

"She wasn't pleased," I said. "Not pleased at all. Christ! She was happier about Joe going to Vietnam than me going fishing."

Mitkof's words took me back to the ass-chewing she gave me when I told her my plan. "You're apt to make next to no money fishing," Mom said. "And once you're there, you're stuck sitting on the beach waiting for fish, waiting on an opening, waiting for the tide. Lots of waiting, Sam. Not something you're good at."

"Mom, I gotta do this. You know this has been my dream since we left the bluff. It wasn't right for you. It wasn't for Joe. This was me and Dad."

"You were peas in a pod with the fishing," she said. Even after all these years, her eyes got distant and she smiled when I mentioned Dad. "But I'll be damned if a son of mine is going to become one of those worthless bums who goes broke fishing and then lives off poached moose and unemployment all winter. Not a chance, mister."

"He even called me Humpy, Mom, his little salmon."

"I know, but your dad is gone, and there's not much money in fishing anymore—well, you never could count on it. In a few more years it'll be nothing but a hobby for rich folk and dreamers. Face it, you can't afford to go broke setnetting for salmon." Mom was folding laundry and handed me a wad of towels. "Here, make yourself useful," she said. "You want to go back. I know. But I just think you're going to be disappointed—and broke. At your age, Sam, you should be looking forward not back."

I shook out a towel and started folding. "I'm not going back to being a little kid who couldn't go out on the boats, Mom. I want to be like

Dad, maybe even buy back our old fish sites someday." I was selling hard like a door-to-door salesman, but Mom was slamming the door in my face every time.

"Your dad had to work all winter to make ends meet, you know, to support his fishing habit. And fishing was better five years ago than it is now." She grabbed a dish towel from my stack and refolded it, shaking her head as she did.

"Mom, I know you think I'm nuts, but I'm doing it. If it's a bust, that's on me, right? And you'll be able to say, 'I told you so.' But I'm going to prove you wrong." She knew I was going whether she liked it or not.

"Fine, but come fall I want you in school. Even if it's just a community college. You've got a good mind, son, and I want you to do something with it. It's a chance I never had. You need to take it as far as you can." Now she was doing the selling.

"I know. I know."

"By the way," she added, "I've got someone I want you to meet. Maybe we can have dinner tomorrow."

"Oh. Who's that? Oh, tomorrow? I'm leaving in the morning, Mom, first thing." I hugged her. "When I get back. OK?"

For some reason, that conversation nagged at me as I drove down the Seward Highway toward my summer on the beach, my summer with the salmon, the summer I would be Humpy again.

"She'll forgive you," Mitkof said. "Just take care of yourself and write to her. She'll get over it. Just make staying alive more important than catching fish, and you'll be OK." I just nodded. Mitkof waved at a man in tattered rain pants standing by an open dory. "There's your ride."

Rolf Peterson was as round as Mitkof was skinny. He wore a dirty white fisherman's hat, a week's worth of beard, and a scowl that looked permanent. Like the owner, the boat was rough, with peeling paint and dried fish gurry holding it together. He grabbed my duffle, tossed it in the bow, and gestured up the steep gravel bank to a Chevy truck loaded with boxes and gear. "Park your rig and get that shit in the boat. I don't want to lose the tide."

Half an hour later, we were bucking the choppy water of Cook Inlet, following the shoreline past Ninilchik Cape. I huddled in the bow with my back against the wind and spray while Peterson ran the outboard. I could see both shores of the inlet, snowy mountain peaks a hundred miles away to the northwest and the brown bluff on the near shore dotted with cabins and fish sites. I felt the separation of leaving my truck and the familiar boat basin to enter life on the water and the beach where the smell of salt and sea life churned up memories in the frothing boat wake.

Peterson hadn't said a word since his initial order to unload the truck, and I had the feeling it wasn't going to be a chatty summer. Suddenly he turned the skiff ninety degrees and we bounced toward the beach where the surf was running well up the sloping sand. Beyond the sand, I could see a tar paper shack sitting in the alders at the base of the bluff that ran for miles along the shore in both directions.

Peterson landed the skiff on the gravel beach in front of the shack. The skiff lifted with the swell and then settled on its flat bottom. I leaped out and tied it off to a driftwood pole set in the sand. Then Peterson spoke for the second time, "Haul the groceries to the cabin. Everything else gets stowed underneath." He stalked off to a slab-sided outhouse perched between the alders and the sandstone bluff.

My new home for the summer wasn't much to look at even by setnetter standards. The tiny shack was sided in weather-beaten tar paper, and several large pieces were missing so the gray boards showed through. The roof was covered in a ragged tarp. Back in the alders was the crooked outhouse where Peterson was tending his business, and in front of the cabin was a rusty 4x4 truck of WWII vintage and a net rack made of driftwood logs. The look of the place would make most people want to climb up that bluff to the highway and never look back, but for me, it looked like Shangri-La. I was on the beach with the skiff and the sand with black chunks of coal scattered about in the gravel. Behind the beach was the bluff rising like a crude castle, a black coal seam running through it. Cook Inlet stretched away to the distant snowcapped volcanoes of the Alaska Range, and eagles and gulls rode the breeze that blew up the beach from the south, while a raven walked the line of trash left by the last tide.

Somewhere in one of those mountain valleys across Cook Inlet, Iris was helping her father set up a guide's camp on some river and waiting for the first bunch of dude fly fishermen to arrive for their dream week in the wilderness. Iris was her dad's camp hand and cook, substituting for the boy he never had. I let my eyes linger on the mountain horizon, feeling the empty distance between us.

That last week of school, Iris and I spent every free minute together, and only the fishing season could pull me away. Right then, I regretted that choice, but Iris had plans too, and she left the day before I did. Iris wasn't the gushy type that would promise to write every day or expect me to either. She just said, "Stay in touch, Barger. I'm getting used to you being around." I could still smell her on my skin and my clothes, and I didn't want it to fade, but I knew it would, and then I would begin to gather the smells of fish camp. The strongest memory I had from my childhood was the rich odor of salt water, salmon, seaweed, and drift-wood smoke. This was the smell of my father.

I had planned on being a salmon fisherman since my first summer going to the beach and watching Dad work the nets from his wooden dory. I had committed then—when I was too young to go in the boat with Joe and Dad—that I was going to be a fisherman.

I knew how it worked. First I'd fish as a hired hand to get my foot in the door and learn the ropes, and someday I could get my own sites. Come fall I'd have to take some college classes to keep Mom off my back, but that was no big deal. My original plan was to spend the winter at our homestead cabin, but I had to give Mom something.

It took thinking about Dad for reality to hit me. "Cripes! Mom has a boyfriend," I tried not to let any images of that invade my mind. Mom had dated guys the last few years, but she had always kept them away from me, and if I met some guy she was going out with, it was a chance meeting when I was coming from or going to the house. She certainly had never wanted me to meet someone. That's what she meant when she said she wanted me to meet someone. This guy must be special. "Smooth move, Ex-Lax," I said. "You could have scored some points eating dinner with her and her new guy." Oh well.

I shortened my gaze to the water before me and remembered how it looked when the nets were fishing and the salmon were hitting. Soon Peterson and I would be stretching gillnets out from the beach with their cork lines bouncing in the surf, and then more nets beyond them to fish the deep water. The salty aroma filled my nose, and I felt it begin to permeate my clothes and hair. Humpy Barger would become the man his father wanted him to be, a setnet fisherman.

Peterson finally came out of the outhouse, and I watched while he inspected the gear I stowed under the cabin. "Be back later. Keep an eye on the boat." He started the 4x4 and drove away down the beach.

THREE

Peterson's beach cabin was built of rough lumber with a door and three windows, one each north and south, and one that looked out at the water. The outside was battered and gray, but the inside was worse. In the back were two bunks heaped with dirty sleeping bags and old pillows. Raingear, rank with mildew and year-old fish slime, hung on nails by the door, and a dirty table with two folding chairs and a bench nailed to the wall sat under the front window with a view of the beach and the inlet. A bucket parked on the end of the bench, apparently to catch drips from the leaky roof, had caught four shrews, their bodies floating in the gray water. A woodstove made of half of a fifty-five-gallon drum stood rusting across from the door, and a shallow counter held a two-burner camp stove and a clutter of dishes crusted with eggs, beans, and dead flies from last fishing season. The cabin was so dirty that I left the groceries on the steps and started to clean the place instead.

I found a big pot and shook out the dead flies, then filled it with water from a five-gallon jug under the counter and started heating it on the camp stove. While the water heated, I found a broom and swept a mixture of sand, dirt, and dead flies off the warped and stained plywood floor and collected food wrappers and cans into a bucket, then hauled them to the burn barrel nearly hidden in a tangle of pushki and fireweed by the outhouse. When all the dishes, the countertop, and the table were scrubbed and drying, I brought in the groceries and stocked the shelves above the counter. Finally, I mixed a glass of Tang and built a peanut butter and jelly sandwich. I lunched on the cabin steps watching the falling tide.

The waters had retreated down the beach nearly a hundred yards since we had landed, so the clam beds and sandbars were lying gray in the sun. I was reminded of a morning with Dad, watching him bring the skiff to the beach for the last time with the boat on the swell, and him all man and muscle and pride. Less than an hour later he was lying in the back seat of the station wagon on the way to a doctor who couldn't heal his failing heart. I was back now to take his place on the beach and on the water. If it meant scrubbing a nasty old beach cabin or anything else Peterson wanted me to do, so be it.

Peterson didn't show himself at the beach site until the next morning, and by then, I was restless and at a loss for anything to do other than clean, eat, and read from the stash of paperback Westerns I found in a box under one of the bunks. When Peterson climbed out of his 4x4 and stretched his back, my restlessness came to an end. "All right, Barger, I brought you a present there in the back of the truck." He gestured with his thumb and walked off to the outhouse like last time.

The present was four sections of stovepipe and two rolls of tar paper roofing, a bag of one-inch roofing nails, and two cans of black tar-like roof cement. I looked from the gift to the roof of the cabin and put the roll of roofing on my shoulder. I had never put down roofing before, but I had seen it done when I was too little to help. I figured it was just a matter of keeping it straight, spreading tar on the seams, and using lots of nails.

By the time he came out of the outhouse and lit a cigarette, I had the tar paper unloaded and the ladder I found behind the cabin leaning against the north wall. "That's a good start," he said. "There's a half-assed toolkit with a hammer and such under the cabin in a wooden box. You need to strip off the old paper first. Pull any nails you can and drive the others flush. Then roll this new shit out and nail it."

I looked at Peterson with his meaty hands and his big belly, and I knew there was no way he was going to get that round body of his up a rickety wooden ladder. He must have weighed twice what I did. "Yup, Sam, I think you're on your own," I muttered. Peterson quickly confirmed my inference.

"I'll be down here if you need anything, and don't fall off. I don't need that on my day."

I laughed even though it wasn't funny. "I'll try," I said. "I don't mind falling. It's the landing I hate."

Peterson gave me a dirty look and shook his head. "I got nets to mend. You best get to it." Obviously, humor wasn't on the menu.

I put my head down and headed for the cabin and that half-assed toolkit. I found it where he said it would be, but it was covered in dirt and the mummified remains of a dead gull. Armed with a hammer and a pry bar, I scrambled up the ladder and attacked what was left of the shredded tar paper just as clouds passed across the sun, and the warmth of the day blew away on a southwest wind.

I had the old paper off when dribbles of rain began to dot the roof, and I rolled out the new roofing with rain running down my back. By then I was hungry enough to eat about anything and too tired to care what it was. Peterson had spent the afternoon stretching and mending nets, then stomped into the cabin. I hoped he was making something for us to eat, but when I climbed down the ladder for the last time and stepped back to admire the new roof, I could hear him snoring.

That's how the first week of fishing with Peterson went. I worked on the cabin, dug a new outhouse hole, and scraped and painted the twenty-foot wooden skiff that I had ridden in on that first day. Peterson drove the 4x4 when we used it to flip the skiff over. Other than that, he came and went, seldom talked, and offered no pats on the back, small talk, or hints about what was to come the next hour or the next day.

I was getting a lot of reading done, and I had groceries and a roof over my head, but I wasn't making any money, and I wouldn't until the fishing started, and this setup wasn't the way I imagined it. Every time I tried to talk fishing, Peterson just waved me off and mumbled, "We'll cross that bridge when we come to. If the bastards let us fish at all."

The "bastards" were the fish and game biologists who kept track of the salmon migration and set the fishing days for each week. The fishermen were licensed to fish and had their designated sites on the beach where they could set their gillnets, but that couldn't happen until the fish, fur, and feathers fellows were confident that enough fish were running up the inlet. I could remember Dad bitching about the fish cops keeping them off the water, but he admitted it was just grousing. "Shit, if they let us, the fishermen'd catch every damn one o' them sockeyes 'til there weren't enough left for a brown bear's breakfast. We're short-sighted, selfish folks—most of us anyway."

And yes, I was one of those shortsighted, selfish folks myself. I wanted them to let us fish so I could have enough money to pay tuition and maybe move out of the house. I wanted an apartment where I could spend time alone with Iris while she finished up her senior year. She talks about getting outta Dodge in a big way, going off to a four-year college in Oregon. I'd be happy for her but pretty bummed to give her up, but hell, that's a year away, I thought, who knows.

If I was broke, fall meant living at home, flipping burgers or washing dishes, and maybe attending community college while I figured out what I was going to do. This last thing was no piece of cake. I thought when I turned eighteen I'd be a rugged, independent guy making his own choices and striking out into the world without answering to anyone. Ha! Likely story. Mom has been riding me as hard as ever. I had to register for the draft—getting called up next year is a real possibility—and everything I wanted to do cost money. This adult thing is not as easy as it looks, I'm finding out. And now that I had the summer on the beach I'd always wanted, I was even second-guessing that.

FOUR

For nearly a month I sat around eating fried Spam sandwiches and reading Louis L'Amour. Every morning I spent a couple of hours on made-up chores like filling extra sandbags for anchoring nets and swabbing wooden keg buoys with fresh coats of paint, then the rest of the day I was just killing time. All that time alone, all that time with nothing to do but listen to the radio playing the Beatles' latest hit too damn many times made me realize that I didn't want to "Let It Be" like the Beatles said. And all that time to second-guess my summer decision gave me plenty of time to miss Iris.

My view from the beach looked northwest across the inlet where Iliamna and Redoubt poked their snow-covered shoulders out of the Alaska Range. Somewhere out there Iris was running the camp for her fishing guide dad, and I imagined all the rich fly fishermen that were calling her honey and trying to grab her ass during breakfast. Some days those thoughts drove me crazy.

The only calendar in the cabin was a year old, and after asking Peterson twice to bring a new calendar, I gave up and spent a day figuring out what this year's days were and changed the numbers on the calendar for June, July, and August. When I was done, I realized I could have copied the dates out of the tide book instead of doing all that math. Dumbass. Then I marked off the boxes on the calendar until mid-August when I'd see Iris again. I was consoled only by knowing that if I stayed in Anchorage, I wouldn't have seen any more of her than I was now.

When I wasn't missing Iris, I had plenty of time to crawl into the dark corners of my memory. It's there that I found images I had tried to avoid, images from last year. Images of me in the rain-soaked woods and moose antlers moving in the flat light of a fall evening. I could relive lifting the rifle and sighting along the barrel, taking the shot. Pale Polaroid photos flipped before my eyes as the rifle fired and slammed my shoulder, the muzzle blasting, then Joe framed in the antlers. Did I see him before I shot? The Polaroids shuffled, blood-stained and gray, then flashing, so they became a flipbook of action when I shot my older brother. Mom was right. I don't handle downtime well.

Finally, three weeks into this self-isolation, I climbed out of my sleeping bag one morning and said, "That's it, Barger. Enough is enough." I put the coffeepot on the camp stove and pulled my duffel out from under my bunk. While the coffee perked, I packed my change of clothes, brushed my teeth, and packed my meager toilet kit. I rolled Dad's raingear—feeling like a quitter as I did it—and packed myself a lunch for the road. By then the coffee was ready, so I sat and drank a cup while I composed a sheepish note to Peterson. The wind was kicking up whitecaps on the inlet and a gray lid of clouds promised rain. I turned on the radio to confirm my suspicions. It might be cold and wet hitchhiking today.

The top-forty station in Anchorage played "Let It Be" one more time before starting on the news. The first item stopped my note-writing and nearly spilled my coffee. Fishing would be open for setnetters two days a week. I turned on the VHF to see if fisherman chatter would confirm what I had heard. It did, and not ten minutes later I heard the growl of Peterson's 4x4 coming down the beach. The Alaska Department of Fish and Game had officially opened the inlet for setnetting.

Peterson stomped into the cabin and grabbed the coffeepot. "Good, you're up." Then after seeing my gear packed up and waiting. "Where you goin'?"

"Nowhere. Just cleaning up." He drank his coffee and held a suspicious look my way, but I didn't care. We were going fishing, and I wasn't going home to eat crow, not yet anyway.

There were two kinds of fishers in this part of Cook Inlet: the drifters who roamed the inlet in boats and stretched their gillnets wherever they thought they could catch fish, and the setnetters like Peterson who anchored their nets along the shore and sat waiting for the fish to come to them. When the fishing period opened, we would tie off our net to the ropes tied off to stakes on the shore and stretch it out from the beach, then tie the offshore side to a buoy anchored to the bottom. Lead weights on the bottom of the net held it down and corks on the top floated it up, so it rode vertically in the water to snare salmon as they charged up the inlet toward the rivers where they were born. I rehearsed the process over and over in my mind as I whiled away that twenty-four hours until we would finally be fishing.

I couldn't concentrate enough to read, so I started a pot of beans and wrote a letter to Iris. Just like last summer, I wrote her at least once a week. Each a long letter that made fun of Peterson and told about me not fishing. I told Iris that working with Peterson was like living with a bear just out of hibernation. Lots of grunting, eating, and shitting coupled with a fear that at any moment he might turn on me. She sent a postcard back with a picture of a brown bear holding a salmon in its mouth. She wrote across the bottom of the photo, *What are you looking at? Go get your own.* Then on the back of the card:

Miss you, Big Guy. Save some salmon for the fly fishermen, and save your money for a Vista Cruiser. Your Friend, Iris.

Iris only wrote postcards. I guess she never had enough to say to write a whole letter, which made me laugh because if she was sitting beside me she would do all the talking.

I was excited to write this letter because we were finally going fishing, and I might even have time to add more to the letter before Peterson left the beach or the fish truck came by so I could send it on to the post office. I wrote that by the time she got it, my hands would be too sore to write.

Between scrawling sentences, I stared out the window and imagined the string of corks bobbing in the swell and the sharp V that formed in the line when salmon hit the net. The wind was blowing from the south and whitecaps were starting to form on the tips of waves. A couple of miles off the beach, drift boats were cruising south from Kenai to be ready to fish the southern inlet when the opening started in the morning. It was easy to envy the swashbuckling life of the drifters, chasing the salmon schools from one end of the inlet to the other in their nimble wooden boats, but they had their own miseries. Rough water, engine problems, fuel bills, and a lone net hanging off the back of the boat to make the payday made their life a gamble too.

Peterson showed up at 4 a.m. and rousted me from my bunk. "Let's go see if you know anything about fishing, Barger."

I jumped up and lit the burner under the coffeepot I'd prepared the night before. Peterson paced the short length of the cabin back and forth while he waited for the coffee, and I made a couple of fried egg sandwiches. We sucked down a mouth-burning cup of camp coffee and climbed into raingear. I ate my sandwich in four bites, and Peterson left his on the plate.

When the season started at 7 a.m., we were bobbing in the choppy waves with the boat tied off to a buoy for the outside set. A cold breeze crossed the water under a cloudy sky, and I huddled in the bow with the hood of my raingear pulled up against the chill. More waiting. More silence from Peterson. Then suddenly, Peterson stood up and started the engine.

Until now, every order from Peterson was in the moment, short on words, and shouted. Whether we were working with the noise of the outboard and buffeting wind, or we were standing side by side on the beach, he shouted. But this time, he stood with the water washing back and forth around his hip boots, puffed his chest out, and just talked.

"Now I know you learned this fishing business from your daddy, and now you're a teenager so you think you know everything, but I got my own way of doin' things, and that's how we're going to do them. Got it? Yessir would be a good answer."

"Yessir." I looked eagerly at the buoy hanging off the bow bobbing in and out of the water and the nets stacked in the belly of the skiff. Peterson must have talked for five minutes, explaining that my job was to pick up the buoy and secure the net to it and how to play the net over the gunnel so that it's not twisted. Step by step he explained the procedure like I'd never seen a gillnet before. "And don't get your ass dragged into the water with the web," he said. "I don't need that shit. Let's get this net in the water."

After we had set the nets, their corks stretched across the current like strings of pearls, and there was a short time there when I could relax on the steps of the cabin while Peterson took a nap and watch the tide climb up our outstretched net on the beach at low tide. The surge of the tide would cover the net and then lift the corks, each time raising the net higher and higher until the sea swallowed it and only the corks were visible. I waited without moving, watching for the first sign of a salmon catching its gills in the web. A salmon striking the bottom of the net might not show on the surface, but when fish hit the web near the surface, the line of corks would bob or bend to a V. Sometimes a whole group of fish would hit the net and drag the corks underwater. I watched and waited for that moment, and it came with a splash on the cork line, and a big Cook Inlet red salmon thrashed its tail and struggled against the gillnet.

I started to jump up and down and shout like I did when I was a kid, but I was a man now and this was routine, everyday stuff, nothing to get riled about. Eagles crossed overhead as waves rushed up the beach toward me, and fish hit the net with the sun breaking through the clouds and spotlighting the tips of the waves. Everyday stuff. All the sights and sounds of my childhood were here in this moment, and I missed my dad like I hadn't in a long time.

Just before slack tide, I made coffee and woke Peterson. At slack, the tide wasn't fighting us for the nets, which hung slack and would be easier to pick. We started with the beach sets, "The tide is slack here first," Peterson volunteered in one of his more talkative moments. The weather was mild and I wore a sweatshirt with the sleeves cut just above the elbow and Dad's worn and patched rain pants. A wood skiff is stable in calm water, but it is always rocking or bouncing with even the slightest wave and that takes getting used to. I worried that I might get seasick or be unsteady on my feet. I could feel the tension down my back as I flexed with the moving boat and tried to appear at ease and experienced instead of what I was, green and well out of my element. I was pleased that the wind was down so we weren't fighting the waves, and I had the chance to get my sea legs.

Peterson didn't seem to notice the weather or the waves, and he brought the bow of the boat up to the net without comment or direction. He seemed to expect that I knew everything now after this morning's lecture. I was supposed to do the right thing without being told. He didn't know how much I was winging it. I reached over the gunnel and grabbed the cork line and pulled it over the pointed bow of the boat. The web snagged and a few sections of the web hung up, then tore on the gunnel as the lead line fought to pull the net back into the water.

"Jesus Christ! Not like that! You'll fuck it all up!" Peterson let go of the tiller and made gathering motions with his hands. "Bring the net together before you haul it onto the boat. You're fucking my damn web!" Then it came to me what he wanted, and I could remember watching Joe years ago leaning over the gunnel and gathering the net hand over hand until he had the cork line, web, and lead line in his hands then he pulled it up and over the bow. I mimicked my memory.

Once I had the net aboard and the web corks and lead line crossed over the skiff, Peterson pulled the cork line toward him and started pulling the net so the boat moved sideways under it. We worked our way along cleaning sticks and seaweed from the web and hoping for fish.

When the first fish tumbled over the gunnel and thrashed around our ankles. Peterson grunted and jerked the web up with a snap so the fish popped out of the net and tumbled into the belly of the boat. Peterson smiled and spit tobacco juice into the inlet, never stopping the continuous motion of pulling the net up out of the water and across the gunnels. "Let's make some money, kid! Not so tough is it?"

By the time we reached the end of the net, I was sweating, spattered with fish slime, and the muscles in my arms and legs felt like collapsed balloons. We had a dozen red salmon flopping around our feet and three nets to go. I realized that this was going to be a long day. I had spent my summer at half speed while we waited to go fishing, and now I was facing hours of hard work without a break or a meal.

When the beach sets were picked, we went out to pick the outside nets. By the time we started the final net, the tide was running and we had to fight the drag of the sea trying to pull the nets and the boat and us down the inlet. With the tide came snags and logs washed out of the rivers on the shore. One small pole had tangled in the net, and Peterson swore and began to work the log out of the net, cutting web only when he had to. He looked up once and swore again. "Barger! Grab that oar and keep that fucker off our net."

Only then did I see the fifteen-foot log bounding through the chop toward us. I leaped to the eight-foot oar lashed to the inside of the boat, waded through the slippery mass of fish to the bow, and leaned out to the log with the oar but still couldn't reach it. "I can't reach it!"

"Hold on!" Peterson moved faster than I had ever seen him move to lift the small pole he was fighting over the side and pull the boat along the net. "I got it," I said, pushing the log with the tip of the oar. That made the log pivot across the tide and it slammed against the side of the boat and then slid away back toward the net. "Damn it! Don't push the log into the net."

It was my turn to swear. I lunged with the oar and pushed the cork line below the water, but just for an instant, and then the oar slipped and the corks bobbed back to the surface. "What the hell?" yelled Peterson, "The log!" I reached again and again until the corks dove, and the nose of the log crossed above them. "You lucky sonofabitch! Shit!"

More trash came into our net that day, but it was small trash: bull kelp, sticks, dead gulls, plastic bottles, and beer cans. Some crossed through the web and some hung in the net and tangled so that we picked more trash than fish out of the net.

When the fishing period ended, the nets had to be hauled, and because the fishing periods went by the calendar and the clock, we were often fighting the tide as we hauled the net into the skiff. That meant we weren't just trying to haul the heavy net into the skiff, there was a drag on the other end trying to pull it away or turn the boat or push us off our mark. I had only a half-assed idea of what we were doing most of the time, and Peterson just grunted and swore rather than explain anything. I braced my feet and wrapped my sore hands in the bundle of net and pulled just as the boat moved out from under me. I slammed my hip against the gunnel and then fell back into the slurry of fish, net, trash, and seawater in the bottom of the boat.

"Don't fight it! Dance with it," yelled Peterson. He laughed then, the only time the whole summer I heard him laugh. I didn't. I swore. I couldn't just spread my legs and pull. If I did, the boat might be moving in the other direction. I had to work with the rise and fall of the deck beneath me or brace against the side of the boat. It was like dancing with a boat and the sea while they moved to different music. Unfortunately, I never was much of a dancer. By the end of the fishing period, I could only think of bed. I longed for bed more than food, more than another postcard from Iris. But even after the nets were hauled, there were fish to sort and tangled nets to pick free of sticks. Only then could I crawl to my bunk and sleep.

After sleeping like the dead, after eating like it was my last meal ever, after pitching fish to the cannery truck after mending nets, then came the downtime again. I was alone with nothing to do. I wished I was alone anyway, but then the demons in my memory awoke to keep me company. With fishing it seemed we were always waiting. Waiting for the fishing period to open, waiting for the tide, waiting for the fish to hit, waiting for the fish truck. And it was those waiting times that I came to dread. When I had time to relive every damn moment of last fall. Especially when it rained. The rain brought back that night in the woods after I shot Joe, and I could wade through every wrecked minute of shooting him and running and finding him alive and fighting to keep him that way. The downtime was like taking a beating some days, and it wore me out.

After a day or three of downtime, Peterson would show up, and we worked our asses off for a few hours, regardless of the weather or the time of day—those didn't matter. If Peterson was late or hungover or still drunk at the end of the fishing period, we would have to haul the net with fish and trash still in it because the nets couldn't be in the water at the end of the period, and the fish cops in their Cessna Super Cub would fly over and see us, so we would heap the tangled mess in the belly of the skiff. Peterson acted as if he answered to no one, but in reality, he had several masters: the tide, the weather, the fish opening, and the fish cops.

Most of the time when we weren't fishing, which was most of the time, I was sitting on the beach alone with a box of books and an AM radio. I listened to the top-forty stations and sometimes the country station when I missed Joe and Dad. There was lots of talk about the Apollo astronauts flying through space to land on the moon, and I planned to listen to the big event when Neil Armstrong set foot on the moon's surface. But instead, I was rocking in three-foot waves picking sticks out of a net with only enough fish to pay for the week's gasoline. I resented that for some reason, more than I should really. But walking on the moon was big, and I missed it. The tides and the wads of trash that moved along the rips of the inlet didn't care what was happening in the world or outside it. But they ruined another day for me even if they didn't mean to.

Later, lying in my bunk listening to a rehash of the big event, "One small step for man—" I realized that it was the same moon that made the tides also made me miss listening to the moon landing because of the timing of the tides, and I wrote to Iris about the magical coincidence of it. "It's not like it was fate," I wrote. "It's one of those elements of chance when one big thing like the moon can be important in a lot of different ways at the same time. It comforts me to know that we don't have much control over what happens in our lives. It's more like how we deal with what comes along." That was kind of a heavy thing I was putting out there, and I should have thought about it later when all the shit hit the fan because I was learning that the old saying is true that *time and tide wait for no man.*

FIVE

Peterson didn't like storing his dory on the beach for fear that winter storms would drive the surf up and wash it away or smash it against the bluff, so the day after the last fishing period, we loaded it with the nets and leftover groceries. "Climb in," said Peterson. "You take her down to the boat harbor. I'll meet you there. Don't fuck around and miss the channel. You'll see it if you come in straight."

"Okay," I said with surprise, scrambling over the gunnel before he changed his mind. I hadn't been allowed to run the skiff alone all summer. "I'll see you there." I hustled to the stern to start the motor. Peterson held the bow bobbing in the surf. "And stay offshore!" he yelled. "You should pass outside the Sisters."

I nodded and waved. Finally, I was getting to run the skiff on my own. I tugged on the starting cord and the motor fired and then died.

"Half-choke! Half-choke!" yelled Peterson, and he pushed the skiff farther into the surf. I waved him off and the motor barked and started on the second pull. I shifted into reverse and gave it some gas. Water splashed up on me as the square stern pushed against the surf, and the skiff moved off the beach. I was too busy backing and turning the skiff to look at Peterson, but I knew he was watching me, probably a little worried that I'd run aground or hit a rock on the run down to the Ninilchik River.

The weather was kind for my first solo trip with the skiff. A light breeze blew out of the southeast, and the sun kept peeking through the clouds. Loaded as it was with nets and gear, the skiff was plowing a bit through the waves, but when I opened the throttle all the way, the bow came up, and the skiff cut a smooth rocking course heading out toward Kalgin Island. Beyond the island, the mountains were hidden by clouds, but I could imagine their jagged shoulders pushing up into the sky.

When I figured I was a couple of miles offshore, I turned south and watched for the Sisters, a pair of rocks that Peterson worried I'd run into. A few miles south of that, I had to turn toward the beach and find the river channel I would follow into the harbor. The harbor was just a wide part of the river dredged years earlier to make a mooring for boats where the river passed along the bluff parallel to the shore. The water was shallow far out into the inlet, so if I missed the channel, I'd run aground a long way from where I needed to be. I had to find the mouth of the river and run up that narrow channel to the boat basin.

It was an unexpected reward to finish the season this way, running the skiff alone out on the inlet. I was brown and strong, scented with the sea and the salmon, and ready to be off the beach. I had left the beach only two days in the last sixty, and other than the occasional beer tossed to me by the guy in the cannery truck that picked up our fish, I had been living like a hermit. Iris's last postcard had said she'd be home on the fifteenth of August, and I hoped that on the sixteenth I'd be knocking on her door, showered, shaved, and ready to wrestle.

When I steered Peterson's skiff past our old Barger fish site, I could see the beach cabin sitting high and square on its pilings the way that Dad had built it. The dory was sitting out in front and nets hung on the rack. The dory looked the same as the one Dad was using the day he died, and I had to relive that day one more time. Dad, Joe, and me together on the beach, shutting things down for the season. Little did we know it was forever. Dad's heart attack came while he and Joe were driving the Jeep up to the house, the house on the bluff above the beach.

From the skiff, I could see the peak of our roof above the trees. I wondered if that was the difference between this summer and the ones I remembered. The setnet sites I remember had a house on the bluff above them with Mom in her garden and kitchen with homemade bread and all of us together in a way that could never be again. And as I looked at that place, I wondered, is that what I wanted for the grown-up Sam Barger, for me and Iris maybe, a log cabin on the bluff with the beach just below? Or did I want something else entirely? I couldn't think about that now, though, I had immediate concerns.

I worried about finding the channel for the Ninilchik River that would lead to the harbor and the end of the season, but it was just like Peterson said it would be, a stripe of milky water making a current through the waves. I motored into the boat basin without incident and pushed the skiff against the boardwalk. Peterson was waiting with the truck. We unloaded the nets and other gear, then we stood facing each other, me with my duffel bag and him with an envelope smudged with grime from his hands and pocket. He held out the envelope. "Here's a piece of your share," he said. "I'll square the rest with you when the cannery settles up. You did OK."

I took the money and shook his thick hand. "Thanks," I said. I was antsy to be on the road, on to the next thing, on to Iris.

Peterson nodded his head and looked past me at the river and the boats in it. "If you wanna come back next summer, let me know by Christmas," he said.

"OK, I'll think about it," I said. "See you around." I walked to my pickup and didn't look back, and I wasn't sure I wanted to look back on that summer just yet. I was too busy looking forward, and that view looked pretty good because I was only thinking of the girl and somehow, beyond that, I hadn't bothered.

SIX

"Holy shit!"

That's what I said when Iris told me she was pregnant. I didn't say, "Holy shit, that's amazing!" Or "Holy shit, that must be scary for you." Either of those would have been a good choice, but I just said, "Holy shit!" and let it hang in the air like a giant voice balloon from some cartoon.

We were sitting in my pickup at Earthquake Park, making out and talking while we waited to see the sunset. I was seriously into making out, but Iris was more interested in talking. She was tense and didn't seem to want to be touched at first. I tried putting my hand up her shirt but, she took it and slid it down to her knee and held it there. First, she talked about school and the war, chasing topics around like she was trying to grab soap in a bathtub. Then she asked, "So how was fishing? Was it all you wanted?"

"Yes and no. There's lots of downtime. I don't handle that well. I think I'd like to go to college and be a lawyer and spend my summers fishing. Mom wanted that, the lawyer part anyway, and I think I did too. Now that I made a stab at fishing, though, I think I want more. It might fit for a couple of summers, but I ain't going to make a living at. I learned that much. I'm not good at waiting, and fishing has lots of waiting."

"Yeah," she said, "I'm thinking this is my last summer at fish camp. Dad'll have to find a camp monkey."

"Really? Is fly fishing losing its glamour?"

"You might say that. Then she sat back against the passenger door and took a deep breath. "Sam, I think I might be pregnant." I jerked my hand away from her leg like I was touching a hot griddle—another bad move—and that's when I said it.

"Holy shit!"

What followed was a long silence during which I rubbed my hands up and down my arms as a fever ran up my spine and my tongue became a thick ball of wool. Suddenly the truck felt small and cold.

"Is that all you're going to say?" She slugged my shoulder. "Did you even hear me? I'm late, you know what that means, right?"

"I get it."

"I stopped having periods, Sam. You don't have to be Dr. Kildare to know what that means." She leaned her head back and closed her eyes. "Yeah, I'm pretty sure, like 99 percent sure that I'm pregnant."

I reached out to pull her close to me. Searching desperately for words, not just any words but the right words for such a moment, the right words for all the ideas racing through my head. She sat up straight and looked me square in the eye. "And don't you even ask, Sam Barger. I know what you're thinking."

My hands came up instinctively to block any blows to follow. "Ask what?"

Finally, she smiled and faked a punch at my face then hit me on the thigh. "Don't even ask if it's yours!"

"Of course it's mine," I said, sounding more confident than I really was. "Wow, this is big. We're having a kid."

"Not so fast, Hotshot." Iris reached down and grabbed an Oly from the six-pack on the floorboards and held it out for me to open.

"You better hand me one too. I'm going to need it." I opened the truck door and used the latch to pop the caps off the beer bottles. I took a deep drink and looked out the window and then looked into those brown eyes and said, "I want to do the right thing." I braced myself as Iris shook her head. I was on thin ice.

"The right thing?" I could feel the ice cracking under me. No, I wasn't ready to be a father, but I was crazy about this girl, and what the hell. Sure, I'd marry her. "The right thing?" she repeated. "What the hell does that mean? Does that mean you'll pay for the abortion?" The ice was breaking under me now. "You'll drive me to the airport and pay the doctor bills? Sam, are you that shallow?"

The ice was gone. I had sunk into ice-cold water and was drowning. "Iris, don't. I'm right here. I'll be here however you want me to be. I want to be part of this. You know how I feel about you. Shit, we can get married." I downed the last of my beer and thought about another.

"Well don't act like it's a job, some chore on your daily checklist," she said. She scooted away from me, putting her back against the door again and her feet up on the seat creating a wall between us. She sipped her beer and looked past me through the window to the horizon of mountains across the water.

"What did I do wrong? What did I say?" I asked.

"You just sounded so flat, like you don't see just how big this is. Shit, I wish I had some weed. I have to walk." With that, she bailed out of the truck, and I followed. We walked away from the other cars steamed up by couples with their heads together and moved down toward the crumpled chunks of earth left from when the shoreline collapsed after the '64 earthquake. Five years later it was still a jumble of giant slabs of mud and dead trees.

"Do your parents know?" I asked, taking her hand. She didn't pull away, and I realized that her hands were so small and mine so broad that we couldn't lace our fingers like lovers usually do. It felt like a child's hand I was holding.

"Are you kidding? Not yet. Dad will kill me—and you too. Mom's going to cry for a week and tell me how I ruined my life."

We were surrounded by the near-dusk light of late summer, and I searched the reddening sky for an answer. "They might surprise you, you know. Sometimes parents get it and actually act like they understand.

Parents were young and stupid once too." I tried to chuckle and lighten the mood, but it sounded more like a clumsy fake cough.

Iris stopped walking and turned to look at me. "What, did you see that on some bumper stickers? Parents were young and stupid once too, really? We know how things go at the Barger house."

I laughed. "Yeah, Mom will shake her head and say, 'For the love of god, Sam. I swear you don't have a brain in your head.' Then she'll talk for an hour, telling me all the things I should and could have done."

"Then she'll ask the question," Iris said. "The question that you were too polite to ask." Two people came down the trail toward us escorted by a black Lab. Iris quit talking and bent to pet him. When the couple and their dog were well beyond us, I said, "Yup, she probably will, but I wasn't being polite. I just knew." We both laughed at that, for different reasons I think. "You gotta tell your folks, Iris."

"Well, I have to sometime, but I want to have a plan first." She kicked some stones. "I want to be able to tell them what I want. Otherwise, shit. They'll decide everything. My dad, for sure." I pointed at the sky turning fuchsia behind the Alaska Range. We stood and watched the wonder of it.

"What do you want, Iris? We gotta talk about it. Yes, I'll even marry you. Is that what you want? I mean that's what we should do, right? If that's what you want."

Iris let go of my hand, and I thought she might hit me, but she patted my chest and leaned in against me. "I want it all. I want it to go away. I want to go to college next year. I want to have this baby and be the best mom. And I don't want any of it."

I was smart this time and didn't say anything. I just held her. For a long time we were sharing our heartbeats but not our thoughts. The closeness was enough for the time in that space by the crumpled earth on the edge of the mudflats where the tide didn't care about two confused teenagers.

We made love again that night, quick and clumsy like we hadn't done it before. I didn't think we would, what with Iris all in a knot about the pregnancy, and me, too, for that matter. But when we were back in the truck holding each other it seemed too easy and natural when my hand slipped under her shirt and stroked her bare back. She stiffened but didn't push me away. Suddenly the fire flared in me again, and my hand began roaming over her body. The truck cab was crowded for lovemaking, but we giggled our way through with passion making up for our lack of legroom or skill. I do remember now that she was less passionate, like she was doing it more for me than her, and she did seem hesitant when I was actually between her legs, so I stopped and looked into her eyes. "It's OK," she whispered. "I want you too."

Iris hadn't said that before, and I could only say the same words back to her. It was as if we weren't ready to say, "I love you," but we could say "I want you." And all that made my passion stronger so that when I entered her, my climax followed almost immediately, and I felt something like an explosion in my head. I flopped back into a sitting position, and she curled her legs up to make room.

"You OK?" I asked.

"Why wouldn't I be, silly?" We fumbled for tissue and buttons.

"I was just . . . I don't know." I mumbled, then kissed her. I tried to reason what was different this time. She was just tense I guess.

I got to thinking about how the first minutes after sex are clumsy and messy in a way that books and movies don't show or talk about. We were welded together for a short, hot time, and then we were apart and alone with separate unspoken feelings. I turned on the radio for company, and we lay against each other half napping, and I tried to pretend I wasn't thinking about what was waiting for us outside our little bubble.

Later, after I dropped Iris off at her house, I lay in bed thinking about that question we asked each other. What did we want? Did we want the same thing? Before, when I thought about being with Iris, I didn't think about being married and having a kid, I just thought about being with her and traveling with her and sleeping and eating and laughing with her. I didn't think about a commitment like marriage and fatherhood.

We never were together long enough to talk about the future. Iris and I had never been the typical high school couple walking hand in hand down the hall to class and inseparable every waking hour. We met in the school cafeteria when she heard I had made a big fool of myself in class talking against the US being in Vietnam, and she tracked me down. She wasn't looking for a boyfriend, but I chased her anyway. Eventually, I won her over—for a while. We got into the anti-war scene, and I got to be that guy with the pretty gal on my arm—that's how it looked anyway. Actually, it was more me on her arm because she was always in the lead, and I was just marching and protesting to impress her and be with her until I got in a fistfight and lost her.

It was a simple thing really, just a fistfight at a school dance when a guy pushed me more than I could take. But Iris was such a peacenik, so committed to nonviolence that me in a fistfight—and then bragging about it didn't help—was enough to drive her away. Then that night at the start of summer when she climbed into the back of the Vista Cruiser everything changed.

I couldn't sleep with all this traffic in my head, so I turned on a light and grabbed a Mike Hammer novel off the table. Spillane's detective stories weren't great literature, but they had a gritty frankness that was uncluttered with circumspection. Mike Hammer acted and never looked back to second-guess himself. I thought how nice it would be to have such confidence.

I read most of the night, and Mom didn't wake me before she went to work. Shortly before noon, I crawled out of bed and heated leftover coffee in the percolator. While the coffee was warming, I put a skillet on the stove and threw in a dollop of bacon grease from the jar. By the time the coffee was hot enough to be tolerable, I had sliced up some potatoes and added them to the grease, covered the skillet, and turned down the heat. I sliced some onion and green pepper and added them to the potatoes and wished I had some ham to throw in. It was the kind of breakfast Mike Hammer would eat. But he'd wash it down with bourbon.

I thought about making an omelet the way I'd learned at the Polar Pizza, but I was too hungry, so I just broke three eggs into the skillet and drank my coffee. Pete owned Polar Pizza, and I had worked for him off and on for a year and a half. Sometimes we didn't feel like eating pizza, so he taught me to make omelets. I learned to whip up some eggs with a little milk and pour them into an omelet pan greased with butter or olive oil. By turning and babying those eggs just so, I could produce a light and fluffy omelet.

Pete said I had a talent and wanted me to join the navy and get trained as a cook like he did. I figured there were easier ways to learn cooking than signing up for four years on the high seas. Besides, there was no way the military was getting a hold of Sam Barger, not while the Vietnam War was still on. No thank you. I checked the potatoes and poured eggs over them and put the cover back on. What I might do was see Pete about a job. I was going to need some money no matter how things turned out.

It would be good if I had a job lined up when I talked to Mom. It had been a while since I pissed her off, so she probably thinks I'm overdue anyway. It's been over a year since I got suspended for protesting the Vietnam War and then again for fighting—there's a little irony. After that, Joe and I went moose hunting and I shot him. Even though it was an accident and Joe didn't die, it was still my fault. At least that's how Mom saw it, just another reckless Sam stunt. And now, I was going to have to tell her about getting Iris pregnant.

About the time my breakfast was ready, my mind was buzzing again, and I had worked up a pretty good fret. How was I going to tell Mom about Iris? What would Joe have to say? What would Iris decide?

Then my mind raced ahead. How would she deal with school when she started to show? I'd seen pregnant girls at school before, and I know people talked about them behind their backs like they were doing every guy around. There were times when I thought that way too, but now that all looked different. I mean, I don't think Iris was a virgin—like I was— but she wasn't the sleep-around type either. Iris was confident, though, and I figured it wouldn't bother her to go to school pregnant. She'd just blow people off for a while, but then maybe she'd just do correspondence or drop out and get her GED. Hell, she was smart and probably didn't need many credits to graduate anyway.

Worrying doesn't hurt my appetite, so all the time I was fretting about school and Iris and Mom, I was working my way through the plate of scrambled eggs and potatoes. I finished the last of Mom's pot of coffee and poured a glass of milk. I needed to call Iris, I needed to call Pete at Polar Pizza and try to get my job back, and I needed to figure out how this whole next year was going to look.

Then the phone rang. Iris was on the other end, sobbing.

SEVEN

It took me a few minutes to get Iris to stop crying, and I was almost crying myself by the time she was down to just sniffling. I had never seen Iris cry—not when she was being browbeaten by the vice principal during our peace protest, not when we were fighting before we broke up. She wasn't a crier, and now here she was, a heap of sobs that I couldn't break through.

"Damnit, I hate crying," she said. "Such a boob I am."

"It's OK," I said. "Tell me what's wrong." I stood over the kitchen sink looking out the window at the backyard and feeling helpless.

"Talk to me," she said. "Just talk to me for a bit about anything."

"OK, I guess. I'm thinking I need to mow the lawn. It's getting pretty long. I think Mom is waiting for me to do it without asking. Uh, let me see. I had a big breakfast, fried potatoes with eggs, and other stuff thrown in. I'd make it for you sometime." I wanted her to talk. I wanted to know what happened, but I figured it was a fight with her parents. No one can make a kid hurt like her parents. "You want me to come over?"

More silence, except for her breathing. Then, "Yes, I want you to come to punch my dad in the nose, and hold me all day, but no. Stay there. This fire doesn't need any more fuel. Mom and Dad were getting along pretty well since the divorce," she said, "but this has them fighting again."

"I take it you told your parents, and it didn't go well."

"No shit, Sherlock. What was your first clue?"

"Well I was hoping your dad would understand. I thought you two were pretty close."

"Yeah, we are, and if I was a boy this would all be no big deal. You know he kinda treated me like a boy all along, but now it's like, *hey, Daddy, your little tomboy is pregnant.* Well, he pretty much freaked out and damn near hit me. Then my mom just started in on me, which got them fighting with each other."

"Oh shit, Iris. What can I do?" I was chewing my lip and pacing. What the hell could I do? I had done enough.

"Nothing, just be there. I know it's no fun listening to me sulk and sob like this." Then we sat in silence. I didn't know if she wanted me to talk more about it, change the subject, or hang up, so I just hung there in the kitchen fiddling with the spiral phone cord, wrapping and twisting it around my fingers.

"Needless to say, I'm grounded." More silence while I imagined a girl mature enough to be pregnant, to be a mom, and still be grounded by her parents. I laughed a silly, involuntary giggle.

"You think this is funny?"

"No, I'm sorry. It's the being grounded thing. You're going to be a mom, but you got grounded. Sorry, I couldn't . . . you know."

"I get it." She'd stopped crying and her breathing had evened out. "It does sound silly."

"I think I should come over and talk to your folks. It might help if they know we're together on this."

"Not if you value your life. Daddy is scary pissed, and I don't even want to think what he might do to you. Hell, he would have slapped me if Mom hadn't stopped him." I choked on a nervous laugh.

"I gotta go," she said.

"Wait," I said. I didn't want her to go. I couldn't end the conversation like this. It felt final and scary like, "I got to GO" as in, *gone for good.* "I'll pick you up for school Monday. I'll drive you, or you cannot go at all. Whatever you want."

"I gotta go, Sam. Really. School? Oh yeah. Oh shit, school, like I feel like that whole parade. OK, just wait out front for me, and don't honk your horn. No, wait. I have to go to the doctor Monday. Mom set it up, you know. To confirm. Oh Christ, Sam."

"I know, Iris." Her voice made me want to cry. My hand hurt from gripping the phone so hard. "Tuesday then. I'll pick you up."

I heard a woman's voice in the background calling, "Iris!"

"Oh, shit. I'm not supposed to talk to you. Bye."

Then nothing but the buzz of an empty phone line on the other end. A woman came on the party line then. "Are you finally done? I've got calls to make."

I looked at the phone and slammed it back on the cradle. "Bitch!" I said to no one. Then I stomped out the door to the garage and hauled the push mower to the backyard and slammed the door on my way out. Mowing the lawn was a one-hour chore when I did it the way Mom liked it, mowed in two directions. I was a half hour in before I quit cussing.

Then I got to thinking about Iris and remembering her face from two years ago when she recruited me into her anti-war protest. I had just made myself public enemy number one when I compared Ho Chi Minh to George Washington during a class presentation. "Are you Sam Barger?" she asked. "They told me to look for a tall guy with a big nose."

She was a year behind me in school, and I had seen her before because we rode the same bus sometimes, but she really caught my attention this time, and it sounds corny, but I was totally done in by those brown eyes and freckles with a ton of black hair falling wild around her shoulders. She was smart and clever, kind of a tomboy but feminine too. It took me months to get her past the 'let's just be friends' phase, and now we were on the way to being parents. My brain was spinning. It was like we just jumped a freight train together, and it was running faster and faster into some dark tunnel with no light at the end.

I finished mowing the lawn and trimmed the edges. I was still in motion, so I headed down to Polar Pizza. A job would be one thing off my list of things to do, something I knew I could fix. Pete liked me well enough that he might take me on again even though I had left on short notice last year. I did know one thing, this whole fiasco was going to cost money, and I was going to need more than the little nest egg I had from fishing if I was going to help Iris, if I was going to marry Iris, or if I was going to do anything at all.

Pete was glad to see me, and we shared a coffee and a slice of pizza. He was trying a new Hawaiian special on the menu, Canadian bacon—which looked and tasted like ham to me—and pineapple. "It's all the rage," he said. "And I gotta keep up with the fads."

"Good for you, Pete," I said. Pete had given me a job two years ago, and I had learned to make pizza and sauces and soups from the man. Mom said I was looking for the dad I didn't have and I should be careful, but Pete turned out to be a stand-up guy who treated me well even when I didn't have my shit together. It was like coming home to munch on a pizza slice—OK, three or four—and catch up with Pete and smell the exotic aromas amid the familiar tacky trailer house paneling hung with old photos of Venice and Rome. "Any chance you need a pizza cook?" I asked, shyly. I had quit Pete abruptly twice in the past, and now I was back again with my hat in my hand.

"Well, Sam," Pete said, eying me across his coffee cup, "it seems we've been here before, and the only reason I took you back last time was because of my daughter. She's always talking me into things."

"How's she doing?" I asked. I remembered the petite redhead that had made me want to work at Polar Pizza the first time I saw her. I had a crush on her for the first months I worked there before I found out that she was married, and even then I couldn't stop looking at her. She was more unpredictable than Iris, and her flirty ways made me nervous.

"Yeah, her husband got transferred, so she's down in the Lower 48 now. Everybody's on the move. Anyway, Sam, I don't have anything for you. Business is booming, and things might change, but for right now I have a waitress and a cook who are pretty solid. I'll keep your number if I need a good hand. Let me know if you need a recommendation. I won't tell them the truth." He laughed at his sarcasm.

I nodded, and said, "Sure Pete, I get it. It's not like I was that dependable, quitting you twice like I did."

"Speaking of quitting, how's your brother? Is he still hitting the bottle so hard?"

Again I nodded. "His wounds healed up pretty good, and he has a limp, but we're at least civil now. He's still drinking off and on, but at least he can keep a job, and Mom doesn't worry so much." I chuckled. "Who would think that shooting my brother would bring us closer together? Funny isn't it."

Pete frowned, "That's in the past kid. That hunting accident could have happened to anyone, and you were close before that. The two of you just didn't know it."

I stood up to leave and extended a hand. "Don't be a stranger," Pete said. "My door's always open. You know that, right?"

"I know it, Pete. I won't be buying my pizza anywhere else. When you talk to Becky, tell her I said hi."

"Will do, Sam. Will do. And Sam, you don't have to buy your pizza, ever. Take care."

I left Polar Pizza with a bit of sulk, even though Pete was trying to be nice. I didn't just need the job, Polar Pizza was like a second home, and Pete was the gruff, loving uncle I never had. I could have used that kind of harbor in the storm right now. I didn't know much about what was coming next, and I wandered home making a plan to pull out the want ads and start the search. There wasn't much I knew how to do except make pizza, maybe be a grill cook, wash dishes, and mow lawns. I walked up the driveway and into the house imagining myself stuck bagging groceries at the Carr's supermarket. That was a picture I didn't dig.

When Mom came in from shopping she went to work in her garden, while I made salmon patties and rice for dinner. I kept a distance as I planned how to bring up the hot topic in the front of my mind. Mom sat down for dinner and looked out the window in the backyard. "Nice job on the lawn. That'll probably do it for the year, I guess," she said. "And it's so good to have you to cook for me again. Dinner by yourself is no fun."

My mind was elsewhere, but I couldn't ignore the guilt trip she was laying on me.

"What about Jake?" I asked. "I thought you had a boyfriend."

Mom's eyes twinkled, and she looked away coyly and said, "Never you mind about that, mister." And I knew she wanted to talk about it.

"Mom," I said, "I know you're disappointed I wasn't around this summer, and I'm glad you found someone to keep you company."

Mom pushed her plate away and lit a cigarette. "Heavens to Betsy, Sam. I was just saying I liked having you around. And yes, since you asked, Jake has been good company to me, something I haven't had in a long time."

"A long time" meant since Dad died, and it did seem fair that she should have somebody close. This was sounding like she wanted me to have Jake close, too, and I didn't need that. I didn't need to talk about it either. So we started talking past each other.

"Well Mom, I've got something kinda big to deal with right now." The room was suddenly hot and uncomfortable.

"Oh Sam, about your fishing, I didn't mean to criticize you for wanting to grow up and go and do the things men do."

I took another salmon patty and the last of the rice. "Sorry Mom, I thought you were guilt-tripping me for not being around this summer."

She smiled and said, "I know, you're going to be off to college soon, and I better get used to not having you around. You won't believe it, but

I like it when you're here. That doesn't mean I want you sitting around here with your old gray-haired mother for the rest of your life." She laughed and got up and poured a cup of coffee.

"Well lots of things are changing, Mom. Believe me."

"There's leftover cobbler in the fridge if you want some," she added. "It turns out Jake's a big fan of my cobbler. . . . Of course, if you go to Fairbanks for college, you won't be that far away, and your sister is there, so you'd have family around. Or if you go here in town you can live at home. That would be cheaper. Have you thought about that? Where you want to go. I guess we're kind of late off the mark it being the end of August." Of course, my mother had no idea what a segue she had presented.

"I guess it's good you'll have Jake to keep you company, Mom, if I'm not here. You won't miss me a bit." It sounded meaner than I meant it, and I know I was just saying things to keep from saying what I needed to. Finally, "Yeah, about my plans," I said. "Things have gotten a little complicated."

I had my head in the fridge by then looking for the cobbler, avoiding the rest of what had to be said. I looked in the freezer for ice cream, but there wasn't any, so I grabbed a spoon and took the cobbler to the table. I don't know why I opened that door, a door that couldn't be shut. We were having a pretty normal dinner conversation—normal if you if two parallel monologues are normal. I couldn't predict how Mom would react, but it wasn't going to be all sweetness and light. I knew that much. She'd know something was wrong anyway because I couldn't eat that cobbler. My stomach was a knotted rope.

"Things are always complicated with you, Sam. What is it this time?" She lit another cigarette and squinted at me through the smoke.

EIGHT

I told Mom everything. No, not the whole detailed story in the back of the Vista Cruiser—that would have been too much. But I did tell her that Iris was 99 percent sure she was pregnant, and I was 100 percent— OK, 99 percent—sure that I was the father. What was my plan? I told her I didn't know what I was going to do, but I wasn't going to shirk my responsibility. Mom just smoked and listened. Finally, I said, "I just want to do the right thing."

"What in the world does that mean?" No rant, no yelling, no disappointed silence. I don't think I'd ever seen Mom like this, and we've been through a lot. Dad died four years ago, and I got kicked out of school for protesting the war plus other adolescent shenanigans. But she never acted like this. When Joe was in Vietnam, she fretted, and then when he came home wounded, she moaned about being a tortured soul, and when I brought Joe home from hunting with another bullet wound, she hit me with the silent treatment, but now, finding out that her teenage son was going to be a father, she was calm as a cucumber. She just asked that one question, "What in the world does that mean?"

I got up and started pacing the kitchen, "That's the thing. I don't know what that means. I do know that I screwed up, and I have a responsibility. I can't just walk away from her . . . from it." I was shaking and could hear my voice breaking. "What do I do, Mom? I gotta marry her, right? I mean should, no, I want to." She didn't say anything, which made me keep talking.

"I was thinking," I said—actually, I wasn't thinking. Ideas just started pouring out of my mouth. All the things that were spinning through my brain came out. "Maybe she wants to give it up. The baby, I mean. Girls do that, right? Or I should marry her, if she wants. Maybe we could move in here. We'd have my room and a baby doesn't take up much space and you could help . . . I mean show her stuff, and I could work and still take some college classes. It's not the end of the world, is it?"

Still nothing from Mom. She just smoked her cigarette and looked out the window like she was waiting for Dad to come walking across the lawn to help her deal with their pain-in-the-ass son. "She's really nice, Mom. She's smart and pretty, and she's tough like you. She kicks my ass." I laughed a silly, nervous laugh. I sat down and stared out at the mowed lawn where Mom was staring and the fence beyond and the trees across the alley with the mountains behind. "That would be a great yard for a little guy, Mom." I could see my mom in that future with a house full of life, and I talked up a lovely image, a possibility just like when I was younger and made up imaginary futures for myself, and it felt so real that it couldn't possibly be anything else.

Finally, she spoke. "Sam Barger, are you listening to yourself? You're eighteen years old, and how old is she? Sixteen, seventeen? You're just kids. You get caught up in your imagination, son, and you dream up things all warm and fuzzy, but that's not how life is. Life is bills and dirty diapers, sick kids, and disappointment."

First Mom killed me with silence, then she wouldn't stop. "Give me a little credit, Mom. I'm not an idiot."

"You've had a pretty good few months, Sam. You got your grades up and graduated, and you worked hard all summer—even if you didn't make any money. You can do something with yourself. Now you come to me with this. For the love of Christ, I don't know what I did to deserve this."

"I know you think I'm just a stupid kid, but I'm not, Mom. You taught me, you and Dad. You taught me to be responsible and how to work hard and be a good person. I know I've messed up a lot of stuff, but—" I was rambling and blubbering like an idiot. "You were seventeen when you got married and you did good, you and Dad. Give me a chance. What am I supposed to do anyway? Just turn my back and act like it's not my problem? Is that what Dad would do?" It was probably shitty for me to play the Dad card, evoking a man long dead to prod her conscious, but I was using everything I had right then.

"Who is this girl anyway? How do you know it's yours? How do you know she's even pregnant? For Christ's sake, Sam."

"Iris, Mom. Her name's Iris Davis."

"The girl who got you kicked out of school? I thought you broke up last year."

"Yes. I mean we did and then we weren't."

"How far along is she?" The calm was coming back into Mom's voice. She ran her fingers through her hair and looked out the window. "I think I need a drink. Make me a bourbon and coke."

I scrambled to my feet, eager to do something other than sit at the dinner table and sweat. I found the liquor in the cupboard above the sink and mixed her drink with ice. When Mom went to the bathroom, I poured a bit of bourbon into a glass for myself and felt the burn as I took in one gulp, then started clearing the table and made dishwater in the sink. It calmed me to get my hands as busy as my mind.

Mom returned, lit a cigarette, and took a long drink. "I asked, how far along is she?"

"Three months I guess. She's going to the doctor on Monday." The dishes were done too soon, and I vigorously wiped the counters with the dishrag.

Mom shook her head, stood, and snubbed out her cigarette. "I need a bath. We'll talk in the morning," She stalked out of the kitchen with her drink in her hand. As she left, I heard, "Well if she's going to do something. It has to be soon."

I was left sitting in a kitchen full of clean dishes staring at the floor and wondering what Mom met by that.

I spent Sunday trying to talk to Iris, but it didn't happen. First I called and got no answer, then I called and her mom answered. "Hi, could I speak to Iris, please?"

"Iris isn't available right now." She hung up without waiting for my reply.

On the third call I identified myself and said I really needed to talk to Iris, and please have her call me. Her mom said, "You won't be hearing from Iris any time soon, Sam Barger, and don't bother calling back. Iris has had enough of your kind around."

"My kind!" I said to the dead phone. "What the hell does that mean?"

I called my buddy David Nelson and told him I'd buy him breakfast. We hadn't gotten together since I got back from fishing, and I could use his energetic distraction. David and I went back a long way, back to middle school when we got each other's jokes and no one else did. I guess we kinda grew up together even though we weren't all that much the same except for our humor. Buddies are like that, I guess, real buddies. I could talk to him when I was pissed and didn't want to talk to anyone, and that's how I felt that day. I picked him up outside his trailer house, and he climbed in wearing new corduroy bell-bottoms and a bright new cotton shirt. His shoes had a shine that showed they were fresh out of the box. "Looking good there, slick," I said, recognizing the contrast with my faded jeans and dusty cowboy boots.

David chuckled. "No law against looking good," he said. "You might want to try it sometime."

"As my mom would say, 'no need to gild the lily,'" I replied. "I'm pretty enough as it is." It was good to be back with David's comfortable banter. We spent most of our conversations putting each other down.

"Yeah, lipstick won't help a pig."

I laughed and let David start catching me up on his summer in Fairbanks. He goes there every summer to live with his grandparents and give his mom a break. I didn't talk about Iris or being pregnant, not any of that. Mostly I let him chatter about the girls he met in Fairbanks while I navigated the traffic and found a parking place at Leroy's Pancake House.

"So, big man, did you and Iris keep it going all summer, a long-distance love affair, or was that a one-night stand?"

I punched him in the shoulder. "It's complicated," I said.

He laughed. "Of course it's complicated. If it wasn't, it wouldn't be you and Iris. I bet with you two even sex feels like work."

We settled into a booth and ordered pancakes and eggs. I watched a couple come in hand in hand, I wondered if David was right. Maybe Iris and I were too intense to be together? "No, we're kinda still hanging out," I said, laughing. "We like the challenge." I wanted to tell him more. I wanted to tell him everything. But a single girl being pregnant was major gossip fodder, and there was no way I could risk it getting out. I trusted David, but he liked to talk and sometimes his mouth was in gear when his brain was in neutral. One slip and everybody would be talking and staring. This shit was complicated.

David looked at his watch after we ate. "Guess we better get our asses movin', Barger. I actually have a job to go to now. Thanks for the breakfast, man."

"Glad you got to see me," I replied.

"So why are you taking me to breakfast instead of having brunch with your lady. Isn't that what couples do? Brunch then go to Penney's and shop for matching jackets? Is she ashamed to be seen with you?"

"She's busy with her family. Tomorrow she's got a doctor's appointment, so you can buy breakfast."

"Farm out and right arm."

"You need new material."

"Nah, just a new friend."

"Good luck with that."

We were in the truck when he blindsided me, "She's going to the doctor, huh? Hope the rabbit doesn't die."

I was halfway into my side of the truck and nearly fell on my face. I knew I was blushing. It had to be just a wisecrack, a typical smart-ass comment like David and I used on each other all the time. He couldn't know. There was no way that Iris's predicament, our predicament, could be out there not yet. I tried to recover and steady my voice. I slammed the truck door. "She's just getting a physical, asshole." I tried to sound casual, but it came out like someone had their hands around my throat choking me. "Any woman going out with me has to be physically fit." I laughed like an idiot who told a bad joke and pretended it was funny.

David just looked at me with his eyebrows raised and shook his head. "Whatever man. Can't take a joke?"

"I took a joke to breakfast, didn't I?"

"That was a half-assed good comeback. You still got your edge."

It took me a while to shake off David's crack about the dead rabbit even though I knew it was just a smart-ass remark, and he had no way of knowing Iris was pregnant. I hadn't said anything, and I knew Iris wasn't spreading the news past her closest friends if that, but it still haunted me, and I went through the day looking over my shoulder.

It's crazy the way we guys had of thinking about sex and pregnancy. Every guy, it seemed, wanted to have sex, and many guys bragged about girls they went all the way with. But if a girl went all the way, she could get a rep for being easy, and sometimes even if she didn't. Girls who showed up at school obviously pregnant wore evidence that they weren't pure. They became pariahs. And now Iris was one of those girls, and those girls usually disappeared. A girl would stop coming to school, and word would get around that she had to leave town. We never knew for sure. It was just assumed that she *got in trouble* unless we knew the family had moved. Where those girls went and what happened I didn't know.

I wasn't sure about anything. Nobody talked about what to do when you got a girl pregnant, and I couldn't go to the library and check out a book about it. It was like trying to fix your car when you didn't know anything about engines and didn't have any tools or repair manuals. Maybe I wanted to do the right thing, but good intentions were only going to get me so far.

NINE

I smelled Old Spice aftershave as soon as I walked in the front door, then I saw the guy with thinning gray hair leaning against the kitchen counter with his hand on my mom's—shit—his hand on my mom's ass. I'm no prude, but that put me off, and I was stumbling over my feet and words when I walked in. Mom didn't help things either, she just turned and smiled, then leaned into this guy while she talked. "Sam, I'm so glad you're here, honey. I want you to meet Jake."
Luckily Mom and Jake were on their way out, so ours was a handshake, hello, goodbye meeting. Mom was taking him to the airport so he could fly off to work somewhere. The farther the better as far I was concerned.

I cooked up a pot of slumgullion and had it on the table when Mom came back. She changed her clothes and then settled herself at the table. She hadn't even taken a bite when she asked, "So did you talk to your young lady—if I can call a girl in her condition a lady."

As much as I hated the conversation this was going to be, it was better than talking about Jake. I needed time to process that graphic image that was anchored in my psyche. "Mom, don't start that way," I warned. "And since you asked, no I haven't. I tried, but I don't think her mom wants me to talk to her." I filled my plate and braced myself.

"Well, if you are the one who got her in trouble, it's no wonder that her mother doesn't want to have anything to do with you." She took a few bites of food and then buttered a roll. "Did you think this family was going to invite you in with open arms? They're blaming you, I'm sure, since they can't imagine their little girl can't keep her knees together. Some girls think that's the only way to get a guy and keep him. It's a shame really."

I dropped my fork on my plate. "Christ, Mom! Is that really what you think? It's them against us, and Iris is just some slut looking for a guy?" I jumped to my feet, "She's smart and pretty, and she doesn't have to do anything to get me. I have been chasing her since the day we met. I love her, Mom! Can't you see that?"

My outburst made Mom calmer rather than riling her up. "Sit down, son. Try to have a civil conversation about this. You're eighteen for the love of god. At your age falling in love is as easy as picking out a new pair of shoes. You don't see it now, but you will be amazed how quickly your feelings will change."

"Not about this, Mom. And besides, it doesn't matter how I feel about Iris. It's my kid too, and what if they never let me in? What if they make her get rid of it? You know, like an abortion."

Mom reached across the table and took my hand. "That might not be the worst thing. She's not far along, and there are ways to get this done, but Sam—" I pulled my hand away and went to lean on the counter staring sightlessly out the kitchen window. "Either way, Sam, this is between her and her folks. This is none of your business, and you are better off staying out of it. They're doing you a favor."

That's when I figured out what Mom had meant before when she said, "'If they're going to do something, it has to be soon.'" "Abortions are illegal, Mom. They just don't want me around."

"There are ways around the law that you don't hear about," she said. "But there are ways. Sometimes it means leaving the country, and it's not cheap."

Somehow I didn't see Iris making that choice, but it could be the way to bring things back to normal. It wasn't like the worst thing in the world, I thought. Maybe then Iris could go through her senior year like a regular kid. But one thing Mom said was true, whether I was the father didn't matter one damn bit. Nobody wanted me in the conversation anyway. That didn't mean I had to shut up.

Tuesday morning I drove to Iris's house in a wooded neighborhood off Debarr Road. The street was lined with newer houses than in my neighborhood, and they were slightly bigger and some were even two stories. I was surprised to see her dad's riverboat on a trailer in the driveway beside a new Ford pickup. I wasn't expecting him to be around. I was about to honk my horn but then remembered Iris's warning, so I parked in front and walked up to the door.

I didn't even get a chance to knock before the door opened and a small muscular man with a crew cut stepped out on the porch and shut the door behind him. "Who are you?" he asked, folding his arms and looking up at me with his chin out. I had met Jack Davis once before, but I figured he didn't remember me. He didn't have much to say that first time we met.

"Good morning, Mr. Davis. I'm Sam Barger. We met last year. I'm here to give Iris a ride to school."

Davis cocked his head to one side and looked away like he wasn't interested. "Barger, huh." Then he hit me.

It was a nasty sucker punch to the jaw that knocked me off the porch and onto my ass. I rolled onto my unsteady knees and tried to get to my feet. My head was ringing, and somewhere, I heard a small dog barking. If you've ever been hit like that, you know that there is no thinking. A person just reacts. I came up fighting—well, I tried to come up fighting. My brain wanted to get up and fight, but my body could only gasp for air. Then Davis caught me with a boot that knocked the rest of the wind out of me. "You stay the hell away from my house, asshole. Keep away from my daughter, and from me, you sorry bastard. Stay away."

I was on my knees trying to breathe when my brain started working again, and I tried to talk. As much as I wanted to stand up and finish the fight Iris's dad had started, I knew there was nothing to gain there. I managed to stand and put my hands on my hips. "I—I just want to do the right thing. We didn't mean—You know, I'm sorry. But please, let me see her."

"Hit the road, Barger, I won't tell you again." Davis stayed on the porch, blocking the door, looking past me like he couldn't meet my eyes. Then the door opened and just for an instant I saw Iris. Her eyes were red and her face tight. "Sam! Dad? What's going on?" Her dad turned, pushed her inside, and followed her, slamming the door as I stumbled onto the porch. I could hear muffled arguments and the barking dog. My lungs had air again, and the fog in my head started to fade as I stood on that front porch feeling like three kinds of fool. I wanted to pound on the door and yell for Iris, but I didn't think some Peyton Place drama would do any good. There had been enough stupid impulses already. I went to my truck and sat there in front of her house feeling sorry for myself.

I must have sat for fifteen minutes before a police car pulled up behind me and flashed his headlights. I watched in the rearview mirror while the driver adjusted his helmet and opened the car door. "Davis, you son-of-a-bitch," I said under my breath. The cop stood for a moment looking from the truck to the house and back, then straightened his gun belt and walked up to my window.

"Good morning, can I see some ID?" The cop was young and tall, lean like my brother, Joe, so that the shiny white helmet made his head look too big.

I handed over my driver's license. "What's the problem? Was I speeding?"

The cop wrinkled his nose like he didn't get the joke. "Mr. Barger, we got a call that you were refusing to leave the premises. Mr. Davis wants you to leave."

"I'm parked on the street nowhere near the premises," I said with a sullen shake of the head, "and this isn't Mr. Davis's place anyway."

He leaned down on the door of the truck and smiled like a guy who didn't have anything to prove. "Probably if you just leave, everybody will be happy."

"He really called the cops?" I said finally. I thought then about reporting that I got punched and kicked, but I didn't.

"Yeah, he did." The cop stood with his hands on his hips looking at the Davis house. "What's your relationship here?" he asked. He sounded less like a cop than just a guy trying to help out another guy.

"It's my girlfriend's house. You can figure the rest. Her dad thinks I'm an asshole, and I'm starting to feel the same way about him."

The cop chuckled. "I get it. Well, why don't you get to school or work, wherever you should be this morning, and let this cool down and try again tomorrow? Can you do that?"

I nodded. As much as I wanted to kick down that door and have a go at Iris's dad, I knew I was outnumbered, and in the back of my mind, I probably knew that fighting with her dad wouldn't help me with Iris at all. Seeing how her dad acted reminded me of why she broke up with me last year. She probably knew what violence looked like.

The cop was walking back to his car when he turned and said, "Next time try calling first. Good luck." He patted the rear fender as he went by. Then he sat in the car and waited while I started the GMC and drove away. I pounded the steering wheel and cussed. "It shouldn't be this damn hard," I said. "It shouldn't be this damn hard."

I kept thinking about my next move and the advice of the cop, *next time try calling first*. It made me think that my frontal assault wasn't going to work. I needed a backdoor. I started looking for another angle, and the next day I was tracking down Iris's friends.

Iris sometimes hung out with the hippies who spent most of the school day in the student parking lot listening to music and smoking reefer. A trip to the East High student parking lot turned up her friend Carol chilling in a VW Bug with Mike Bennett and his perpetual pot pipe. The Bug was so thick with smoke that I got a nose hit when Carol rolled down the window. "Hey, Sam, what's up?" she said. "Or should I say, Daddy!"

"What?" That comment popped into my head right behind the blast of reefer smoke. I jerked the car door open and pulled Carol out with a billow of smoke following her. "Iris told you?" I hissed, looking around to see who was listening.

"Cool it, Sam, of course Iris told me she was knocked up. I knew it had to be you, after seeing you two playing hide the salami back in May." She pushed my hand off her arm. "But you gotta chill. Haven't you caused enough trouble?"

I leaned back against the car and let my breath return to normal. "What trouble? I'm the one who got punched."

"I can see that. So you don't know?" She reached out to touch the small cut under my eye, but I stepped back.

"Don't I know what? Oh, come on, Carol. Where's Iris? Her folks won't even let me talk to her. You talk to her, right? I'm sorry I'm rambling. Just a little frustrated."

Mike got out of the car still holding his pot pipe. Carol stepped around the car and growled, "Cool it, man. We gotta get to class. Put the pipe away." Then she turned back to me, whipping her hair out of her eyes as she did. "God, Sam, you are crazy. You've been calling her house every day, and then you even went over there. That's not how it works, stupid."

"Come on, Carol. What was I supposed to do? I'm trying to do the right thing here. Nobody will even let me see her."

"Do you even know what you did?" She lit a cigarette and paced back and forth behind the car.

"I got punched in the nose if that's what you mean. I got pushed around and treated like shit. Nobody will let me do or say anything." The lunch warning bell had rung, and kids were leaving their cars and heading for the doors to the school.

"She's gone, Sam. Yeah, gone. Like out of here."

"Gone? You mean like out of town?"

"Like out of state, dipshit."

"Her folks sent her outside?" My heart was racing. "But she said she was going to stick around."

"Yeah, clueless. She's in Washington now. I gotta go." Carol grabbed her books and started across the lot toward the school. If Iris had left Alaska, things were really getting twisted. I followed, and she kept talking. "You spooked them, Sam. That's what happened. Iris's folks were thinking of letting her stay here in town and have the baby and just work it out. But no, Sam had to start acting like he could make everything OK and marry her. Seriously?"

"Yeah seriously." I held the school door for her and followed her down the empty hallway, with our boots clattering along the tile floor and echoing off the lockers. "You made me late."

"Sorry, Carol, but this is a little more important than a damn tardy slip."

Carol stopped walking and turned and looked me in the eye. The foggy, weed stare was out of her eyes, and her voice was intense and serious. "Yeah, well, she probably already left, her and her folks. She called me last night, really scared. She waited until like two in the morning when her folks were asleep. She said they were worried you two would do something stupid and get married. Do the whole elope thing, I guess. Yeah, you scared the bejesus out of her folks, and now she's heading for Walla Walla to live with Aunt Sally."

TEN

Joe's apartment was so clean it was hard to tell that anyone lived there. The tiny living room had a side chair, a couch with a poster of a bright red Mustang GT above it, and a TV on a metal stand. In the same room, the kitchen was an L-shaped nook with a plate and a coffee cup resting in a plastic dish drain. I flopped on the couch and stared at the order of it all. "There's some burger and other shit in the fridge if you want to throw together some slumgullion while I'm in the shower," Joe said. "I gotta wash off some of this grease."

By the time he had finished his shower and traded mechanics coveralls for clean Levi's and a western shirt, I had a pan of burger, macaroni, and canned tomatoes simmering on the stove.

"So, what's up, Humpy," he asked, walking out of the bathroom and combing his hair. "Speaking of which, did you meet Mom's new boyfriend? How 'bout that shit."

"Too weird for me. Don't even go there. What's this, a midlife crisis or something?"

Joe laughed. "She's old, not dead." He grabbed a couple of plates and silverware from the dish drain and set them on the table. "This looks pretty good. Maybe you ought to move in."

"You obviously forget what a slob I am."

"That's true. So what brings you here, Sam? You need to borrow some money, or do you need me to kill somebody for you?"

"How did you know?" I said, trying to be clever and oblique like Joe. I hadn't seen Joe since being back from fishing, and he seemed at ease and healthy, neither of which was typical Joe. It eased the guilt I had about the scars on his face and the pain I knew he still carried.

Joe did a partial tour in Vietnam, then got sent home when he was wounded. It turns out getting shot was the least of his problems. The place messed with his head big time, and he got pretty goofy. He drank too much and went off the deep end for a while. Seeing him like this was a big relief. Of course, my screwing up on the hunting trip didn't help.

"You make any money fishing?" he asked. "As if I need to ask. I guess nobody made a killing this year." Joe filled his plate and buttered a slice of bread.

"It was OK. A lot different than I remember. I spent most of my summer sitting around waiting," I said while I loaded my plate. We ate in silence for a few minutes, then I couldn't be quiet any longer. "Joe, you know how you gave me the truck?" He nodded. "I need the title so I can sell it."

"Sure," Joe said. "But why? You love that pickup. Don't make the same mistake I did and spend all your money on a new car. Just drive that ol' GMC until you're out of school. I'll help you keep it running."

"No. I need the money, Joe. I gotta sell it. Dad's rifle too." I watched as he got up and grabbed two beers out of the fridge and handed one to me.

"The Model 71? Why would you sell it? That's the rifle you shot me with." He laughed, then stopped. Our minds both went back to the hunting accident and the cold night in the woods. "Shit!" he said, "You knocked some girl up, didn't you? And now you gotta pay to get rid of it. Is that it, Humpy?"

I sat up straight and stared. I couldn't believe that Joe could guess so fast what was going on. "It's not that simple Joe. It's not like that." Then I told him my plan, the plan I'd thrown together that same day.

Joe washed dishes while I complained about the Davis family keeping me from seeing Iris and how they took her to Washington because of me.

"So you knock some girl up and then you go over and pound on the door after she told her parents. How did that go?"

"Not very well."

"I bet." He laughed again.

"Her old man punched me in the face as soon as I said my name. Shit, Joe. I never saw it coming."

Joe laughed again. "Oh my Humpy, only you would complain about the predicament you're in. Most guys, any guy, would be tickled shitless that he could get some girl pregnant and her family wants nothing to do with him. They are doing you a favor. Hell, Sam, you don't even know it's yours. You were gone fishing for two months. Don't be a dumbass."

"I know, Joe. Trust me."

"Famous last words."

I gotta do it, Joe. I'm not letting Iris deal with this alone just because of her parents. Screw them. I'm going to Washington to see Iris, so we can work this out. It's between us, it's our kid."

Joe got up and went to the bedroom shaking his head, and I could see him rummaging in a drawer. He came back and handed me the truck title and a hundred-dollar bill. "Here you go, Humpy. The hundred's for the rifle. Don't sell or hock it, you'll kick yourself later. Leave it in your closet. Pay me back when you can. I ain't one to hand out advice, but Mom is, and she's going to kick a lake in your ass and stomp it dry when she hears this plan."

"She ain't going to hear anything. I gotta do what I think I should." My talk was brave, but inside I was in turmoil. Without telling Mom, I was going to hop a plane to Seattle and hitch my way to Walla Walla, find Aunt Sally, and sit down with Iris face to face. Simple plan, but I needed money to travel and the nerve to follow through with it. My small bankroll from fishing wouldn't last long, and the only things I had worth selling were my stereo, Dad's rifle, and the GMC pickup. My nerves were already a tangled mess.

"Let me check around," Joe said. "Call me at work tomorrow. Maybe I can sell that truck for you."

The next day I tracked down pothead Carol again, wondering all the time how she and Iris were friends. Yeah, Iris smoked a little pot and drank with the rest of us, but Carol was a walking hash pipe who lived in the ozone. The mystery was solved when I tracked her down the second time. She was in Mike Bennett's VW again rocking out to Led Zeppelin's "Whole Lotta Love." I went straight to the point. "Carol, I need to know where Aunt Sally lives," I said, sticking my head through the veil of pot smoke around her head.

"I told you. She's in Walla Walla." Carol grinned foolishly, then looked at Mike and rolled her eyes.

"What's her address?"

"Her address? Oh yeah, that's a thing, isn't it? Where does Aunt Sally live?" Her head rolled like it had come loose from her shoulders. "Like I write Dear Aunt Sally letters every week."

"Carol, it's kind of important."

"I know, Sam. I know, but I don't know her address."

I started pacing between the parked cars. I needed more than *Aunt Sally in Walla Walla* if I was going to find Iris. "Come on, Carol, I need more! I'm not some private eye like Mike Hammer. How about Aunt Sally's last name?"

Carol looked indignant. "Of course, I know her name. She is my aunt too."

"What?" I thought the pot was talking or she was messing with me. "Are you related to Iris?"

"Related? Shit man, we're sisters." She started giggling. "I thought you knew."

"Sisters? Oh, bullshit, Carol." I was about to walk away and find someone else to help me find Aunt Sally.

"I'm not shitting you, Sam. My Daddy is married to Iris's mom. We're half-sisters anyway. Oh my god! I can't believe I'm going to be Aunty Carol!"

I shook my head. "OK, *Aunty Carol*. What is Aunt Sally's last name?"

"Oh, that?" Carol smiled. "Here I'll write it down for you. Suddenly clear-headed and helpful, she ripped a page from a spiral notebook and wrote, *Sally Martin Walla Walla, WA*. "And," she said, "here's my phone number. If you need anything, Sam. You just call Aunty Carol." She laughed in a spooky make-me-nervous way, but I took the paper, folded it carefully, and put it in my pocket.

"Thanks, Carol. You're a lifesaver." I turned to go when she yelled at my back.

"That's *Aunty Carol*, from now on." Her laughter rang in my ears like a fire alarm.

That evening Mom opened with an interrogation. "Well, Sam, has your young lady been to the doctor yet? I should hope so. Have you talked to her parents? Don't promise them anything. In fact, you should probably just stay away from that girl. There's nothing to be gained by getting involved, Sam. Are you even listening to me? Sam?"

I had a mouthful of meatloaf, so I waved her off, which gave me valuable seconds to think of a response. I decided on a half-truth. "I haven't talked to her, Mom, and I really doubt her parents want to talk to me. You know how people are; I bet they are blaming the whole thing on me."

Mom pushed her plate away and shook her head. "She should know better. She has an obligation."

"Gosh Mom, that's harsh. What obligation?" I scooped the last of the fried potatoes and thought about my plans for the next day. Was I really going to do it? Was this my last dinner at Mom's table? "It was my fault, too, Mom. It's not like she held a gun to my head."

Mom started clearing the table and from the rattle of plates, I could tell she was irritated. "A girl can run faster with her skirt up than a boy can with his pants down," she said, dismissively.

"Come on, Mom. Give me a break. Is that really how you feel?"

"It's her good name, Sam, her virginity. Everybody knows how you boys are, in a constant state of rut. A girl should look out for herself." She moved on, and I could tell she had been thinking about this all day.

"Take your sister" she continued. "She and Peter had been dating for over a year. It's no big surprise that she got in the family way, they wanted to get married anyway. It's a whole different story for this girl, Sam. What on earth was she thinking? Unless she was looking to get you to marry her, and don't you even think about that, mister."

"So, what do you expect me to do?"

"The hardest thing in the world for you, Sam Barger, do nothing. You need to do absolutely nothing. If you were Joe's age, that would be different, I'd expect him to do the right thing and marry her, but you're just a kid, Sam. Trust me, I know what I'm talking about."

By now I was about to swallow my fork. Doing nothing was the last thing on my mind. I had put plans in motion that were the complete opposite of nothing. I didn't like pissing off Mom, but after listening to this diatribe, I knew we were not going to see eye to eye, not ever. I couldn't keep my mouth shut either though.

"It's my fault, too, Mom. It's not fair to just blame Iris. I've heard you say many times, it takes two to tango."

Mom stopped washing dishes and leaned on the counter. She was wearing yellow rubber gloves, and she shook a yellow soapy finger at me. "That may very well be true, but you have no idea how many tangos that girl has been dancing. That's not what you want to hear, I know, but you need to hear it."

ELEVEN

The boarding agent looked at my ticket and smiled. "Student standby, huh? Where are you headed?"

"The ticket says Seattle," I answered with a bluster that really was just a cover for being scared shitless. He glared at me and wrote in large letters on the ticket, *23A.* "Here you go," he said. "Don't wander off. We'll be boarding soon."

I took a deep breath and found a seat where I could look out at the planes squatting on the tarmac while men scurried around their wheels pumping fuel and loading baggage. I spied my duffel in a big cart full of suitcases, and I watched with a sense of finality as the khaki canvas bag was lifted and tossed on the conveyor belt. Most everything I owned was riding that conveyor belt into the belly of the plane. I had already taken my stereo to a pawn shop. Except for clothes and a few books, there wasn't much left in my closet back home. I was banking everything I had on this trip to find Iris.

Joe did sell the truck. I dropped the GMC off at his shop, he handed me two hundred-dollar bills and a fifty, and I took the city bus to the airport. I had a full duffel with a change of clothes and clean underwear, a toiletry kit, and a sleeping bag wrapped in a nylon tarp. My only coat was a whipcord wool jacket that had been Dad's. It was light and durable, and now that I had grown into it, I felt like I was wearing his armor. I told myself Dad would understand and that this is what he would want me to do. "Do something, Humpy, even if it's wrong," he used to say. I was sitting around doing nothing. I wasn't going to know if this was wrong until it was too late, but I couldn't just sit and look at the calendar.

Joe didn't like what I was doing and said so. "I think this is a hare-brained plan, even for you, Humpy, but here." He had pulled a twenty out of his wallet and stuffed it in my jacket pocket. "This is an emergency stash. Don't spend it until you have to. And hide it somewhere away from your other money. In your boot or the watch pocket of your Levi's. You never know."

I nodded with a lump in my throat. "You're a good brother, Joe."

"Yeah," he said. "Whatever. Mom's going to give me hell for this, you know."

"Nothin' you can't handle. Her bite is worse than her bark." We both laughed at the twisted axiom.

This move was one Mom might never forgive me for. It doesn't mean she didn't influence me. I spent the night tossing back and forth on my bed, reliving all the things Mom had said, and more. Mom's final words made me imagine Iris with other guys, but that didn't fit, and I refused the image. But I also remembered every detail of the night together in the back of the Vista Cruiser and felt Iris pressing against me with her bare skin under my hand and the feel of her breath on my neck, the sweet, musky smell of sweat and marijuana smoke. I remembered how I was uncomfortable after we'd done it, and I was thinking, *OK what now?* Then we lay there together in the half light of a June night talking about what was coming this summer and beyond.

I tried to look ahead at the two of us, married and living in my room in Mom's house, and Iris with her belly swollen and her face pale and tired. In another breath, I tried to imagine us giving the baby away and watching a pair of TV-perfect parents carrying our child to their station wagon and driving to a future we couldn't see.

After all that thinking, I couldn't see any way other than the one I chose. If I didn't do this, if I didn't jump on a plane and go find Iris, she was gone forever, pregnant or not. If I stayed home and acted as if nothing had happened, I would have to forget Iris and let that night be just a framed, sweet memory. That didn't carry over into my soul. I couldn't do it. If it hadn't been for me, Iris would still be here in town, accessible, local, and close. Now she was gone because I scared her parents and they didn't want me involved. They didn't want me around at all, but I decided they weren't getting their way. I told myself I could live with all the hassle that came with that decision and hoped I was right.

I boarded the plane and worked my way toward the back. The walk down the aisle felt like going down a tunnel that grew narrower and narrower. I passed row after row of people chatting and looking out the windows. Everything was close, and I couldn't seem to move without bumping someone, and while the other passengers didn't seem to mind the jostling and bumping, the whole experience made the tunnel even narrower. And if there weren't six men behind me waiting to get to their seats, I could have easily turned and run. I could have bailed on the whole trip and gone back home to be safe but guilty and alone.

Then suddenly I was seated and buckled in and looking out the window at the last of the luggage going up the conveyor belt, and a pretty stewardess with a beehive hairdo was taking drink orders from the two GIs sitting next to me. Then the plane was taxiing. With a roar and a thrust that pushed me back against my seat, the plane left the ground. It felt like I was in one of those adventure movies where the hero gets chased to the edge of a cliff and has to jump into the raging river below. The whole flight to Seattle was me free-falling after jumping off my own private cliff.

By the time I had relaxed a bit and the jet had leveled off, the two GIs were smoking and flirting with the stewardess when she served them whiskey and Coke. I ordered a root beer. The one next to me gave an elbow and said, "Here, want a drink?" He poured one of the little bottles of whiskey into my cup and grinned while I sipped cautiously like it might be poisoned.

"Where are you headed?" he asked. He looked to be a couple years older than me, tan and buzzcut like Joe had been when he came home from basic training. "Walla Walla," I said. "Going to see a girl."

"That's a long way to go for a date. She must be special. You got a better ticket than we did." He laughed nervously. Then his buddy leaned over and explained, "We report tomorrow and ship out to 'Nam the day after. Hell of a deal, huh."

"Holy shit," I said. I thought about how this could be me next year. Instead of taking a plane to find Iris, I might be saying goodbye to her for the last time.

"How about you?" the GI asked. "What's your draft lottery number?"

"Not yet," I mumbled. "But it's coming."

"Maybe you'll draw high, and you can stay home. And there's always the three Cs: college, Coast Guard, or Canada." He laughed like he wasn't sure if he should be proud of being drafted or not. I had already made up my mind. Why miss another chance to disappoint Mom.

The other fellow shook his head, "Yup, two dipshit draftees too stupid to go to college and too proud to run Canada." They finished their drinks in one swallow, and I stared out the window, wondering what trajectory our three lives were taking.

My seatmate waved his arm at the stewardess and called, "Hey Sweetie, how about another round?" He elbowed me then, "We'll take care of you too." I nodded and stared down at the mountains and glaciers that stretched away as far as I could see, and the world suddenly seemed much bigger than I had ever imagined.

The GIs kept drinking, and I guess would have, too, if I had their itinerary, but after two whiskey and Cokes, the lack of sleep caught up with me, and I didn't wake up until we were on the ground and people were filing off the plane. One soldier leaned over and patted my shoulder and shook my hand before they left. "You be good to that gal of yours," he said, "and go to college!" He laughed a scared, nervous laugh that was too loud, and I saw him stumble a bit as he moved down the narrow aisle of the plane.

I felt woozy, too, and waited until the other passengers were up and moving before I left my seat and started toward the exit at the front of the plane. The long fall after my jump off the cliff had ended, and my walk off the plane into a warm, rainy August Seattle day felt like landing in the raging river that waited below. There was no turning back now, I thought. Then I remembered Joe's advice. "Call Mom after you land," he said. "Don't keep her worrying. Yeah, she'll be pissed, but she'll be worse if she doesn't hear from you. Call her. Let her rant, then promise to call again. Don't argue, it's a waste of time. Just call her."

I entered the terminal and looked for a pay phone.

TWELVE

The flight to Seattle had been my first, and the jet had a bright and modern feeling, full of the speed to carry me to the future. The bus ride was a whole different story. Walla Walla is far enough south to almost be in Oregon, and the Greyhound made it seem like we were traveling halfway across the country. Every few miles, the bus would leave the highway, weave through some narrow dark streets of a small town, and stop with a groan of brakes.

The whiskey I drank on the plane left me with a headache, and I hungered for the sleep I'd missed the night before I left. I knew I was doing the right thing, but I still couldn't sleep that last night in Anchorage. I was excited to think I would see Iris the next day, but even that anticipation wasn't stronger than exhaustion, so I leaned back in my seat and fell asleep, but I woke every time the bus turned off the highway. Sometimes the stops were quick, and I didn't even come fully awake. Other times I'd leave the bus to pee or buy a candy bar, standing bleary-eyed among other silent, sleepy passengers who didn't have anything to say.

The sun was peeking over the horizon when we pulled into Yakima, and I washed up and bought a couple doughnuts and a coffee. The driver was walking around the bus looking at tires and checking the bus lights, sipping coffee from a paper cup.

"How far to Walla Walla?" I asked, finally feeling awake and ready for the next thing.

"We'll be there before noon," the man said, kicking a tire. "It's going to be a nice day after that rain."

"Feels hot to me already," I volunteered.

He laughed, "You are in for it then, son. Going to be hot tomorrow. Today won't be bad after the rain, but tomorrow. She'll get up there." Then he looked at me and added, "You must not be from around here. Seattle?"

"Alaska," I said.

"Well, hell son, you got a right to be hot," he said. "Let's get you to Walla Walla." He gestured toward the bus. "Load 'em up!"

I climbed on the bus suddenly amazed to realize I had left Alaska for the first time in my life. I had flown on a plane for the first time, and now I was on a Greyhound bus traversing the state of Washington on my way to be a father and a husband maybe, and even with my vivid imagination I couldn't conjure up what that might look like.

I could imagine Iris, though, meeting me at the door of her aunt Sally's house with the surprise on her face and her belly starting to show—as if she would change that much in a few days. She wouldn't hug me; she'd punch me in the shoulder instead, and she'd call me a dumbshit for coming all this way, but she'd really be glad, and maybe Aunt Sally would have a porch with a swing on it like they do in the movies, and we could sit there together in the shade on this hot August day. Iris would look up at me and say, "What's next, big guy?" The movie I'm running in my mind freezes right there, maybe because it's the perfect thing and maybe because I don't know the answer to that question, and there is nothing beyond it that I can see. What would the Hollywood ending to our movie look like?

I turned my attention out the window of the bus, following the lines of apple trees in the orchards we passed and fields full of crops I couldn't recognize. I could see corn turning gold and some pumpkins, more fruit trees, barns like the ones in kids' picture books, and pastures with horses and cows and sheep. "You're a long way from home, Sam

Barger," I heard myself say, and I felt a chill run up my spine because there was another movie running inside my head where Iris didn't smile when she saw me, and she just turned away after saying, "What the hell, Sam, are you kidding?" And that movie goes on with me going back to Alaska alone with my tail between my legs looking like a fool. Was I apprehensive? Maybe just a little.

The phonebook in the Walla Walla bus station looked like somebody's dog used it for a chew toy, but I was able to find the Ms and locate an "S Martin" on Poplar Street. I considered calling first but thought the better of it. I might have a bright fantasy of my arrival, but I had to remind myself that there was no reason to think I would be any more welcome at the Martin house than I was at the Davis's.

I found a street map in the bus station, figured out that Aunt Sally lived about a mile away, and then went to the toilet to wash and put on a clean shirt before I set out to walk the last leg of my journey under the hot midday sun.

I walked along tree-lined streets through neighborhoods with smooth green lawns and old-fashioned houses with porches and shiplap siding. My duffel wasn't heavy, but it was hot against my back and sweat ran down my spine before I'd walked three blocks and realized what a waste it was to put on a clean shirt. Across the street, I noticed that the trees shaded the sidewalks, so I crossed and sought the shade of those trees all the way down the street.

I wished I had a canteen of water, but I hadn't planned that well, so I walked on trying to ignore the blister starting to form on my heel where the right boot was rubbing. I figured I was halfway to the Martins' house when I passed a baseball park with a restroom and water fountain, so I called a pit stop and dropped the pack for a few minutes while I drank and took a leak.

Ten minutes later I walked up the steps to a house on Poplar Street and knocked on the door. Indeed, the house had a porch with a swing and flowers decorating the margins of the small yard. My stomach churned and my mouth was dry. I reminded myself that the last time I knocked on someone's door like this I got punched in the face. I touched the scab by my left eye.

A pretty, middle-aged woman in a flowered blouse and blue Bermuda shorts answered the door. She looked at me through the screen door and asked, "Can I help you?"

"I hope so," I said, taking a deep breath, "I'm Sam Barger, and I'm here to see Iris."

THIRTEEN

The woman behind the screen door, who I dearly hoped was Aunt Sally, looked over my rumpled clothes, long hair, duffel, and cowboy boots like I was a secondhand chair at a yard sale. "Iris Davis?" she asked. "What makes you think she'd be here?"

Her response was full of promise. She hadn't slammed the door yet, and she seemed to know who I was talking about. My breath quickened as I realized that I hadn't taken this trip in vain. I pressed my advantage. "Are you Sally Martin, ma'am? Aunt Sally?"

She smiled. "I am. Though I don't think I'm your Aunt Sally." She cocked her head to one side studying my face, waiting for me to sell myself to her like a door-to-door salesman selling vacuum cleaners.

"Well, yes ma'am. I mean no ma'am. I'm Iris's—uh friend from Alaska, ma'am, and I came all this way to see her." Under Aunt Sally's scrutiny, I was sweating even in the shade of the porch. I wiped my face and wished I could drop the pack, which was digging into my shoulders. "I came all this way, ma'am hoping we could talk. You see I'm—"

Suddenly, she pushed open the screen door and held it wide open. "I know who you are, Sam Barger, and you're about to *ma'am* me to death. Come in here and let's you and I have a glass of iced tea."

I nearly fell into the open doorway, but first I dropped my pack on the front porch. "Thank you, ma'am." Then I laughed nervously.

"No need to leave your rucksack out here unless you're planning a fast getaway. Bring it in with you. The neighbors will think I'm taking in hobos." She grinned and I got the feeling she wouldn't care what the neighbors thought anyway.

We passed through the living room, with its brown plaid couch and wooden end tables settled on a tan shag carpet. The kitchen was bright white except for the flowered oilcloth table cover and red curtains on the window. The dish drainer was full of clean dishes, and I tried to imagine Iris having breakfast at this very table.

Aunt Sally handed me a glass of water that I drank in one swallow. Then she took a pitcher of tea from the fridge and settled us at the kitchen table. I looked around, hoping to see Iris or some sign that she was there, but the bright and tidy bungalow gave me no hint that Iris might be about.

Aunt Sally looked over her glass of tea with a grin and asked, "So what on earth brings you to Walla Walla, Sam Barger?"

Something told me she was having a bit of fun at my expense, and I willingly played along. "I'm from Alaska, Iris and I go to school together. Or at least we did. I graduated last this spring." I felt a lump in my throat, so I took a drink of tea. "Now I guess she's here living with you for a while."

"I see." The face never wavered. She wasn't going to make this easy for me.

"Yes, ma'am. Well." I paused and felt cornered. "Here's the deal. Me and Iris—Iris and I never got a chance to talk things through, and I couldn't just leave things hanging like that, so here I am. And I really need to talk to her. Is that OK?"

Aunt Sally stood up and pushed in her chair. I started to rise like Mom tried to teach me, this thing where guys should stand whenever a woman gets out of her chair. "Sit down, Sam. I thought you might eat a bite. Pour yourself some more tea."

"Wow. Yes. Thank you."

"So you and Iris are close then," she asked.

I couldn't help smiling at her feigned ignorance. "Really close. Well, I guess you know. I got her—you know, uh, pregnant." The word hit the floor like a muddy boot, and I knew I was blushing bright red and so glad Aunt Sally was working with her back to me building bologna sandwiches.

Aunt Sally spun around and leaned back on the counter, wiping her hands on a dish towel. Thank goodness she was smiling. "There. That wasn't so hard was it? I just wanted to hear you say it."

"Ma'am?"

"I wanted to hear you announce your part in this little soap opera."

"I guess it kinda looks like one, but it's not—"

"And I'm sorry, Sam, but Iris is not here and that's my fault. Let me finish these sandwiches, and I'll tell you all about it."

I slumped in my chair and looked at the floor. Suddenly, I was tired. It was like she had cut a vein and drained the blood out of me. What a stupid wild goose chase. I had to wonder, then, how I talked myself into it. I had traveled all this way, pissed off my mom, and spent half my summer wages, and here I was sitting in Walla Walla, Washington, eating lunch with a total stranger. I wanted to run, but Aunt Sally did promise to tell me all about it, and I was hungry.

I was at least in a good news–bad news situation. The bad news: I hadn't found Iris. But good news: I hadn't been punched in the nose, and Aunt Sally didn't seem like she was going to throw me out on my ear. Besides that, she was about to tell me what was going on, and no one had done that for a while. I pushed aside my disappointment and tried to keep my mind from racing ahead. That bologna sandwich couldn't come fast enough.

"I hope you like onions. We're famous for our onions, you know." There were in fact two bologna sandwiches. White bread, onion, tomato, lettuce, and two slices of bologna. In spite of my misery, the food made me realize I was hungry. "Thank you, those look delicious," I said. "I think I missed breakfast, and maybe supper too. Just had some doughnuts in Yakima."

"Well, eat hearty, Sam, you've got a long road ahead of you." I thought she meant the road back home, but she didn't. With that introduction, I ate sandwiches, and Aunt Sally brought me up to date on the adventures of Iris and Sam.

"First off, Sam, you need to know that Iris is a sweet girl, and I love her dearly. Her father on the other hand, well, he's quite a piece o' work. Anyway, Iris's mom called me in tears one night telling me how her life was ruined, Iris's life was ruined, and she'd never be able to show her face in public again. It took a while, but she told me what happened and how this terrible young man was trying to steal her daughter. She was terrified that Iris was going to run off and marry you, but she made it sound like you were going to kidnap poor Iris and spirit her away. *You aren't a kidnapper, are you?*" Aunt Sally was a lively storyteller who used her hands and voice to add drama to the telling.

By then I had inhaled one sandwich and was gulping iced tea. "No ma'am. Matter of fact, I have never been able to get Iris to do anything she didn't want to do." I added, "She's really forceful. My mom would call her a willful child."

Aunt Sally chuckled. "Good, I'm glad to hear it. Her mother was so convinced that you were going to ruin all their plans that they decided Iris should come to my house for the school year and go through her pregnancy far away from the circle of gossip and, especially, far away from the evil Sam Barger. You really worked them up."

"I know. I found out the hard way."

"So you've talked to them? Iris's parents, I mean."

"I tried, but all I got was hung up on. Then one day, I went to the door and got punched in the face."

Sally shook her head. "That son of a bitch, I wanted to punch him. You see they showed up here with the plan in place, which was fine with me. I'd love to have Iris for the winter. What do I care if she's pregnant? Anyway, to make a long story short, they show up and poor Iris is a mess. She is not happy at all about leaving Alaska and being here, and they won't let her call you. Her parents are ramrodding this whole show and have this expectant mama on a short lease.

"Well, I open my big mouth and say that Iris needs to have a voice in where she is and what happens to the baby when it comes, and so on and so forth. Her daddy got up on his high horse and made Janet—that's Iris's mom—throw a fit at me for stirring the pot. I finally told them that if Iris was staying with me, it was going to be my rules, and no, I wouldn't keep her from talking to you, and I even suggested that we all decide together what happens to the baby."

I had eaten through two sandwiches by then and wanted to hear the punchline. I wanted to yell, "Where is Iris?" But I didn't. I just nodded and listened.

"That all went over like a fart in church." Aunt Sally continued, "And with not so much as a by-your-leave, they were gone. It was like a tornado come through here. Whoosh! And here I am with egg on my face knowing full well I should have kept my mouth shut and then Iris would be here with me watching you eat bologna sandwiches. Do you want another? It's no bother."

I smiled at my answer and nodded. "Thank you, ma'am. I was so hungry my stomach thought my throat was cut. But I'm good now."

I was trying to imagine Iris sitting through all of this, and how she must have really felt cornered. "So Iris just went along with all of this?"

Aunt Sally placed a plate of store-bought cookies in front of me and patted my shoulder. "I don't think the poor girl had much choice," she said, "and her daddy had a firm hand on her the whole time. I mean he had his hand on her shoulder making sure she stayed where he put her. Iris has a lot of spunk, Sam. But right now she's a scared little girl with two parents leaning hard on her. And nobody's asking her what she wants. Shoot, I didn't have five minutes alone with her to find out where her head was at."

I was feeling antsy and got up to pace the kitchen and fill my water glass from the tap. The kitchen looked out over a large yard with a vegetable garden in the back. I was near to crying looking out there imagining Iris in one of those summer dresses that girls who live in houses with front porch swings wear, picking fruit off the trees that shaded the fence along the alley. I felt weak and helpless and alone, yeah, and a little stupid. It was how Mom warned me it would be. A dead end with the only road leading back to Alaska without Iris. Maybe I was going home with my tail between my legs.

I breathed deeply and turned to Aunt Sally. I could tell she was giving me room to gather all this into my brain and heart. "I don't know what to do now," I admitted. "I had it all planned up to this point, and I never imagined something different. I mean I just knew she would be here."

"Well, she said, "How do you think Iris is feeling right now? You know her. What do you think she wants?"

I shifted in my chair and looked at my hands. "She's probably scared and nervous like me I guess. And last time we talked, she was still trying to figure this out. We didn't plan this, you know."

"People rarely do. And you are certainly not the first to end up in this predicament. Why do you think they have these maternity homes all over the place? There are lots of kids out there having babies before they are ready."

"Maternity homes? Like hospitals?"

Aunt Sally poured herself more tea and sighed. "No, they are like boarding homes for unwed mothers. They go there when they are a few months along and stay until they have their babies." She stopped and looked out the window with a face gone sad like she'd seen something out in the yard.

"And?"

"And the mom stays with the baby for a few days, then it gets adopted, and the girl goes home. Or sometimes she never sees the baby at all. Just whisks them away, they do. That's how the fight started with Iris's dad. We were just getting Iris settled when he told me that was his new plan. Iris put up a fight, and I took her side."

"So, old man Davis had it all figured out, and Iris didn't have any say. That's how I feel. Why don't I get to be part of the discussion? Don't I have a chance to weigh in?"

Aunt Sally chuckled. "You are special, Sam. Most guys in your situation tend to run the other way, fast. Most guys make themselves scarce or claim the baby isn't theirs. But here you are trying to elbow your way in. That's pretty classy, but dear boy, if they won't listen to what Iris wants, do you think they'll listen to you?"

"I just want to do the right thing."

"Don't we all. Don't we all. But Iris's dad thinks that means the baby goes away, and everyone moves on like it never happened."

We both sat quiet for a few minutes, treading water in a pool of sadness.

"Sam," she said finally, "why don't you get your rucksack and put it in the room down the hall."

"What?" I was confused and only half listening.

"You just stay here tonight. It will give you time to think, and I will send you off with a good breakfast tomorrow."

I slumped back against the kitchen counter and looked around like I had just awakened in a strange place. "I can't just stay here. I—"

"Yes, you can. It will give us time to talk more. Now go get that rucksack." She pointed, and I obeyed. I had no compass, no map, and no guidance, so I just parked myself in Aunt Sally's guest room and pouted.

When Aunt Sally went out to run errands, I wandered into the backyard and picked an apple off a tree and ate it, something I had never done before. Then I picked a tomato, it was hot from the sun, and I ate it with the warm juice running down my chin. I took off my cowboy boots and let my sweaty feet dry in the sun and walk on the cool grass. Aunt Sally's was a quiet neighborhood, and I felt alone there without the interruption of cars or kids or barking dogs. I sat in a metal lawn chair and the knot in my stomach loosened, and I began to think more clearly. I realized that I had only two routes to choose from. Go home or go on.

With that realization, the lights came on in the control tower of my brain. All I had to do was turn left or right, home to Mom's I-told-you-so head nods or on down the road to find Iris. It wasn't really a choice at all. The whole process took less than a minute, and it injected me with adrenaline that jacked me up, so I couldn't sit still. I paced the lawn and then wandered into the garage and found a lawnmower. I mowed the lawn—both ways like Mom likes it—then went to the kitchen for water. Going out the backdoor, I found loose hinges on the screen door and used tools I found in the garage to fix them. Then I mowed the small front lawn and edged the driveway.

By the time Aunt Sally returned, I was sunburned and smiling, ready to convince her to help me find where Iris might be. It was a sure bet her folks didn't take her back to Alaska, and that meant there was probably some relative out there somewhere willing to open their door to a pregnant teenager and her parents.

Lucky for me, Sally Martin was a willing ally, and we soon narrowed the possibilities down to an uncle in New Mexico and a distant cousin in Nebraska. After a couple discreet phone calls, Sally turned to me with an impish grin and said, "It looks like our girl is in New Mexico."

FOURTEEN

The main road heading south out of Walla Walla is Highway 125, and that's where I was standing with my thumb out with the early morning sun peeking over the horizon and the traffic moving briskly in both directions. I had only been standing for about fifteen minutes when a farm truck with two men in the cab stopped and the passenger rolled down his window. "Where you headed, kid?"

I pointed with my chin, "New Mexico. I can ride in the back." I looked hopefully at the empty truck bed. I had enough experience hitching at home to know that there was a pretty good chance that hitchhiking would be a faster way to get to New Mexico than taking a bus that would meander through the countryside stopping at every small town and wander deep into the heart of any big city. I had no patience for that.

"Well, we ain't going to New Mexico, but we can get you to Oregon. Hop in the back. Bang on the cab when you're set."

That's how I got on the road to New Mexico and one state closer to finding Iris. Not only did I have a ride out of Washington but I had the name of a town I could head to—Las Vegas in northern New Mexico. But none of this is as simple as it sounds in the telling. We had narrowed our search to Bob Davis in New Mexico, but we had no address and no plan on how to get there. I only knew that Iris's dad wasn't going to give our baby away without me and Iris having a say in it. At least we had Aunt Sally on our side.

However, hitchhiking southbound at the crack of dawn was not part of Aunt Sally's big plan. Her idea was going to involve endless phone conversations, getting Mom, Iris's folks, me, and Iris to all agree that I actually should have a say in this whole thing. Ha! She had the idea that we would work the phone lines to track down where Iris was and then actually get Iris on the phone with Aunt Sally and then with me. But first, she put me through the third degree. "So Sam, I'm guessing you left Anchorage in a bit of a hurry, and I'm betting you are skipping school to do this."

I squirmed in my seat. "I've graduated, but Mom wanted me to start college. So yeah, you could say that."

"And your parents? Do they even know about this? Do they know where you are at all?"

We were sitting in the living room of Aunt Sally's, surrounded by fragile china knickknacks and spindly looking end tables. "My dad is dead," I said. "There's just Mom."

Aunt Sally was sipping tea out of a fine porcelain cup with a rose on it. It reminded me of the kind of things Mom liked around her. "And?" She said, skeptically, "You are here with her blessing?"

"Well—"

Sally set her cup down firmly. "Just as I thought. Young man, can you imagine what she's going through right now? My goodness, Sam. You can't just run off and not tell your mother."

I could feel the heat on my back. She had gotten to me that time. I had seen Mom upset enough over the years since Dad died that I knew what that looked like, and it hurt like hell when I couldn't do anything about it. I had been the source of Mom's angst enough times that it shocked my soul that I had done it again. "I left her a note," I said with the guilt spilling out of my eyes as I did. "And I tried to call when I landed in Seattle."

Sally nodded. "Your mother needs to hear from you. And you'll get no help from me until you do." She stood, smoothed her dress, and picked up her tea cup. "I'm going to the kitchen and make us some dinner. You know, Sam, my mama always said, 'Look at how a man treats his mother, and you'll know how he'll treat his wife.'"

I could only nod. I got the hint though. Sally started toward the kitchen, then stopped in the doorway and turned back to me, her face stern. "There is a phone right there." She gestured at the phone on a table by the window. "Call your mother, Sam, tell her you're OK and that you'll be home in a couple of days."

I jumped to my feet—that standing thing when a lady stands up. I almost fell over before I sat back down. "A couple days? What do you mean? I'm going to find Iris."

"Oh Sam, honey, you can't do that. No, no. I said we'd find her, and we will, but you can talk to her on the phone that's all. Then I expect you to go home to your mom and school and start being a teenager again."

Mad this time, I stood up. "I thought you were on my side, on our side. I'm a part of this, you know. How come everybody wants to cut me out?" I felt myself getting hot and ready to say mean things, but I was also embarrassed to be talking so rudely to this woman. "I'm sorry," I said, "I'm just—"

"I know. Simmer down and call your mother." Aunt Sally shook her head. "Dinner in about thirty minutes. Don't call collect. This one's on me." She disappeared into the kitchen, and I was left alone with my frustration and a black telephone staring me in the face.

The phone was cold against my ear, and I was so nervous I misdialed a couple times and had to start over. Then I heard Mom on the other end and felt warm and comforted by that. "Hey. It's me, Mom. I'm in Walla Walla, Washington."

"Sam? My word, you sound just like your brother. Are you OK?"

"Yeah, Mom. I'm fine. I know you're mad, but as I said in the note I left you, I had to do this." When I stopped talking, my mouth was dry and my throat tight. Mom didn't say anything. I imagined her cradling the phone against her shoulder while she lit a cigarette and let the silence bludgeon me.

When she spoke her voice was dripping with disappointment. "So what have you accomplished with this little escapade of yours? Are you two getting married? Is that what this is all about?"

"Mom." She didn't stop.

"I imagine her parents will have something to say about that—though, obviously, I don't have that luxury. I'm surprised you even bothered to call."

"Mom."

"You know I had a call from this girl's parents. They had the nerve to tell me they didn't want you around their daughter. Can you believe that?"

"Mom, would you listen?"

"It's like they want to make it my son's fault that their daughter is a little tramp."

"Mom! Stop it!" I was nearly yelling into the phone, and I was sure Aunt Sally could hear me. Finally, Mom took a breath, and I was able to get a word in edgewise. "Listen, her name is Iris, and she's not a tramp. I never said I was going to marry her, and I wouldn't without telling you first. In fact, I think I need your permission." I was making things up as I went along. "I just wanted you to know that I'm OK and that I'm not going to do anything stupid. I just want to be a part of whatever happens with Iris and, you know, the pregnancy—the baby." I had to stop and control my breathing before I cried or something stupid like that.

"You're not going to do anything stupid?" The sarcasm was as thick as cold gravy. "You mean like running halfway across the country after some girl?"

"Mom, that's not helping." What it was doing was making me feel homesick and vulnerable. I suddenly felt so remote from all things familiar that I felt paralyzed, frozen in place like a rabbit surprised in the woods. I sat forward on the edge of a big easy chair and stared out the window without seeing the kids riding bikes on the sidewalk and the cars passing on the street. My mother's voice seemed to drone on like a fan in the background of this empty scene.

"By the way. You got a postcard."

"What? I'm sorry, what? A postcard?"

"Yes, a postcard. Sam, are you listening to me at all? It has a picture of a very large and very old hotel. The caption says Montezuma's Castle. Shall I read the back?"

A postcard! I jumped to my feet, the freezing spell had broken. "I'm here, Mom, what's it say?"

"The postcard. Not much. It's from a girl I'd guess from all flourish in penmanship. It says '*The weather is here. I wish you were beautiful. Haha. from: That Girl you Knew once.*' That doesn't make any sense at all. I take it this girl you knew once is Iris."

Iris! I knew it. "Where's it from, Mom?" I was restlessly pacing around the room as far as the phone cord would let me.

"I'm sorry, Sam, there is no return address."

"The postmark. Look at the postmark, Mom."

"It's too smudged to read, Sam. Maybe New Mexico. But the city, forget it. And who doesn't sign a postcard?"

I took a deep breath. I felt like a guy in a detective novel, scrounging for clues wherever I could. "The postcard, Mom. Is there anything printed on it . . . like where it came from?"

"My gracious, calm down, let me look. Wait, I take it you didn't find what you were looking for in Walla Walla. Is Iris not there?" It was the first time Mom had said her name. She wasn't "the tramp" or "that girl" anymore. She was Iris.

"No, Mom, she's not here. I just want to find her and talk to her and be responsible, so she knows I'm not running out on her." I flopped on Aunt Sally's couch.

"I do understand, son, I do. You just don't realize that I have a bit more experience with these things than you do. Someday you will. And the postcard, it just says, Montezuma Castle, Las Vegas, New Mexico. I thought Las Vegas was in Nevada. You want me to spell it."

"Got it, Mom." Aunt Sally was right! In my mind, I was already on the highway with my thumb out heading south.

"I suppose that's where you are going next." She said it like a question.

"Yup, and, no, I won't do anything stupid." Probably another lie. "I'll be catching the bus in the morning, and I'll call when I get there." Another lie.

The conversation ended with Mom checking if I was eating and had money. Finally, an admonition to be safe.

"OK, Mom. Gotta go. Iris's aunt has dinner ready."

"Behave yourself and turn a hand while you're there."

"Yes, Mom. I already mowed the lawn . . . both ways." I was nearly bouncing off the ceiling. Iris was in Las Vegas, New Mexico. How far could that be?

"Oh, Sam. You got another letter."

Another letter? I didn't get mail except for Columbia Record Sales, and Mom usually threw those out. "From the Selective Service, probably reminding you to register for the draft."

"Got to go, Mom, thanks." Yeah thanks, Mom. I really needed to be reminded that Uncle Sam might want my ass too. Talk about good news–bad news. For now, though, forget Uncle Sam, Young Daddy Sam was heading for New Mexico.

"Sam, how about some dinner?" came the call from the kitchen. I played it cool all through the meal and fidgeted restlessly with my mind racing ahead. I wouldn't wait for Aunt Sally's plan for playing phone detective, and I certainly wasn't going back to Alaska. I spent the evening making polite small talk, doing the dishes, and taking out the trash before I went to bed. Well before daylight I lit out and headed for the highway leading south out of Walla Walla.

My farm truck ride dropped me at a crossroads with a gas station and fruit stand. I bought a candy bar and picked up a map at the gas station, then visited the fruit stand and left with an apple in each hand and one in each pocket. The apples were hard and pungent with the smell of the orchard still on them. If I wasn't so driven to get down the road to New Mexico, I could have hung at that fruit and vegetable stand until they ran me off as a nuisance. I stuffed three apples in my pack and stuck my thumb out while I ate the other one. The apple was so crisp that it cracked when I bit into it. It surprised me that it wasn't soft and mushy. I thought how different this was from the old tired apples I knew back in Alaska that were brown, spotted, and soft like the dead carcass of an apple compared to these fresh, ripe beauties I balanced in my hand. I thought about going back for more.

I had barely finished the apple when a Ford Econoline van passed me and pulled over to the shoulder. A friendly face with a half-assed beard stuck his head out, "Hop in, dude."

"Thanks," I said and popped the back door, tossed in my duffel, then climbed in. The van was set up with a mattress and sleeping bags that reeked of pot smoke and cigarettes. A pair of long-haired heads with scraggly beards turned and grinned at me.

The driver was named Kurt, and he had a round face with a wispy beard that didn't have much hair to it, and the passenger went by Ziggy and was a lean guy with thick curly hair and a beard that most guys would envy. "Wanna finish this roach?" said Ziggy, holding out an alligator clip on a leather thong pinching the stub of a joint.

"No, I'm good," I said. "It's early for me."

Kurt pulled the van out into the highway behind a truckload of potatoes. "You ain't a narc, are ya?" He looked over his shoulder and laughed.

Ziggy slapped his shoulder. "God man, look at him. Narc-shark. You in the dark? He's cool. I can read it."

Kurt giggled, "Now you a poet, Zig man?"

"Poet smo-it," said Ziggy. "You back off. Look at him, man. Clean-cut country boy."

Kurt jabbed a thumb in my direction, "Could be a junior G-man. Undercover cowboy."

I laughed, "Yeah, that's me. An undercover agent sent to podunk Oregon to arrest guys smoking pot in a Ford van."

Ziggy put his hands in the air. "You got us, man." Then we all laughed together in a way that made me feel like none of us really trusted the other. Through the morning, I learned that Ziggy was on the run from the draft board, and Kurt had to leave Seattle in a hurry for some other reason. He never said why, and I didn't ask. I sat in the back on the dirty sleeping bags and listened to the banter.

"So Zig, what do ya think? Cruise due south and get to Mexico? Score some mushrooms, and you know they got some serious weed. It's like everywhere down there."

Ziggy rolled a joint while he talked. "I could do that. I could seriously do that. But how are you an expert on Mexican weed." Crosby, Stills, and Nash were strumming guitars in the background. "But, ya know, they got that peyote shit over in Arizona, and we don't speak Spanish, amigo."

"I hear you can talk to God when you take that peyote," said Kurt. "And he doesn't speak Spanish, I know that much, but you gotta find that peyote like out in the desert right? In Mexico, you can buy shit right on the street like chewing gum." The joint was being passed back and forth fast. I didn't even ask for a hit, but I was getting high from the smoke filling the van.

"Talk to God? What the hell do you want to talk to God for? You know you're making Mexico sound a lot better now," said Ziggy. "There ain't no God in Mexico, I figure . . . and no draft board. Just women and weed."

"That's what I need!"

"Need smeed. We could go to New Mexico with Sam the sham here. They speak English there, don't they, Sam?"

"What? Me? Yeah, I think so. It is a state, you know." I leaned forward, feeling more a part of the conversation. "They can arrest you there, too, for draft evasion. Just a thought."

Ziggy looked confused, "So it's like Mexico, but it's not?"

"Just go to Mexico," I said. "You can always learn the language."

Kurt nodded and smiled. "See, I told you. Mexico, here we come!"

I napped part of the morning, laying back on a dirty sleeping bag with my jacket keeping my face off the toxic fabric. As I dozed before sleeping I reveled in the miles I was covering that were bringing me closer to Iris. Yeah, I might have trouble finding her once I got to Las Vegas, but I was still in that confident delusional state that had led me down this path in the first place. I would figure something out.

I woke to find Kurt asleep beside me and Ziggy driving. Kurt smelled worse than the sleeping bags, so I helped myself to the empty front seat and peered around at the fields and barns flowing past. "Yeah, ol' Kurt gets sleepy when he smokes," chatted Ziggy, over the music of Crosby, Stills, and Nash on the cassette player, the same tape playing over and over. "Look at those farms. Imagine all the pot you could grow there."

I dug an apple out of my pack. "You want an apple?" I offered. "They're amazing." I held it out to him.

He took it and bit into it. "What's so damn special? It's a damn apple. You ain't from around here are you?"

I bit the other apple and felt young and naive. "No shit. I'm from Alaska. By the time we get apples, they are pretty old and beat up."

Ziggy waved at the fields we were passing. "Guess you got nothin' like this up there in the land of ice and snow. Why in the hell are you going to New Mexico?"

I was suddenly self-conscious and didn't want to tell the story of chasing my pregnant girlfriend across the continent. The Iris thing was mine and a private sort of quest for me, and somehow I didn't want Ziggy to hear about it. I imagined him making fun like he did about the apples—and those were amazing apples. "I'm just going to see a friend there, checking out the country. You know." I tried to sound cool and confident, but even to me, I sounded fake.

"That's cool, man." Then Ziggy pulled the van off the road for gas. The gas station sat alone at a crossroads, a cinder block cube with a Texaco star on the post out front.

Kurt woke up confused and swearing when the van stopped, and Ziggy shut off the engine. "Just in time," he said when he realized where we were. "I gotta piss like a racehorse."

Ziggy laughed as Kurt bolted from the back of the van. "I don't figure a racehorse pisses any more than any other horse, do you?" The gas station attendant pulled the nozzle off the gas pump. "Fill 'er up?" he asked. He was a gray-haired man in greasy coveralls and an old-style flat top.

When I saw Ziggy fumbling in his pockets for money, I spoke up, "Yeah, fill it." I pulled out my wallet and handed Ziggy a ten-dollar bill. "You're all right, my man," Ziggy took the ten and passed it under his nose before handing it to the attendant while I stuffed my wallet back in my jeans and then headed off to drain my bladder. By the time I got back to the van, the boys were ready to roll, and Kurt had a lap full of candy bars.

"These were on sale," he laughed, "five-finger discount." Then he laughed and tossed me a Snickers bar. I was halfway through it before I realized he had lifted them, and I started looking cautiously out the back window.

"You always find the bargains, Kurt," said Ziggy. "You do have the knack."

"Call me five-finger Jack 'cause I got the knack." Kurt was dancing in his seat and eating candy bars while I fretted in the back seat and waited for the sound of sirens. I realized then that the attendant probably hadn't even realized he'd been robbed. That stolen candy bar didn't sit well in my stomach though, and I didn't ask for another.

That evening we pulled in to an empty campground just off the highway. Several giant cottonwoods shaded a stream that ran between a steep bluff and the highway. I gathered fallen branches and built a fire.

"Well, you're a regular wilderness scout, there, Alaskaman," said Kurt. He sat on the wooden picnic table and opened two cans of pork and beans. "Look at him build that fire, Zig. Ain't that somethin'." Zig was rolling a joint and grunted.

"I got some hot dogs in my pack," I said. "I'll cut some sticks." I wandered into the brush to find some willow wands for roasting hot dogs. These two were not the kind I'd choose to hang out with, but it was good to have some company, and I did like camping out and cooking over a fire. I had a pot and some oatmeal and coffee for breakfast in my duffel and a sleeping bag that was plenty warm for eastern Oregon in September. I had looked at my map and figured we'd be in Utah by tomorrow, and with any luck, I could be in New Mexico by the next day. But that depended on which way Kurt and Ziggy would decide to travel. Then all I had to do was find a ride to the town called Las Vegas and take a gamble that I could find Iris there.

After a dinner of canned beans and hot dogs, we sat around a fire smoking pot and sipping whisky from a bottle Kurt had under the driver's seat. Mostly conversation consisted of a Kurt and Ziggy debate about the virtues of going to Mexico versus the chance of scoring some peyote somewhere else. It was a rerun of the conversation in the van but flavored with alcohol and pot. They wore me out enough that I went right to sleep in my bag rolled out on the ground with my jacket for a pillow.

The next morning all that wondering about Iris and New Mexico was pushed to the back of my mind when I woke up and couldn't find my pants.

FIFTEEN

The bright sun of a late summer morning nearly blinded me when I woke and shoved my throbbing head out of the sleeping bag. I reached for my pants but didn't find them, so I reached for my bag thinking they might be in there. No luck. In fact my duffle was missing too. "OK guys," I said, "very funny." No answer, but then I noticed that the dirty Ford Econoline was also gone. "What the hell?" I said. I would have yelled, but my head was pounding. Even my eyes hurt. The campground was empty. No van, no Kirk, no Ziggy.

I was pissed, hungover, and cold, so I sat at the picnic table and pulled the sleeping bag over my legs. "Did those two really rip me off?" I asked myself. I could see my boots on the other side of the campfire and hobbled over to grab them and pull them on. It was starting to dawn on me that my friendly shoplifting, draft-dodging, pothead buddies had robbed me of everything I had except my beat-up cowboy boots, a sleeping bag, and the jacket and shirt I had rolled up for a pillow. "You dirty sons a bitches," I yelled at the empty campground, letting the words beat on my tender head. I was shivering by the cold campfire and trying to calm my temper enough to figure out what I was going to do when I heard a vehicle pull into the campground. I scrambled back into my sleeping bag and watched as the sound grew closer. Maybe I was wrong, maybe the boys just went to get coffee or breakfast. Maybe they were coming back with breakfast, and taking my pants was just a joke.

No such luck. A blue station wagon stopped at the toilet, and a lone man made his morning pit stop. I needed to do the same, so still in my sleeping bag, I hopped over to the picnic table and sat down to wait my turn. While I waited, I looked around the campsite. Maybe some of my stuff was still here somewhere. Maybe the two bastards hadn't taken everything. Who steals a guy's pants, anyway. I wondered how long they had been gone. Like it mattered. It wasn't like I had any way to chase them across southern Oregon.

When the station wagon left, I walked over to the toilet for my turn at a morning go. My head was pounding and my stomach churned as I sat on the john and plotted how to solve the problem of being broke and pantsless in the middle of Oregon.

"Broke is bad," I said to no one at all. "And being stuck out in the middle of nowhere is a pain. But going without pants is really going to present a challenge." I was going to have to try and hitchhike in this condition. The best I could do was tie my flannel shirt around my waist and hope some driver would give me the benefit of the doubt.

Needless to say, it didn't take long to break camp with only a sleeping bag to roll and my shirt to tie around my waist. I was just leaving the campground when I took a hopeful look in the trash can by the toilet. Lying on top was a pair of blue jeans, my jeans. I pulled them out and shook them free, looking for my wallet, hoping it tumbled to the ground. No luck. The garbage can was half empty, so I dug through the paper cups and bean cans until I got frustrated and dumped the contents of the can on the ground and started pushing around the potato chip bags and beer cans.

I heard a crunch of tires on gravel again and lifted my head to see a pickup truck with an Oregon State Parks logo stop beside the toilet. The driver's side window opened, and a face appeared above an elbow pointing at me. "What the hell do you think you're doing?"

The man wore a baseball cap with a logo matching the insignia on the truck door.

"Well, I guess from your perspective this looks pretty screwed up."

"That's an understatement."

"Doesn't look so good from where I'm standing either."

He nodded and scratched his cheek. "Why the hell are you digging through the trash in your underwear?"

"I guess I could put on my pants."

"Good idea." Then he took off his aviator sunglasses. "Are you shopping for breakfast or looking for treasure?"

I tried to put on my pants and nearly fell over. "Well, if I find the treasure I'll be able to have breakfast." I realized then that I was still a little drunk.

"Do I have to get out of the truck?"

"No. No. I'm sorry. Two assholes ripped me off. They stole my wallet and left my pants in the trashcan. They took my pack too. I thought my wallet might be here."

He rested his arms on the door and leaned out to look at the pile of trash. "Is that it, there by the pork and beans can?" Feeling dizzy and dry-mouthed, I bent over with my hands on my knees.

"That's it!" The money was gone, but my driver's license and picture of Iris were still tucked in the worn leather wallet. I stared longingly at the photo, a Polaroid cropped to fit in the plastic photo sleeve. Iris was sitting on the tailgate of my truck in cutoffs and a tank top and giving me that don't-take-my-picture look. The day of that photo seemed so far in the past now. I checked the pants pockets and found three quarters and a dime; my pocketknife was gone. The Boy Scout knife I'd carried since I was twelve, the same knife that Joe teased me about because I was never a Boy Scout was now with the two jerks in a Ford Econoline van. I got pissed one more time.

"Thanks again," I said to the park ranger. "After I pick up this trash, can you give me a ride into town or wherever?"

"No can do. Can't have civilians riding in a state truck. I'd lose my job." I saw him dig for something, then he reached out the window with three one-dollar bills in his hand. "Here's some money for breakfast."

I took the money and thanked him a third time. "It's a nice morning for a walk anyway." The prospect of hitchhiking was more appealing now that I had some pants to wear.

He smiled like he was reading my mind. "And with your pants on, you should be able to get a ride pretty easily. Maybe stick your hair under a hat or something."

I nodded and started picking up trash while he drove away. "I'm knee-deep in shit now," I said. "Maybe it's time to stop digging." Just as the sun peeked over the bluff above the campground, I shouldered my bedroll and followed the gravel road out to the highway.

Traffic was slow, and I stood for quite a while on the shoulder trying to look clean-cut and harmless. I didn't have a hat so I combed my hair flat and tucked it behind my ears. I put my thumb out, smiled pitifully, and watched the eyes of drivers as they passed me. Some looked at me like I was an alien dropped from some unknown planet, and others gave me a fearful gaze like I might jump in the back of their truck if they weren't careful, but most weren't looking at all. They only watched the road ahead as if eye contact would give me recognition of their guilt for not stopping.

In spite of my attempts to look friendly and hopeful, I knew that my long hair and just-slept-on-the-ground appearance were strikes against me, but eventually, a big Buick sedan stopped, and a man with a white shirt and black tie invited me to put my bedroll in the back seat and climb in. "You look like a young man that's a long way from home," he said. "Where are you headed?"

My head was still buzzing, and I blinked into the morning sun for a moment before answering, "New Mexico, I guess."

The man smiled at me and then turned back to the road. His hair was cut high above his ears and oiled into place with a ruler-straight part. "You don't sound too certain? A rough night was it, brother?" Beside him on the seat was a worn, leather-bound Bible, the kind with the zipper around the closure, and I noticed on the dashboard a four-inch-tall statue of Jesus.

"You might say that." I wasn't ready to talk about it, and there wasn't much this guy could do anyway. I looked at the plastic statue and chuckled. "Like the song," I said, not thinking at the time how rude I might sound.

"What's that?"

"Your Jesus statue on your dashboard," I said. " I've never actually seen one before. It reminds me of a song."

"A song?"

"Yeah, there's a song about a plastic Jesus on the dashboard."

"Really. Can't say as I've heard that one. Do you mean a hymn of some sort? How's it go?"

I thought for a minute, then regretted that I'd brought it up. "Let me see, *I don't care if it rains or freezes, long as I got my plastic Jesus*," I said, kind of half-singing. That's all I remember. "Silly song, I guess, about a guy with a plastic Jesus on his dashboard."

"Well, this Jesus, plastic as it may be, does give me comfort," the driver said. "It helps remind me to follow his way. So what gives you comfort, young man?"

We were driving through arid land now with few trees and a few scattered cows grazing in the distance. It reminded me of the scenery in Westerns, sagebrush and sand. "I don't reckon I've got much comfort right now," I admitted, looking wistfully at my hands. "Pretty uncomfortable, actually."

"Well, son, I'm a minister, and it's my job to counsel those in need, so if you want to, you can unburden your soul right here."

I looked at the plastic Jesus and the Bible and the man at the wheel, and I wondered what he would say to me if I told him everything. I tried to imagine telling him how Sam Barger came to be hitchhiking on this country road in Oregon. How last night I got drunk and stoned and robbed, how my girlfriend was pregnant even before she was my girlfriend. How I'd run away from home to chase her down. Yeah, he'd really see lots of chances for redemption in my story. What I said was, "I've been unburdened already. A couple guys in a van took care of that."

The driver accelerated to pass a station wagon pulling a camp trailer and said, "I don't understand."

"Two guys gave me a ride yesterday, then they robbed me. Even took my pants. Luckily I found them in the trash." I blushed when I said it, feeling like an idiot for being so reckless.

"Were these friends of yours or were you set upon by thieves?" The preacher's voice filled with a certain excitement like he'd been asked to play the role of the Good Samaritan.

"Well, I was hitchhiking, and they gave me a ride. I bought a tank of gas, so they saw I had money. Then when I was asleep, they snuck up on me and took my pants and duffel. Bastards cleaned me out."

"I'm glad I happened to give you a ride then. Perhaps I was sent your way to ease your burden. The Lord works in mysterious ways." Then the man started praying in earnest, calling for God to support and guide me and shelter me from harm and bad weather. I sat quietly, a little spooked by his manner but glad that I had been given a ride by a preacher with a generous soul who would give me a little help. I couldn't ask, of course, but I hoped that he might offer me some money or maybe spring for a meal at least. Instead, he pulled in at a gas station café at a crossroads and said, "Well, I'm turning here. I wish you the best."

I was turned out in the parking lot of a place that looked to be on its last legs with only a prayer to help me. Before he drove away, the preacher rolled down his window and extended his hand. "This is for you, young man. A little help on a cloudy day."

I reached out hopefully, but all that was in his hand was a pocket New Testament with a red plastic cover.

"No thanks," I said and turned away without saying more to this preacher looking for a flock. I looked at the forested mountains around me and the pastures running up to the forest edge where cattle were feeding along the strings of barbed wire with sagebrush growing up through it. All I needed was a horse, a cowboy hat, and a country song, I thought, but I had neither. I was a long way from home, and it did look like it might rain.

I moved to the shoulder of the road and half-heartedly stuck my thumb out. I stood for probably fifteen minutes and five cars passed before I gave up and followed my stomach to the tiny diner that shared a cinder block building with a gas station. Only one car was parked out front though it was almost noon. The driver was coming out as I was going in, and he gave me a critical once over then jerked a thumb back toward the café door. "It's OK if you like canned chili and crackers," he said without turning around.

"Thanks." I held the screen door so it didn't bang when it closed. This was your average café with a counter and six stools and four small tables. A Black man in mechanic's coveralls and grease was making notes by the cash register. "Welcome stranger," he said. "Have a seat here at the counter. Coffee, pop? What'll it be?"

"Root beer. And a glass of water." I reached for the plastic-coated menu tucked in the back of the holder for salt and pepper and condiments.

"Don't bother with the menu," he said. "Don't have anything but chili today. And it's out of a can. Sorry, I lost my help, and as you can see I'm in the wrong part of the building. I got flats to fix next door." The mechanic chuckled and shook his head.

"Chili it is then," I said.

The man set a glass of ice and a can of root beer in front of me, then filled a water glass from a pitcher on the counter. True to his word, he smelled more of garage than kitchen, and he looked tired. The chili was hot and unremarkable, but he brought diced onions and saltines that helped me fill in the gaps. From my stool, I could see into the kitchen where sinks full of dirty pots and pans and bus trays full of dirty dishes waited for washing. The twenty-dollar bill still safely tucked in the watch pocket of my jeans reminded me that I was living on a shoestring with still a long way to go. I might be looking at an opportunity, and I silently thanked Joe for the money and advice.

"Looks like you need some help around here," I said.

The man poured a cup of coffee and moved toward the garage. "That's an understatement." Then a car pulled up at the pump and a bell by the front door rang. He set down his coffee. "See!"

"I'll clean that kitchen for my lunch," I said as he stepped to the door. He didn't even look back. "Help yourself!" I ate my chili and looked over the kitchen I had just volunteered to clean. The back wall was taken up with a long stainless steel counter with two big sinks full of pots and a little dishwasher tucked in the corner. It was like the one Pete had back at Polar Pizza. Dishes were loaded into square plastic baskets and slid into the dishwasher, then it was closed and soap and high-pressure hot water did the trick. Big pots and pans had to be washed in the sink. Then there would be garbage to haul and the floor to sweep and mop. "Better have another bowl of chili, Sam," I said aloud. "You're going to earn it." And I did, serving myself from the pot and dropping in a dollop of chopped onions.

While I ate, I read the menu. The Crossroads Café offered burgers, BLTs, chicken salad, and hot roast sandwiches, turkey or beef. There was a daily soup and a lunch special like meatloaf, baked chicken, chili, or spaghetti. A plan started to form in my mind, and I thought how that stingy preacher might have done me a favor by dropping me off where he did, and I knew full well that he'd smile and say, "The Lord works in mysterious ways." And maybe he does, but I had a kitchen to clean, so I waded into the mess and looked for an apron.

When I was standing on the side of the road hitching a ride, I had plenty of time to fret and dream and stew about seeing Iris, about what I'd say, and what she'd want from me, like maybe nothing. But when I was cleaning that kitchen, I was too busy to think of much at all. I loaded the dishwasher with plates, bowls, and glasses, filled the big sink with soapy water, and scraped chili and god knows what else off of pots and pans. Mom always said, "Idle hands are tools of the devil," and I had to admit it felt good to be working again even if it was just pearl-diving, as Pete used to call it.

I was just getting started when the owner stuck his head in the door to the kitchen. "By the way, I'm Harold, I'll be next door if you need anything. If a customer wanders in, the chili's a dollar, and the coffee's twenty-five cents. Whatever else you need is on the menu."

I walked out toward the lunch counter, drying my hands on a towel. "I'm Sam, Sam Barger. I got this."

Harold grinned, "God, I hope so." Then he left me to the dishes, pots, and pans. I fed a trucker that came in looking for lunch and a fill-up for his thermos. I served him two bowls of chili and brewed a fresh pot of coffee while he ate. He left smiling and I made a quarter tip. I now had twenty-three dollars and twenty-five cents to get me to New Mexico.

And yes, all I had to go on was a town called Las Vegas, New Mexico. No names, addresses, nothing. Sam, the impulsive one, had dashed off from Walla Walla bound for New Mexico on nothing but a wing and a prayer, and now I didn't feel like I had either. I slipped the quarter in my pocket and turned back to the sink full of pots soaking in hot dishwater. A shelf ran along the wall above the sink, and I assumed that the pots were stored there since the shelf was empty and the sink was full. In less than an hour I had that reversed and was putting away clean plates, glasses, and silverware when a couple about Mom's age walked in and sat at a table by the window.

I brought them water and repeated Harold's line about the chili. "We've got chili and that's it. And it's out of a can."

"Chili it is then," said the man. "That work for you, hon?"

Hon lit a cigarette and wrinkled her nose. "Chili? You're kidding, right?" Then she looked at me and took a drag off her cigarette. "Do you have a sandwich? Chicken or turkey maybe. A BLT?"

She was a pretty woman, slender with smooth skin and bright red lipstick. "I'll see what I can find," I said confidently, drying my hands on a kitchen towel and not feeling confident at all. "You want coffee?"

"Seven-Up for me," she said. "My, you have beautiful hair for a man. Your girlfriend must be jealous." I pushed my hair behind my ears. The man shook his head and said, "Make mine a Coke."

Back in the kitchen, I ran my fingers through my hair and thought I better tie it back. Pete always made me cover it with a hat or bandana when I worked. It wasn't a big deal when I was washing dishes, but I didn't want my auburn locks flying when I was cooking and ending up on someone's lunch plate. While I was looking for some canned tuna or something else to make a sandwich, I found a box of paper hats like soda jerks wear and fitted one on my head. My hair wasn't quite long enough for a ponytail so I stuffed it behind my ears.

I wasn't sure what I could do for a sandwich the woman wanted, but I had seen bread and mayonnaise in the pantry. The fridge offered up a turkey breast and some lettuce and mayonnaise, but the only cheese I found was moldy, so turkey was the only option. I did find some potato chips to serve with the sandwich. The couple ate and left a five on the table when they walked out without comment. I checked the prices on the menu and figured I had earned a dollar tip. I had twenty-four and a quarter to get me to Las Vegas, and I had only been at the diner a couple hours. I was getting the idea that I might get more than a bowl of chili and some spare change out of Harold's Crossroads Café.

I needed traveling money, and Harold needed a cook. Maybe I could make this work for both of us. It would take a little exaggeration on my part, but I knew enough from what I'd learned at Polar Pizza and from Mom to handle the basics, and there were cookbooks on the shelf in the pantry.

SIXTEEN

Harold was the biggest man I had ever seen, and it didn't take me long to figure out that he was big all over, especially his heart. I tracked him down in the mechanic's bay of the gas station after I finished in the kitchen and watched silently while he finished installing a fan belt on a Plymouth station wagon. I could hear a ballgame on the radio in the background. When he crawled out from under the Plymouth, I noticed his bad leg. The left leg was stiff and didn't seem to bend much when he walked.

"You like baseball?" he asked. "The Reds are up by two and they better stay that way, or I might think you're tramping bad luck into my kitchen like this." Then he laughed, and somehow that made everything seem better.

"My dad liked the Reds too," I said. "I was born in Ohio, so obviously—"

"No kidding, well hell. You might be my lucky charm. 'Cause these boys could use some help this year."

That's how I met Harold Jackson, and we settled pretty fast into a routine. He taught me about baseball, and I taught him—well, I guess I didn't teach him anything, but he seemed to like the company. There was an acceptance in him of the world as it was. A lesson for someone like me who was always fighting against it and getting mad as hell when it didn't change. When I walked into that café and ate his canned chili, I never knew I was grabbing a life preserver in the wide ocean of my life.

"Harold, I got your kitchen cleaned up and served some customers that came by."

"That's good, Sam. Thanks." Harold wiped his hands on a rag that used to be a T-shirt and looked me in the eye. "You can see I'm kinda treading water here. This is my side of the operation, and the wife runs the restaurant. I'd hate to have to close it up. I been lagging on that side of it, and we're losing customers."

"Maybe I can help with that," I said. "I worked in a restaurant back home, and I bet I could turn out most things on your menu. You got some burger and other meat in the freezer and there's burger buns and bread. I can do enough to keep your doors open and keep the customers coming." I was feeling warm around the neck from stretching the truth the way I was. Making pizzas and meatball sandwiches was the extent of my training at Polar Pizza, and everything else I implied was pure invention.

"You askin' for a job?" Harold leaned on the fender of the Plymouth. "Well, shit. I don't know. See, I had a guy set up to cook while my wife had surgery, but he didn't last a week and then my waitress got sick or something, so she ain't been in. I've been running back and forth these last few days, and that sure as hell ain't workin'."

I had a feeling I needed to sell myself harder than I was, so I tried honesty. "Harold, here's the deal. I'm on my way to New Mexico. I hitched a ride with these two guys in a van. Well, they seemed nice enough, so I camped with them last night. While I was sleeping they took my pack and all my money even threw my jeans in the trash." I held my arms out for effect. "All I got is this and my sleeping bag. I reckon I can help you, and it would sure help me."

Harold didn't say anything. He just closed the hood on the Plymouth and walked around to the driver's side and got in. He started the engine and leaned in like he was listening to the engine. Then he backed out of the garage and parked the car. He limped back in with his head down. Then he looked me in the eye.

"Grab a couple beers out of the fridge there in the corner," he said, "and meet me out back."

Beers in hand, I wandered through the kitchen for a bottle opener, missing my Boy Scout knife for the first time. Out back I found two metal lawn chairs under an apple tree and Harold sitting in one of them and lighting a cigarette with hands still coated in grease.

"What's in New Mexico, Sam," Harold asked after a pull on his beer.

I sat down and looked at the mountains in the distance, then up at the apples in the tree. "Got a girl there. I'm going to see her." I reached up to touch a ripe red apple just above my head. "Can I?"

"The apples? Sure. Take all you want. We can't use them all. This girl, she waiting to see you? Or is she runnin' from you?" He didn't laugh when he said it.

"Well, that's a good question. Hell, I think she does want me to come. She sent a postcard. And if she doesn't, I want her to tell me to my face." I picked the apple, polished it on my shirt like I'd seen in the movies, and took a bite. It was tart and crisp. "It's a long story."

I started thinking of apple pie.

"How does a guy from . . . where the hell are you from?" Harold drank and puffed on his cigarette, looking at me as he waited for the answer.

"Alaska."

"Well holy shit. No wonder you want to pick apples." He laughed then.

"My first. Not my first apple but the first I picked from a tree." The juice was running down my chin as I ate.

"What's a guy from Alaska doing with a girl in New Mexico? Sounds more like a pen pal than a girlfriend?"

I had a feeling that Harold was going to milk me for the whole story, so I told it to him straight out. I told him about Iris and me being pregnant and her parents not liking me and the whole story of Aunt Sally and how I got here. Well most of the story anyway. It wasn't like me to spill my guts that way, but Harold was one of those people who made you want to tell him everything.

He listened with his head nodding, and then he said, "That's how I ended up married to Betsy. Her daddy told me there was no ifs, ands, or buts about it. What they call a shotgun wedding, but he didn't need no shotgun. He was bigger than half a cow and was all muscle. As soon as he found out she was in the family way, he drove us down to the courthouse and stood there to make sure we followed through. I guess it worked out all right. Been twenty years now. I don't know that life would be any better or worse if things had gone the other way."

"Yeah, I guess it's hard to predict the future. I wish it had been that easy for us, but here I am." I sipped my beer and watched the light changing on the mountains in the distance as the sun moved closer to the horizon. I reached up and touched the cut on my eye that had just started to heal.

Harold finished his beer and studied my face. "That cut on your eye got anything to do with this girl?"

"I told ya her dad didn't like me." I picked another apple. "This is amazing," I said, gesturing with the apple. Harold chuckled. "I guess he didn't. Who got the best of it?"

"Shoot, there was only two hits in that fight," I said. "He hit me, and I hit the ground."

"That's a fight you couldn't win either way." Harold leaned forward. "I'll give you twenty-five bucks a day and a place to sleep if you give me a week of good work and keep the café open for me. Now I know you're antsy as hell to get on the road, and I can't blame you. But the last thing you want to do is show up on her doorstep looking like you've been bucked off and stomped flat like you did when you walked in here. You'll want some money in your pocket when you get there, and a week of working here would give you that." He gestured with his hand. "There's an old canned ham camp trailer there you can bunk in. What do you say?"

What could I say? I was over a barrel, flat broke, and too proud to call my mom for money, so I shook the man's hand and started scheming on making that week more like five days. We finished our beers without talking. Then Harold limped off to the double-wide trailer house behind the café. He stopped halfway and said, "Call your mother, or the deal's off, use the phone in the café. Then lock up the front and leave the back open so's you can come and go."

The place Harold had made under the apple tree was shaded from the evening sun and gave a view of mountains in the distance. I tried to imagine what was beyond them for that was the way I would travel when I left. I'd wind through the Blue Mountains, into the southwest corner of Idaho, then south through Utah to a corner of Arizona and in to New Mexico. I tried to imagine the road ahead of me based on photos from *National Geographic* magazine and TV news. I sat there a few more minutes realizing how tired I was. But I knew Harold was right. I needed to call Mom and Iris's aunt Sally, too, if I hadn't burned that bridge.

I walked back to the kitchen, finished my cleaning, and dialed Mom on the café phone. I had myself braced and ready, but when there was no answer, I called Aunt Sally. Sally tried to be tough with me and answered with words bitten off like bites of a crisp apple. "I'm sorry I left like I did," I said, "but I got a tip where Iris was and couldn't wait."

"You couldn't wait because you were afraid I'd try to stop you. And I would have. You didn't trust me."

She knocked me off center with that. "Well, I'm—I'm sorry," I said. "I talked to my mom, see, and figured out where she was—Iris I mean, and I had to go."

"You missed a good breakfast on top of it all. And I talked to Iris's dad. He called me."

The phone felt hot against my ear, and I touched the cut above my eye. "Oh. Is Iris OK?"

"She's fine. Her daddy's fit to be tied though. Somehow he knows you're on her trail."

"Too bad," I said. "He sucker punched me once, but he won't again." I could feel my stomach churn as I made my boast.

"I wouldn't be surprised if he was in New Mexico waiting for you."

"Yeah, me either. Thank you, Aunt Sally, and sorry for being a jerk."

I was about to hang up the phone when she spoke again. "Sam, you bring that girl back here if you want. She's always welcome here . . . and you, too, I suppose . . . if you don't pull another stunt like that."

"OK," I said. "Good night."

I was on a roll, so I called Mom.

"Hi, Mom. It's me."

"Sam? Is that you? You know I can't tell you and your brother apart on the phone."

"Yeah, Mom, it's Sam."

Silence. Then. "Where are you? Are you OK?"

"I'm fine, Mom, I'm in eastern Oregon."

"Why are you in Oregon? I can't believe you just up and left like that, though I guess I should have expected as much from you." Flat, tense, feigning indifference. I could see her set jaw, and I heard her light a cigarette and take a deep drag.

"Can you believe it, Mom? I got a job cooking in a restaurant—just for a few days. They needed some help, and it couldn't hurt to have some traveling money I figured."

"I see. Iris's aunt called me. You left her place in kind of a hurry, it sounds like. She sounded nice enough. Where are your manners, Sam? That lady was trying to help you."

"I know, Mom, I called her just now. She's nice, and I was a jerk just leaving like that, but I needed to."

"Well, you obviously didn't get very far anyway. She was pretty disappointed that you basically ran off in the middle of the night."

"I know, Mom, you said that already." I looked at the mouthpiece of the phone like I could see her through it, and I could in a way, having watched her talk on the phone to Joe this way. She would light a cigarette with the phone cradled against her shoulder. With a cigarette hanging from her lips, she would doodle on the notepad she kept by the phone. I knew she was doing that now while she tried to figure out what to say to me that would actually have any effect on what I did.

"You got another postcard from that girl."

My heart immediately zoomed in. "You mean Iris, Mom? She has a name."

"Yes, I know her name, Samuel. She seems very strange. It's just a postcard from some drive-in burger joint with the slogan, "Saddle up for a round-up." I could hear someone chuckling in the background, probably Jake.

"Well, what's the message, Mom?" My hands were shaking, and I paced back and forth at the end of the phone cord.

"Hold your horses! It just says, '*Sam, Our burgers are the best, and I know you'll like our buns.*' I suppose she thinks she's quite clever. But that is not lady-like language. No wonder she ended up—oh never mind."

I chuckled and grabbed a pencil. "Say that again, Mom. There was static in the line." I wanted the words exactly as they were written. I knew now that Iris was reaching out to me, sending me these coded messages on postcards that read loud and clear, *Come get me, Sam!*

"Oh my word, you are stricken, aren't you, son," Mom said with the first hint of tenderness I'd heard in her voice. And then she read the card again. "And. Yes, the postmark is Las Vegas, New Mexico. Did you know there was a Las Vegas, New Mexico? I never heard of it. Sam is everything all right? I can hear it in your voice. It's like there's something you're not telling me."

As much as talking to Mom made me feel young and homesick, there was no way I going to admit to her that I was broke and as stuck as a pig in quicksand. "Mom, think about it. What might be wrong? This is all so hard, and it's all uphill, and nobody's on my side." I knew I shouldn't have said that, should have kept it in.

"Sam, you know that's not true. I'm on your side. Right, wrong, or indifferent, I'm here. I think Iris's aunt, too, what's her name, Sally. Even after you ran off like you did, she spoke well of you. Things like this are just hard, Sam, and you don't make them any easier being so stubborn and independent about it."

I said goodbye and hung up without letting her know I was broke or needed anything more than her acceptance of my decision, and that wasn't likely to come until I had proven myself right.

Returning to the camp trailer, I rolled out my sleeping bag and tried to sleep, but it was early for that and soon I was poking around the cupboards and cabinets of my new home away from home. I found a broom and swept out the camper and set an old folding chair outside the door. I found myself writing scenarios in my head for when I got to New Mexico. In one scenario, Iris was pretty and bright and eager, her body curved and sexy, with a little bulge the size of a baseball cap under her blouse. I dressed her in a white summer dress in a field of flowers like Linda Ronstadt or Merrilee Rush on a record album cover. She rushed into my arms, and everyone knew then that this was right and good, so good that we got married and were a family. In that scenario, all I had to do was get there, and everything would be fine. This possibility intrigued me, and I fantasized about myself as a father, like my dad was a father and my Papaw Barger. I was still too much of a kid to be able to imagine the Dad job being that difficult. What I did know was what it was like to be without a dad, and there was no way I'd wish that on any kid.

When I finally lay down to sleep, though, a dark and less hopeful scenario came to mind and made me toss and fight with my pillow. This was the worst of the what-if scenarios with a swollen, sallow Iris, who wasn't sure she wanted to see me at all and who carried her pregnancy like a malignancy that was slowly taking over her body. She wasn't sexy or warm but cold and angry, like my sperm was an infection that attacked her body and soul. In this meeting I was on the defensive, and Iris was looking for a way out, serving her nine-month sentence, after which she would move on, and the baby would stay, finding a home with someone else. That made for some crazy dreams when I did fall asleep, and I woke up feeling like I had lost a wrestling match.

SEVENTEEN

By noon the next day, Harold's Crossroads Café was open for business. Meatloaf with mashed potatoes and gravy was on the luncheon special, and three long-haul truckers bragged about how good it was while they finished their coffee.

Harold wandered through the café and gestured at the trucks parked outside. "Them's better than a freeway billboard, you know. People see them semis parked out front, and they know it's the place to eat."

"I'm doing my best," I said, making a fresh pot of coffee. Without a waitress, I was cooking, serving, and cleaning up, which was fine as long as it was slow. The café had been basically closed for a week, and the locals had stopped coming.

"Business is picking up," Harold said. "You're going to need some help here, you know." He turned to look at the calendar. "I got a waitress, but she got sick right after my wife had her surgery. Shoot, I think I told you that. I hope she'll be back tomorrow or the next day. She's a good enough waitress, but she ain't much of a cook, so I didn't even try havin' her run the place. But with you cookin', I'll give her a call."

I immediately thought ahead to when I could leave with some money in my pocket. In a week with pay and tips, I should be able to leave with $150. Sure, I was antsy to be on the road to Iris, but I didn't have much of a choice but to stay. Harold was right. I could get to Las Vegas, New Mexico, but did I want to show up like a hobo without two nickels to rub together? That was never far from my mind, and when a pregnant woman came into the café with her husband for lunch, I kept staring at her bulging belly and imagining Iris shaped like that, and I got blue about it all over again. Luckily it was a busy lunchtime, and I had more to do than stare at that pregnant woman and get sad.

That evening at closing time Harold showed up with two beers and nodded his head toward the backyard where the metal lawn chairs felt like a featherbed. For a while, we sipped our beers without talking. I was waiting to see what Harold had to say, but he just sat and looked at the mountains.

"I found some cooks' uniforms in the storeroom," I said. "Hope it's OK I'm using them—as if he hadn't noticed I was wearing white pants and shirt instead of my jeans and flannel. And I need to do some laundry." I didn't say I also needed to buy a change of clothes and some underwear and socks.

"Sure," Harold said. "Take your clothes up to the house tomorrow. Betsy's up and about enough she's doin' some laundry and such. Anything else you need?"

"No. I'm OK."

"There's a shower in the head at the back of the garage."

I blushed. "Yeah, I guess that would be a good idea. Were you in the navy or marines?"

"Marines. Why?"

I drank and looked at the man sitting next to me with his bum leg and a short-cropped haircut. He had the look of a guy who would have called me a hippie and given me a bad time about my hair hanging past my collar, but he didn't seem to even see that. "My brother, Joe," I said. "He was a marine and came home saying *head* instead of *toilet*."

"Vietnam?"

"Yes," I said, remembering the wounds Joe carried that were deeper than the ones of the flesh. "Is that how you got crippled?"

"This?" He slapped his leg. "Nope. I was drafted during the Korean War, but I never saw combat. A bumper jack slipped and a car fell on me. Thought I was going to lose this leg. It's about half there. Yup, you just never know." Harold finished his beer in one swallow and pushed up from the chair in a way that showed that leg wasn't much help. "Have a good night," he said as he moved off toward home where the lights were on in the kitchen.

The camp trailer was old, beat up, and mildewy, but it was out of the weather and better than sleeping on the ground. Alone and looking at the mildew on the warped plywood ceiling, I had time to think of Iris and imagine her showing like that woman in the café. I wondered how I would feel then, how she would feel then. That thought carried me back instead of forward, and we were back in the cafeteria at East High, where she tracked me down that spring day. From then on we were partners in crime, fighting the war on the northern front, trying to throw our voices to DC with the other students against the war. I followed her because I wanted to be with that brown-eyed, freckle-cheeked girl who didn't take crap from me or anybody. Then we weren't a couple anymore until that night when we couldn't keep our hands off each other. I wonder now if maybe that's how we'll always be, on again, off again, and only good together in spurts. Maybe the best thing that happens is that I can't find her.

I tried to turn my attention away from that and thought about the café and what I had to do the next day. On the shelf above the hand-washing sink, I found a spiral notebook full of handwritten reci-pes. I brought it to bed with me and studied it for recipes that seemed simple and could be made from what Harold had on hand. I was going be preparing dishes I'd never cooked, like roast beef and chicken-fried steak. Luckily Pete had taught me to make soup, and Mom taught me to make gravy, so in two days I had most of the menu figured out, and I even made potato salad that was fit to eat. Of course, most people were ordering burgers and sandwiches at lunch, which was no big challenge even for me. While I was eating leftover meatloaf for dinner, I had decided to have spaghetti on the menu the next day. I would make Pete's pizza sauce, add some ground beef, and call it spaghetti sauce. A big box of spaghetti was literally gathering dust in the storeroom, so we were set.

Just before lunch the next day, I started a pot of water boiling and cooked two handfuls of spaghetti. When it was a little firm, I strained it out of the pot and dumped it into a stainless steel pan. Well, it turns out that if you cook your spaghetti ahead and dump it in a pan like I did, it sticks together into a solid, stiff wad. I was standing in the kitchen scratching my head and staring at a brick-shaped block of pasta while four hungry truckers waited for their spaghetti and meatballs. I was about to throw my masterpiece in the trash and start all over rather than try to offer it as anybody's lunch.

"Put it in a pot of hot water then add some cooking oil," said a voice from the back door of the kitchen. A round, curly haired woman stood in the doorway wearing pajamas and a bathrobe. "Don't tell Harold," she said. "He'll kill me if he knows I'm down here. I'm Betsy."

"Hi, Betsy." I looked over my shoulder as if checking for Harold. "Hot water, huh?"

"Yes, it'll loosen up the spaghetti so you can serve it." She smiled and looked around the small kitchen. "It smells good here and things look good too. Harold said you were a lifesaver, and I just had to see for myself."

I grabbed a pot off the shelf and filled it with hot water from the faucet, then set it on the stovetop. "Thanks, let me try this. I've got four hungry truckers out front waiting for spaghetti."

Betsy leaned on the stainless dishwashing counter looking pale, "Your sauce smells wonderful." Harold had told me she had surgery, and I didn't expect to see her up and about. She suddenly looked like she shouldn't be. "I'm going to head back now," she said. "Just put it in that pot and turn the heat off. It'll loosen right up. In fact, that spaghetti's probably ready now."

I turned to the stove, and she disappeared out the back door. The spaghetti came out of the pan loose and tender like I wanted it, and I was able to serve the truckers their lunches. In fact, the spaghetti special turned out to be a hit with truckers and the locals. The Crossroads Café was back in business, which meant I was up at six in the morning to open the place, grilling bacon and hashbrowns and flipping eggs. People would ask, "Where's Betsy," and I would say something clever like she was gone to cook for the president, then act sincere and say she needed a few days off. I didn't know what was wrong with her nor was it my business, so I was winging that like everything else from cooking steaks and fried potatoes to patty melts and chicken soup.

After three days at the Crossroads, I was already feeling comfortable being there with Harold and the little trailer. But working in the kitchen was pushing me to the limit. I had sold myself a bit high and had to cover my bet. Most of the time I didn't know what I was doing, and my only salvation was that I rarely had more than two customers at once. Unlike fish camp, there was no chance for boredom. I could always find something to do. Trying to make the meals and serve them after I figured out how they should be prepared kept my brain and body in constant motion. Being in this friendly place and sleeping in an old camp trailer, evening beers with Harold, this was all so easy that I found moments in my day when I wanted to stay here. Yup, I wanted to put New Mexico on hold, put it all on hold. And maybe that was the attraction. Here at the Crossroads Café, I didn't have to make choices that mattered much beyond how many slices of bacon to put on a BLT sandwich. I was feeling guilty as hell thinking that way, but a part of me didn't want to leave.

I wanted to do the right thing by Iris and be a part of it all, but what was the *right* thing? What was best for everybody? In a few days when Harold put some cash in my hand, I could decide, but until then, being robbed gave me the coward's gambit of doing nothing for now.

EIGHTEEN

At six o'clock the next morning, I was cooking up some bacon for breakfast when a lean brunette unlocked the front door and blew in like a gust of wind with her long hair flying behind her. "Who the hell are you?" she asked, slapping a massive shoulder bag on the counter. She was in her twenties and was nearly as tall as me and wearing a waitress uniform with more leg than skirt.

I was dressed in whites and cooking bacon, so it was obvious I wasn't a burglar. "I'm your cook, Sam. You must be Cathy." I walked out of the kitchen to greet her. "I'm happy to have the help. I heard you were sick."

She dug a cigarette out of her purse and looked around. "I know who you are. Harold called me." She ran her hand over the counter like a health inspector as she worked her way down the counter and picked up a coffee cup. "Good. You made coffee. No, I wasn't sick, just bleeding to death. I can't handle this place and my damn period at the same time."

My eyes widened, I nodded and turned back to the kitchen. "OK then. Nice to meet you. We've got everything on the menu except biscuits and gravy."

"Well, you better have that fixed by tomorrow. I don't want to start Sunday morning without biscuits and gravy. They'll be whining from here to next Christmas."

I didn't answer. The conversation she started seemed to be doing fine on its own, and she chatted up a storm the whole time she was filling salt and sugar shakers and wiping down the tables. Only once could I tell her words were directed at me. "You didn't put bleach in the water for wiping down the tables last night did you? Gotta use that bleach, Sam! Don't be a slacker."

I rattled a stack of plates so it sounded like I didn't hear her and smiled when I realized I could work in the kitchen today and not worry about serving. But when the first pair of truckers came in for breakfast, I found I had other things to worry about.

I had an order of eggs over easy with bacon and hash browns and sunny-side eggs with ham and hash browns. They were barely in the pass-through window when Cathy came flying into the kitchen with the plates on one hand and the other hand waving like a signal flag. "What the hell shit is this? Where's the damn garnish?" She moved past me like a snowplow and grabbed parsley and two oranges and slammed them on the worktable by my grill. "A slice of orange twisted in a curli-cue and sprig of parsley! Every damn breakfast plate!" She flounced back out the door, and the two breakfast plates sat on the table before me. As soon as she entered the dining room her tone changed to charming, "You fellas want some coffee while you wait for breakfast? It won't be just a minute."

That's how I met Cathy, the waitress tornado, who seemed to have known intuitively that I was half a fake with no idea as to what I was doing. She was duty bound to set me straight on all things Crossroads Café. I quickly learned that she could go from frowning to flirty faster than any person I ever saw. I was suddenly twelve again with a sister who was more than glad to take over my life and guide me on the right path. Harold only came into the café for coffee in the morning and for lunch at about one o'clock, so he was never available to referee. I was on my own, and suddenly I was looking down the road again and thinking about leaving.

After the lunch rush of two ranchers, three truckers, and a family on vacation, I asked if Cathy wanted something to eat.

"I hate sandwiches," she said. "I'm a breakfast person."

I was pouring myself a cup of coffee, "Hams and eggs? Pancakes? What?" This could be a make-or-break moment for Sam Barger.

She flopped onto a counter stool and put her head on her hand. "Oh, Sam, I'd really love some French toast."

I sighed with relief, afraid she'd be wanting eggs benedict or something else I hadn't mastered. "French toast! You got it."

I whipped up three eggs with cream and cinnamon and poured them over four slices of bread. While those were soaking I cleaned my grill, and by the time I spilled clarified butter on the hot steel, the bread had soaked up the egg mixture. "Thanks, Mom," I said aloud, as I lay the bread in the pool of hot butter on the smoking grill. I flipped the toast at just the right time and served a plate of luscious golden toast sprinkled with powdered sugar, and a curlicue of orange slice with parsley. And so I won the day, sending Cathy home smiling. I decided that keeping her fed would be the best salvation, for after eating she was much easier to deal with and almost pleasant.

The next day, of course, she was back in my face. She leaned on the counter watching me make a sandwich. A certain routine had settled in for me, and I was starting to feel in control of all things kitchen-related, but Cathy seemed bent on breaking any chance at self-confidence. "You aren't really a cook, are you? In fact, just who are you really, Sam? I can tell you're not a cook."

I kept building the sandwich, then cut it and set it on the plate. "What do you mean I'm not a cook? Who's putting out this food? The Galloping Gourmet?"

Cathy delivered the sandwich and started in again, "Oh you're cooking, but you're not a cook. I can tell. You just talked Harold into letting you work here, but you don't belong in the kitchen."

I gave her a nod to let her know that two more customers came in and took a table by the window. She gave them a look and said, "They can wait 'til I finish. You're just trying to change the subject, Sam. Where did you cook? Before here, where are you from? We know nothing about you, really."

I laughed, "I'm on the run from the mob, okay. Don't spread it around."

She was still talking when she turned and took water and menus to the two ranchers who were checking her legs as she sashayed across the room. She put a hand on her hip and leaned toward the table as she talked to the men, then giggled at their jokes.

When she came back with their lunch order, she continued, "You shouldn't try to make jokes. You're not funny. So where are you from? Did you just fall off a sugar beet truck and land on our doorstep?"

"I'm from Alaska," I said. "No big mystery. I was on my way to New Mexico when two guys ripped me off, and I was stranded here. Turns out Harold could use a hand, so here I am."

"So you just suddenly appeared to help Harold out? What are you some guy like on the TV shows wandering from town to town helping people out, like *Route 66*?"

I tossed two burgers on the grill and set the plates with potato salad and pickles. "I'm a cook. See me cooking. I worked in a restaurant for almost two years."

Cathy stepped in beside me and pointed to my plates. "See that, it's a mess. Put the potato salad on a piece of lettuce with an ice cream scoop and it looks better." She pushed me aside and set up the plate the way she wanted, talking the whole time. The plate did look nice with the rounded scoop of potato salad on the lettuce bed dusted with a bit of paprika, and I tried to set the cheeseburgers on the plate artfully too.

"So why are you going to New Mexico anyway? Are you really from Alaska, really? I don't believe any of this."

I couldn't help but laugh. "You are nonstop," I said. "Where do you think I'm from? And why would I be here unless it happened just as I said?"

Cathy looked at me over the top of her nose and went to tend to her customers. She cycled back and said, "I guess you're right. Maybe we're all stuck here. Harold kind of inherited this stupid gas station café. That's why he's here, and I'm stuck 'cause I can't keep my knees together."

"You wanna eat?" I asked, looking over her shoulder at the last of the lunch customers leaving.

"Just eggs, scrambled, please. If I had kept my pants on like a good girl, I'd be in Boise by now, but some guy I didn't even like knocked me up—he was handsome though."

I scrambled the eggs, put them on the grill, and chased them back and forth with a spatula. "Did he marry you?"

Cathy laughed, lit a cigarette, and perched on a counter stool. "Are you kidding? He never stood still long enough to get married. He started running as soon as I told him I had a bun in the oven, and shit, he's probably still running."

"Toast?"

"No. But I will eat some of that potato salad."

"My mom's recipe, best I could guess at it anyway," I said, putting the plate of eggs and potato salad in front of her. I poured some chili over a plate of french fries and sat down beside her.

Somehow she managed to eat, smoke, and talk at the same time without losing pace or running out of breath. "Yup, there's just me and the spawn now, she's almost two. My mom keeps her when I work." Cathy talked about the trailer house out on her parent's ranch and how she wanted to go to vet tech school, but now she was just getting by waitressing until something bigger and better comes along. "Or some cute trucker sweeps me off my feet and takes me and the kid to live somewhere else. Funny though, a lot of guys don't want to be raising some other guy's kid. Dumbasses. Like it matters. Shit, kids are kids."

"I'm a pizza cook," I said.

"What?"

I finished the last bite of chili fries. "You keep asking if I was a cook. I was a pizza cook back in Alaska, and I made other stuff, too, but mostly pizza. You like pizza?"

"Pizza? Hell yes, I like pizza. If you can make pizza, I might let you live."

She got up then to straighten the dining room and wipe the tables before she left for the day, and I cleaned the kitchen while I schemed on making pizza. It would be fun to bring a bit of what I really knew to share here. That was on my mind when I wandered into the garage where Harold was still working. Johnny Cash was crooning country ballads in the background, and I sat and watched while he changed the fan belt on a Ford sedan. "How are you and Cathy getting along?" he asked.

"Good, I guess. She might not say the same." I went to the fridge for beers and set one on the fender for him.

Harold wiped his hands and tossed the rag into a trash barrel. "She does take some getting used to. She don't want to be here, but she's got a kid and can't just hit the road footloose and fancy-free like you. I bet she was telling you how to do everything, wasn't she?" He chuckled when he said it like he could imagine the whole scene with the breakfast plates. He sipped his beer and looked thoughtful, staring a hole through the back wall of the shop. "She's got her quirks, but beggars can't be choosers. Even out here in friendly Oregon, there aren't a lot of folks who will work for a Black man. Know what I mean?"

"Shoot. I never thought of it that way. Really?"

Harold chuckled and started sorting his tools into their drawers. "I noticed it don't seem to bother you, but lotsa White folk don't want to call a negro boss."

I didn't have any experience with this sort of thing, and it made me uneasy thinking about how Joe and other guys would talk about Black people. Even Mom would say things disapprovingly, like *they should stay in their place.* Harold seemed at ease with the topic. "I guess you live with stuff like that every day," I said.

"Most every day. But at least here I don't have to keep my head down like down South where a Black man is 'supposed to know his place.'" His voice went all southern when he said the last part, and I saw the tightness around his eyes. "Here, if people don't like me, they just stay away. Or they come and get their biscuit and gravy and an oil change 'cause that's OK for Black folk to do that kinda work."

I sat and listened with my beer forgotten in my hand. I was embarrassed at his brashness, but it was like he was respecting me by talking that way. I nodded my head to show I was listening.

"You got many Black folks up your way?"

The question caught me off guard somehow, and I stumbled over my words. "In Anchorage, yeah. There were Black kids in my high school. Lots of military people I guess. We got along mostly. But it was like we were sorta divided. I mean we'd talk in class or do sports together, but we didn't hang together much." I was blushing, I think, and I drank my beer with a nervous twitch.

"Well, brother, that's a damn sight better than life was in my younger days. Maybe things are getting better. Of course, when you read the newspaper, it seems like everything's going to hell."

That night I went to sleep thinking how it would be to live where people didn't like you or thought you were less than them. Of course, that thinking got twisted around in my dreams, so I was surrounded by Black people telling me to learn my place. It being a dream, things didn't match because the people were in the woods with me and Joe and the dead moose, and they were yelling and chasing me in a chaotic dream-warped, slow-motion way. I woke in the dark, confused and scared. I was little-kid scared like I was five years old again and worried about bears coming into the house after me.

Once I was awake, all the buried blame about Joe rose to the surface, and I lay in my sweaty sleeping bag and waited for morning, looking out the smoked glass window at the glowing yard light and listening to the late-night truckers downshifting as they headed up the grade north of the crossroads.

It seemed the knot in my stomach came at night when I had time to think back to last fall. Was it only a year ago that I ran off to the cabin on the bluff after fighting with Mom and Joe about the war. Then there was Joe, showing up like everything was good and fine, and we were hunting buddies again. My memory was so vivid that I could smell the morning coffee and the moose blood, and Joe's blood, and then the knot in my gut would be so tight, and my legs would kick at the covers on the bed, and I could feel Harold's little trailer rocking from my thrashing. The first few nights I slept like a baby, but then my mind started chasing ideas around, and I would lay awake until dawn, staring in the dark or reading one of the books I found in the camper.

I spent the day working like a zombie, and Harold noticed when we settled ourselves that evening in the metal chairs under the apple tree. "You went out on the town last night?" he asked. "Son, you look like nine miles of bad road."

"I wish. There were too many demons running around in my head, and I couldn't sleep. You know what I mean?"

Harold slapped his leg, "Hell boy, I'm a Black man in rural Oregon and got a leg that ain't worth a nickel anymore. So, yeah, I got my share of demons. Some demons you gotta kill before they kill you, and some you just have to drag along with you like this bum leg."

"I think I've got one of each. I guess it'll get better."

"I thought you were haunted by what happened with your girl Iris, but it sounds like you got more eating you than that. What got a young fellow like you frettin' so much?"

Harold was one of those guys who makes you open up and spill your guts. And that's what I did. I told him about Joe and me fighting about the war and both of us trying to make up and be brothers. And I told him how I shot Joe when I thought I was shooting a moose, and finally I admitted the one thing I'd never said out loud. "I just worry that maybe I did it on purpose."

"I thought you said it was an accident."

"I did—I mean it was, but I keep seeing it in my mind. And sometimes when I roll that movie in my head I can see Joe's face before

I pull the trigger. It's like I knew he was standing there, and I shot anyway."

Harold laughed, "Good Lord, son. You can't trust your memory or your brain on stuff like that. It can make up stories and memories to make you believe whatever you want to. That's how the demons work. They get in your head and read your worries and feed them. *Do you want something to feel guilty about? Try this buddy.* And in comes some wildly different images of how things were."

I tried to see how Harold was telling it, that my brain was just creating a memory to match my thinking.

"Like my Daddy. He's passed on, and I miss him. Like to think about all the good times."

"Yeah."

"Hard to figure though," Harold said, "cause my daddy used to beat my ass, and I'd be so mad I could taste it. But now I tell that like I wasn't ever one bit mad at him, and I laugh to remember something that wasn't funny at all."

"Yeah, I see what you're saying."

"Hell son, cut yourself some slack. I bet everybody has forgiven you for shooting your brother except you."

That was one of those comments that kept me thinking for a while afterward, especially since I missed my dad the same way he described it.

NINETEEN

Without paying attention, I settled in at the Crossroads Café. Out in front of me, Iris was waiting, but I couldn't move in that direction. A routine quickly formed with rising early and working in the kitchen all day and then sitting with Harold under the apple tree and drinking a beer. Some afternoons when things were quiet in the café, I wandered into the garage and tried to make myself useful. Sweeping up, hauling garbage, and pumping gas. One slack day Harold gave me a hard look when I wandered in, and I could tell he had something on his mind. I didn't say anything and waited instead for him to speak.

A car pulled up to the gas pump. "I'll get it," I said and walked out to the pump and pumped five dollars' worth, wiped the windshield, and checked the oil. When I came back, Harold was wheeling a motorcycle out of the storeroom. It was a black Honda 350 with a coat of dust on it. "You ever ride one of these?" he asked. "I can't since my injury."

I ran a hand over the domed fuel tank and the dust came off and made a little cloud. "Nice bike," I said. "Just once I rode one back home. My buddy had a Honda 50. Called it his rice rocket. My mom was terrified of them. She thought motorcycles were sent by the devil to kill teenagers."

Harold laughed. "They have killed a few, usually people too stupid to stay alive." He opened the gas tank and peered inside. "Want to ride it? It's no good to me to just sitting in the garage. I do start it up now and then just to hear it purr." He replaced the gas cap and wiped the tank with a rag. "Bought this baby three years ago," he said. "Then I had my accident, and I can't ride anymore. The doctor said, maybe never. We'll see."

"That's a shit sandwich," I said. Then I stood there feeling apprehension.

"Sit on her and start 'er up." He pointed out the throttle, shifter, clutch, and brake and stepped back with only one hand on the fender. I swung a leg over and took the handlebars. He showed me how to start it and shift the gears by squeezing the clutch and tripping a lever with my foot. In what seemed no more than a blink, I was riding the empty highway with the wind tugging my shirt and the hot engine throbbing under me. Fences and houses swept by, and bugs struck my face, and I even swallowed one. The bike had felt heavy at first when I walked it out to the edge of the road, but once it was moving, it seemed to get lighter. I practiced shifting and felt the machine lurch beneath me and lunge forward.

I took Highway 201 where I didn't have to deal with traffic while I got the feel for driving with only two wheels. The highway flows southwest in a loose, meandering path, almost like a river, and at each curve of the road I felt the pull of gravity and motion that intensified the speed, heightened my senses. It was a mix of balancing on a bicycle while managing the speed and power of a car. I flashed an image of New Mexico and Iris and wondered for a moment, what if? What if I just kept going on this road until I found a road heading southeast toward New Mexico? What if I rode this motorcycle straight to Iris and found her serving burgers at that drive-in and took her up behind me on the bike back to this place. All those ideas flooded my head, and the highway suddenly was an empty, lonely place, and I was scared to ride it alone. It wasn't the dangers on the road I feared, it was me. I wanted to be back at the café where I was safe and broke and stationary.

By the time I got back to the garage, that trepidation had passed, and I didn't want to give up that bike and the freedom it represented.

I wanted this motorcycle, and I schemed on how to make it mine and imagined how it could open the whole country to the freedom of unfettered travel. I knew, then, why a motorcycle had the reputation it did, the aura, the stigma attached to it. It was a machine-age horse, a mechanized wild mustang, and riding it made a guy feel like an outlaw, a cowboy, a knight errant, a wild barbarian gunslinger riding alone on the steppe.

I coasted the bike back to the front of the garage, and I saw my reflection in the windows across the front of the shop. There was no rugged biker there in the glass, just a tall kid in fry-cook whites and cowboy boots straddling a motorcycle. I looked awkward and undramatic.

"Quite a ride, isn't it," asked Harold, standing in the doorway with a grin on his face.

"I could get used to that," I said. I wanted to jump up and down like a little kid.

"I sure miss it," he said. "Can't bring myself to get rid of the bike, but I should." I just nodded and felt bad for him. "It hasn't been ridden for almost three years. I kept telling myself I'd be able to ride it again, but I won't." He patted the tank, then I pushed the bike back into the rear of the shop. After I parked it, I gathered rags and a bucket of water and started washing it. I started with the gas tank where the dirt was mostly dust from sitting, and it didn't take much to bring out the shine.

The bike wasn't dramatic like the Harleys with big handlebars I'd seen pass on the highway. It was black and chrome with a flat leather seat and regular handlebars that seemed to fit my frame just right. I polished the chrome casing on the engine and wiped a bit of grime off the still-warm chrome exhaust pipe that ran along the left side of the bike.

"Be careful," said Harold. "She'll steal your heart." He set a beer on the floor by the front wheel. "Thanks for wiping her down like that." Then he walked out of the shop, locked the gas pumps, shut the lights on the Texaco sign, and slipped the deadbolt on the door. He didn't look back at me and the bike.

The next day, I told Cathy about riding the motorcycle, but she just turned up her nose and went stomping off to make more coffee, then she cycled through the kitchen, "Gosh, Sam, you got to ride a motorcycle all by yourself. Am I supposed to jump up and cheer? Jesus, did it have training wheels?"

"Sorry," I said. "Guess I was kind of silly about it. There's a lot of new things in my life now, and—oh never mind."

She scooped coffee grounds into the big percolator basket and put the lid in place and turned to me with a hand on her hip. "Oh my god, you are a dork! You want me to be your big sister? Is that it? That's all I need. And to think I was probably going to hit on you . . . eventually." She shook her head, and I turned back to shredding potatoes for hash browns. I hoped the heat of the stove helped cover the bright red I could feel in my cheeks.

TWENTY

That evening under the apple tree, I could feel the cool of the night falling faster, and Harold wore a jacket and pointed out the leaves turning colors on the trees. "Feel that chill in the air?" he said. "Fall has arrived."

"Yeah it's probably snowing back home," I said.

"I get all the winter I need right here, thank you." Harold leaned forward in his chair and looked at me with a tight face. "So, Sam. Did you change your mind about that gal in New Mexico?"

"What do you mean?" His words came out of left field, and I was suddenly embarrassed.

"You've been here a while, and every day I figure you'll pack up and move on. Shoot, stay here till Christmas if you want. I was just thinking you might feel obligated to stay."

"No, I'm still heading to go see Iris," I said. Silently, I counted the days I'd been here and remembered how this was just going to be a quick stop to make a little money. "Well, I gotta have my shit together when I go. I can't just fall in there on the Greyhound bus and say, "Here I am!"

"It looks like cold feet to me." Harold stood up, stretched, and turned his head toward the house, then stopped. "You need to figure out what you want and then go get it. You stayed on here to help out. Now it looks more like you're hiding out."

I looked up at the profile of the hills behind the house. "You're right. I guess. I like it here, and I don't know what to do. Maybe Iris is better off if I just stay away. I don't want to do the wrong thing. Or maybe I already did."

"So, you're going to do nothing? Can you live with that? In a month, two months, are you going to be fine with this?"

He left me, then, and walked away into the falling evening light toward the gold rectangle of the kitchen window with his wife's silhouette waiting for him. The cold of the evening worked its way into the metal seat of the chair, and I was suddenly chilled and uncomfortable. The chill got me moving and heading to my trailer, which wasn't warm and inviting like Harold's house. On the table where I left them were a detective novel and an unfinished crossword puzzle from the newspaper. I reached for the book but pulled back when I realized what I was doing. It was so easy. Pick up the book and read for a couple of hours and then try to finish the crossword before bed. I could go all evening every evening that way without thinking about Iris or the next steps. I could forget about shooting my brother and getting my girlfriend pregnant and disappointing my mom. I could just disappear into a make-believe murder in the fake city some author conjured up. I could pretend to be the divorced, alcoholic detective who gets the girl and the bad guys. I threw the book across the trailer, and the brittle pages shattered like fall leaves.

I spent most of the night wrestling with my conscience, chasing foolish ideas down rabbit holes. I remembered how it felt on the motorcycle, rolling down the highway, and it tempted me to keep moving. I thought a lot about the motorcycle, how it could carry me to New Mexico to find Iris. I could see myself on the open highway crossing the deserts of Utah, Arizona, and New Mexico bound for Iris. I even found a road map in the gas station and plotted the route and the distance I would have to travel. According to my best calculations, the trip would be about 1,200 miles, and I could do that in two days. I could camp for a few hours somewhere in Utah then ride on into Arizona and then New Mexico. I figured I didn't need much money if I made some sandwiches to take, then I'd just have to buy gas, and a motorcycle didn't use much gas. I knew all these little details that could make such a plan work, but something held me back as if actually seeing Iris now would break the fragile fantasy I carried of us together.

Sure, I could see myself riding up to that hamburger joint in New Mexico and sitting on that Honda in my jeans and white T-shirt like Marlon Brando, just waiting for her to come out and see me. But then what? That's where my imagination stalled, and the fear cloaked the future. I couldn't see beyond it. I couldn't know the feeling I was supposed to have now much less in the six months. Iris and me, and then Iris and me and a baby.

The past was hard enough, and the real prospects for the future were fraught with pitfalls. I kept scrolling in my head, What am I supposed to do? What do I want to do? What does she want?

I could see the world her father and mother wanted—and my mom wanted it too—a world with no baby. A baby that came and then was gone, a world where we didn't have one damn word to say and our parents' children, Iris and me, stayed children, and our child became part of another family. What would Iris and I be then?

Would we be a couple, friends, enemies? Maybe she would blame me and never see past anything but that. Yeah, I could move on. If I never see the baby, if I never experience that whole bringing life into the world event—which from the movies suggests that I'll be boiling water and then pacing the floor chain-smoking—would there ever be a baby for me to miss, to imagine, to grieve? Iris would have that. She would go through that lying in bed screaming from labor pains, she'd hear some doctor say, "It's a boy!" or "You've got a healthy baby girl!" And then, according to my local expert, Cathy, the baby would be whisked away, and Iris would be left empty and alone with all that afterbirth stuff and no baby.

Amid my turmoil, the days at the café continued miles covered on a highway while distracted by something else. I kept cooking, squabbling with Cathy, and avoiding the pay phone by the front door. Each evening after the café and gas station closed, Harold and I met under the apple tree to greet the evening. One night before I locked the café, I wrote up a shopping list for Harold and brought it to the chairs under the tree. It was a cool day, and the breeze dried the sweat on my back and made me cold. I went to my trailer for a sweatshirt while Harold opened beers and looked over my shopping list.

He put the list aside and drank. "You called your mom lately?"

I drank, too, and looked at him, chuckling as I said, "Yeah."

"Good. You laugh, but it's important. Women care about that shit. Callin' and checkin' in. And you gotta tell 'em your troubles so they can fret over you a bit. Now your dad. If you call him, he'll just think you're in jail or something where ya need help."

"My dad's gone. He died quite a while ago."

"That's tough. But your mama, she wants a running commentary."

"So you know my mom then."

"No. Just moms in general. It's their way." He drank again, then lit a cigarette. "And that gal in New Mex. You call her?"

"Wow. Did you have a bad day? I feel like I'm in the principal's office."

Harold just looked at me like he was waiting for more. I scuffed my boots on the grass and looked at the apples scattered around and starting to rot.

"Sam. What are you doing here?"

"What do you mean? I'm cooking and running the kitchen. Is there a problem?"

"No, no problem for me. I just want to know what you are doing here? It's been another week and you're still here. Why?" He leaned forward and looked hard into my eyes. "You said you had this girl, a pregnant girl, that you couldn't wait to get to. And here you are sitting under my apple tree drinking beer."

That set me back in my chair, and I drained the rest of my beer. "So you want me to leave. Is that it?"

"Like I said the other night. Stay as long as you want, but—" Harold stood up. "Shit! I'd love to keep you here. But what about you? What's keeping you here? Cold feet? Lost your nerve? What's going on?"

I stood up, too, shuffling restlessly, pinned by the question that he somehow knew I needed to hear. "I don't know," I said. "I got stopped here. You know when those guys ripped me off, and now. Shit. I can't start."

"Hold that thought," Harold said. "This is a two-beer night. I'll be right back. He headed to the house, and I watched his broad shoulder and shuffling limp as he crossed the lawn to the sliding glass door to the house. I could see his wife moving around under the lights of the kitchen and heard their muffled voices as they greeted each other.

The sun dipped below the peak of the hill behind the house, and the breeze slackened, bringing stillness to the evening. I suddenly felt alone in that twilight of the cooling evening and surrounded by the reality of my turmoil, and I realized that I was far from home, far from Iris and her freckled cheeks and growing bump, far from Joe and his critical eye and tasteless jokes. Joe would know what to do, I thought, and he'd do it without looking back. I knew what Mom wanted me to do, too, and my sister, too. She would know. But I was the one who had to decide, and I was the one who didn't know.

When Harold returned, he was carrying two plates with a beer in each armpit and forks in his shirt pocket. I jumped up to take a plate and beer. "She made shepherd's pie," he said. "And she's as good a cook as you, Sam. You'll love it."

We ate in silence until I realized that Harold was waiting for me. He had pushed his nose into my life, but he wasn't going to tell me what to do. I started talking, "I don't know what's holding me back. Heck, I haven't even called her. I could get the number to the place where she works and call her I guess. But she's not like other girls—like I would know. She might not want me there, or she might jack me around because she doesn't want me to do anything just for her. It's not like she sent me a note and asked me to come to rescue her."

Harold set his empty plate on the ground. "First off. From my limited experience, no girl—or woman—is like other girls. There is no operator's manual. You just have to feel your way along and pay attention. But not talking, or talking like you know what they should do, that'll get you nowhere fast."

"I know, but I haven't been over this ground before. I came all this way, and now I wonder if she really wanted me to. If I wanted to."

"So why did you come? Why did you jump on that plane and hightail it all the way from Alaska?"

I thought about that before I spoke. I ate the shepherd's pie and wondered, what made me do it? Then I knew. "I wanted to do the right thing. Not be that guy who bails on a girl when she gets pregnant. And yeah. I'm crazy about her. I think. Shit. That sounds stupid when I'm just sitting here."

Harold chuckled. "No. It's a scary time. When I was in your shoes. There was no time to think. Betsy told her parents, they called my parents, and the wedding was a month later. No discussion for either of us. It was either that or one of those homes for unwed mothers."

"A what? Oh, they have them, really? I heard about them, but it's kinda creepy sounding."

"You think we are the only ones this ever happened to?" He gestured with an unlit cigarette at the two of us. "Yeah, they have these homes where they send girls that get *in the family way*. The girls stay there until they deliver, then they leave without the baby, and everybody hopes no one knows that daddy's little girl got herself in trouble."

"No shit."

Harold leaned back in his chair and smoked like he'd said all he had to say. I stared into the growing darkness and wondered what lay beyond. I tried to identify the choices. Go home, stay here, go to New

Mexico. What else was there? "I thought about joining the Coast Guard if my number came up."

"What number?" I hadn't realized I said it out loud.

"Oh, sorry. My draft number. If I was going to be drafted I figured I would join the Coast Guard. I don't mind serving, but that Vietnam shit really sucks."

"So now you're thinking you could run off and do that now. Leave this girl on her own? You need to tell her that, to her face." Harold stood up suddenly. "You need to go. It ain't easy to do the right thing, but you need to look her in the eye and say whatever you got to say and hear what she's got to say." He gathered up the plates and beer bottles. "Hell. I'll fire you if that's what it takes. But you need to get your ass on the road." He didn't wait for an answer. He limped off toward the house with his load and didn't look back.

TWENTY-ONE

I had to ride south on Harold's Honda for about a hundred miles before I realized, I mean really understood, how exposed a motorcycle rider is. And even though I knew this going in, I was suddenly scared shitless. I was speeding along a highway doing sixty miles an hour with nothing but air between me and the pavement or the shiny fender of an eighteen-wheeler. What the hell was I thinking? I was going to ride across three states like this? Besides the prospect of becoming a blood stain on a truck fender, I was learning to manage the throttle, clutch, and shifter. I was assaulted by the sun, bugs, dust, and the blasts of wind that wanted to knock me off the road into the sagebrush every time someone passed me.

A motorcycle rider always looked to be just a laid-back cruiser, an exquisite sculpture of chrome and leather, indifferent to their surroundings. Now that I was one of them, I felt like a tangle of knotted ropes had replaced the muscles of my shoulders and back. My hands hurt from the death grip I kept on the handlebars, and my face was chapped and spattered with dead bugs. I wasn't sure I had taken a breath since I hit the kick-starter in front of Harold's gas pumps. I rode halfway across southern Idaho before I could relax and enjoy the ride.

Once I calmed down, I was having a great time. I was blessed with a clear, warm day, and the road southeast from Twin Falls was nearly empty of traffic, so I concentrated on relaxing my hands, lowering my shoulders, and breathing. I practiced shifting gears with the foot lever as I navigated the rolling hills and curves of the state highway, and as each mile passed, I was more confident. By the time I left Idaho, I was sure that I would take this bike all the way to New Mexico, and I could stand in front of Iris and say, *let's do this*. I just had to figure out what *this* was.

When I turned south onto the highway toward Salt Lake City, I saw a girl in jeans and a white T-shirt standing on the shoulder with her thumb out. There was just enough breeze to move her long blonde hair off her face so I could see she was tan and lovely. "Another time, another place," I said aloud, and I cautiously lifted a hand and gave her a little wave. I toyed with her image for a while, thinking guiltily of how it would be to have a girl like that riding behind me with her arms around my waist and her blonde hair streaming as I rode through the bleak, arid country of northern Utah. I thought of Joe who would have jabbed me and said, "What's the big deal? Just because you're on a diet doesn't mean you can't look at the menu." And Joe would have ordered off that menu I'm sure.

A couple miles down the road a big Chrysler passed me with the windows rolled down, and there was that girl waving and smiling as she passed with her blonde locks streaming in the wind like cirrus clouds— just as I imagined. She looked a lot more comfortable in the car than she would have been on the back of a motorcycle.

Not long after that, I found a pull-off at the top of a ridge and stopped to eat a ham sandwich and drink a root beer while I looked at the miles of highway stretching out to the horizon like a broad line of black ink drawn with a giant's pen across the brown desert. Dusty green sagebrush and rabbitbrush shaded the sparse tufts of grass under a pale blue sky, and thunderheads were building in the west. It was a lonely, desolate scene, and I was eager to cross it and leave it behind me. The day had grown hot, so I took off my jacket and rode in only my T-shirt, wishing I'd brought some water.

An hour later I had more water than I wanted for the thunderheads had raced in to bring me rain. I saw it ahead of me like a gray curtain, and as we converged, I could see the border of wet pavement waiting. In an instant I left the hot and dry and entered a cold downpour. I let off the throttle and squinted through the drops forming on my goggles. My shoulders tightened again. The empty country offered no shelter, not even a tree or an overpass, and after a couple of miles of misery, I pulled to the shoulder of the road and squatted on my heels beside the bike as the rain washed over me. I was still in my T-shirt and starting to feel chilled, but I knew my jacket would only get soaked if I put it on.

Then as fast as it came, the rain passed to the east. I pulled off my shirt, wrung it out, and used it to wipe some of the water off of the seat. I dug out a dry T-shirt and my jacket. I was chilled but the sun was out and the pavement began to steam. Back on the highway, my clothes began to dry, but the drying chilled me, and even though it was hot and sunny again, I was shivering. Finally, I stopped at a gas station and filled the tank. A block farther I found a café and had a bowl of watery chicken soup and coffee. The waitress must have seen my misery because she brought me another bowl of soup. "No charge," she said. "We have plenty. It doesn't taste like much, but at least it'll warm you up. You must 'ave gotten caught in that rainstorm."

"Yeah, I did. Thanks."

The restaurant was nearly empty, and she stayed and chatted while I gulped my second bowl of soup and a third cup of coffee. I felt revived by the food and the flirty chat of the waitress. It took me back to the days at Polar Pizza when I thought I had chance with the boss's daughter. I must not a been in that café thirty minutes, but it uplifted me somehow, like a good night's sleep. I got up when I saw the pay phone on the wall outside and knew it was time to call Iris. "Come back and see me," the girl said, twirling her hair and tilting her head like I had a camera to take her photo. I did sort of take a snapshot with my mind, then I turned my attention to Iris. I had been telling myself to call her for three days, but I always found a reason to give into my hesitancy. "Procrastination is the thief of time," I said to myself, and I asked the waitress for quarters when I paid my bill.

The long distance information operator had a Southern accent, and I had to ask twice how much money to put in the phone to pay for the call. Then the signal traveled through the wires and a phone was ringing in New Mexico and a young woman's voice answered. "Round-Up Drive-In. How may I help you?"

I heard the coins fall into the bottom of the phone. My heart was pounding, and I nearly hung up the phone in a panic, but the coins were gone, and the phone had been answered. I was committed.

"Hello? Is anyone there?"

"Ah, ah. Hey." Deep breath. "Is Iris there?"

"Hold on." I paced back and forth as far as I could with the phone to my ear. I watched the cars on the highway like they were my competitors in a race leaving me stuck in the pits.

"Hello, this is Iris." Her voice sounded distant and metallic. In the background, I could hear the rattle of more voices and shuffling feet.

"Hey."

"Sam? Is that you?"

How did I end up on Harold's Honda 350 riding through a rainstorm in northern Utah and dialing the phone to talk to Iris? It went something like this: I was finishing the last of the breakfast orders the day after my little talk with Harold and starting to wipe down the workstation behind the grill when Harold's wife walked in the back door of the kitchen. She was dressed in a sleeveless summer dress and her curly black hair was tied up in a scarf. "You must be Sam," she said. "With that bandana and long hair, I thought you were an Apache warrior. I'm Betsy."

I stepped toward her, wiping my hands on my apron. "Hello. Yeah, we met. Remember the spaghetti. How are you feeling?"

"Yes, that's right. Well, I'm here." She looped a flowered apron over her head and tied it in the back, and looked around the kitchen. "Things look to be in good order. Harold said you were doing a good job, but what the hell does he know? He'll eat anything that doesn't eat him first." She chuckled, and I could see her eyes roving over the pots on the shelves above the stove and plates stacked by the grill. She leaned over the large pot simmering on the stove back and sniffed. "Lamb barley soup?"

Not sure why I was nervous, I scooped up a clean spoon and held it out for her. "Your recipe," I said. "I found some lamb in the freezer that looked like it needed to be used."

She dipped the spoon in the soup, tasted it, and smiled. "Nice. Thanks for bailing Harold out of this jam I put us in."

"Kinda saved my bacon too, ma'am." I was still nervous. This was her kitchen, and I could feel her eyes taking everything in. I kept wiping even the places I had already cleaned.

"Now, young man you need to get out of here." Her voice was warm but firm, and she reached into her apron pocket.

"You want me to leave? Just like that?" I stopped wiping and leaned on the counter. "I don't understand."

"Harold and I talked and—"

"Harold and I talked, too, but he didn't talk about firing me." I took off my apron and rolled it on my hands to hide their tremors. "Well, he did, but I thought he was joking."

"It's not like that, Sam. You did good. Here's a hundred dollars." She put an envelope on the table." I kept rolling that apron. "This should be enough to get you to New Mexico and back." She smiled. "Go see that girl, Sam. Then come back and give me a hand in the kitchen. I'm not up to full speed yet."

I breathed a sigh of relief. "But who's—?" Betsy was pushing me where I was afraid to push myself, and I was still looking for reasons to stay.

"Sam, go change your clothes and pack your stuff. Harold's got the bike out front gassed up and ready to go. Bring it back in one piece, and I'll give you the rest of what I owe you."

My heart and mind were racing. Harold's bike and me and Iris? I had only ridden the motorcycle the few miles to Sears and back. "Are you kidding?" I heard myself say, "I can't take Harold's bike. That's his baby. And—"

"And you need to get your ass out of here—pardon my French. Get changed, get packed, and get down the road. I'll make you some sandwiches. You like ham?"

I had no excuse. The door was open, and I needed to walk through it. I went to the trailer and changed into my jeans, rolled my sleeping bag, and packed a satchel I found in the trailer. All I had was a clean T-shirt, some socks, and underwear. It hit me hard when I realized that it took someone else to get me back on the road. How long, I wondered, how long would I have stayed if Harold and Betsy hadn't moved me off the dime. I was excited, but I was scared too. I was going to have to face Iris now, Iris and the future.

I came back through the kitchen, and Betsy handed me a bag of sandwiches and two cans of root beer. "Now get going," she said, "and don't break Harold's bike or your neck." She smiled.

"Are you going to be OK here? I can wait until after lunch." I looked around the kitchen and saw that Betsy had already set up the workstation with slices of onion, tomato, and lettuce for sandwiches.

"You think you're the only person that can grill a burger and make a BLT. Shoot, you set me up with soup already. Now go." She turned her back and started shaping hamburger patties from a bowl of seasoned ground beef. I touched her on the shoulder as I walked past the counter, headed for the front door, and the next big step.

Cathy stopped in the middle of the room and put a hand on her hip. "Where are you going, hotshot?"

I patted her on the shoulder and grinned. I could see the Honda waiting out front with a helmet and goggles resting on the seat. "Don't you know? I'm going to Hollywood to be in the movies."

TWENTY-TWO

"So you guess you want to order a burger and fries? Is that why you called?" Iris said with her serious voice. Then phone line interference broke in.

Her humor caught me off guard, but that was her way. Iris seemed always to push me off my center, but I could play along. "Ah. Something like that. Do you have onion rings?" A loud truck passed on the highway, and I plugged one ear with my hand.

"Of course, made fresh right here. They are the best. But don't order onions if you're planning on kissing any girls."

"I wish I knew a girl! Guess I'll have the onion rings then."

"Want anything else?" Even with the static on the long distance line, her voice was like listening to music, the high notes on a piano. Oh boy, did I miss her.

"Got any brown-eyed girls with lots of freckles?"

"She laughed, and I imagined her eyes catching the light like a crystal hanging in the sun. "Just a fat pregnant one."

"That sounds perfect," I said.

"Oh Sam. You're so sweet. Where are you?"

"Heading your way, lady. With any luck I'll be there tomorrow."

"You're what? Oh my god you found me! Where exactly are you?" Her voice exploded through the phone with the excitement I wanted to hear.

"I'm in Utah. Of course, I found you."

The operator interrupted us. "Please deposit sixty-five cents for another three minutes."

I fumbled in my pocket, but I knew I was out of change. "Hold on," I said, "I need more change for the phone."

"Sam, hurry, we don't have much time. My dad—"

"Iris? Iris?" I was talking to a dead phone line. Time? Did she mean time on the phone or time before things changed for her?

The Southern accent was back, "I'm sorry your time has expired."

I slammed the phone into the cradle and kicked the wall. "Dammit!" I headed to the café for more change, then turned toward the parking lot instead, and straddled the bike. *Sam, hurry. We don't have much time.* What else did I need to know? I knew where she was, and I had the means to get there. What about her dad? Maybe that son of bitch had found out I was on my way. Sure he had. Aunt Sally owed me no confidence. She must have told them.

It would be a waste of time to try and call Iris back. It wasn't like she could just sit by the phone and wait for me to call. I turned the key and kicked the starter. I strapped on the helmet, still damp from the rain storm and wiped the fog off the goggles. I pulled out on the road, calculated the number of miles between Iris and me, and ran formulas through my mind—time distance speed. Miles, miles per hour, rest time needed. Distance divided by average speed equals travel time. The math kept my mind away from those words, *We don't have much time,* away from looking too far down the road and the next big question, what was I going to do when I got there? I kept crunching the numbers.

The traffic picked up as I approached Salt Lake City, and once more I felt exposed and vulnerable on the motorcycle in the rushing stream of cars, pickups, work vans, and long-haul trucks.

I was wound up now and the adrenaline hounded me to leap out into the fast traffic in the left lane of the divided highway. *We don't have much time!* But I was too fearful and kept riding like the naive rider

I was clutching the handlebars until my hands hurt and hugging the white line on the shoulder. I was barely able to keep up with the slowest traffic. I rode through Salt Lake City in a turmoil of traffic, time, and frustration. At a town called American Fork, I pulled over and found a gas station, got two dollars in quarters, and called again.

It was a total waste of time. Iris had finished her shift and left for the day. I hung up the receiver, filled the bike with gas, and bought a sandwich. I had wasted fifteen minutes, and I didn't like to think about how much farther I could be if I'd kept riding. "No matter," I said, "I'm on the road now, and I've got lots of time to figure out the next step. If I ride all night I can be there by noon. Then we'll sort this thing out."

Saying you'll do something is one thing. Actually doing it is another. By the time I got to Green River, I was sore like I had ridden a horse bareback the whole way from Oregon. To be honest, I had never ridden a horse, but it couldn't feel worse than the ache in my back and shoulders and the cramps in my hands. It was dark, and the only place open was a truck stop where I bought gas and coffee. I made myself drink two cups as I walked among the parked semitrucks with their engines idling like sleeping dragons and their big sleeper cabs casting shadows from the street lights. I stretched and moved, trying to keep myself awake and loose. The day had started early, and my mind hadn't rested since Betsy had walked into the kitchen. That seemed like days ago, and now I wanted rest for the mind and body. I wanted to sleep. But I put that out of my mind and returned to the motorcycle. Rest would have to wait. As Joe would say, I can rest when I am old.

TWENTY-THREE

"Can I take your order?" The voice on the speaker wasn't Iris; it was a girl that sounded like Texas.

"I'm here to see Iris."

"Iris? She's off today."

"Oh."

"Do you want to order something?"

"Um. Just a minute."

"Haha. OK. Hit the button again when you're ready." I hit the button.

"Are you ready to order?"

"Yes. I'll have some onion rings and a root beer."

"Anything else?"

"No, wait! Yes. Do you know where Iris lives?"

"Who are you?"

"I'm Sam, her—uh friend from Alaska." I had made it to the Round-Up Drive-In in Las Vegas, New Mexico, just after noon. The Round-Up Drive-In had parking places under a sloping roof with intercoms for ordering, and the menu was on a placard above the intercom. I drove the bike under the aluminum sunshade, turned off the engine, and pushed the button on the intercom. I put down the kickstand and sat astride the bike letting my muscles sag against my spine. I was stiff and sore and tired and windburned and scared and excited and hungry and thirsty, but mostly I was here and I knew why.

In five minutes a blonde woman in her twenties walked up in a denim skirt, white cowboy hat, and checkered blouse. She carried a tray holding a basket of onion rings and a tall paper cup rattling with ice. "My god, you must be Sam. You did come. Iris said you were coming, but holy shit, who would believe it? Damn, Sam!"

"Yup." I took my root beer off the tray and put my money in its place. At that moment, significant as it might be, I was so thirsty I could drink out of a puddle—if I could find a puddle in this brown desert. I pulled out the straw and poured the icy soda down my throat, feeling the ice against my teeth and the tingling of the bubbles against my pallet.

"Yup? You travel all this way and all you can say is *yup?* Who do you think you are, Gary Cooper?"

I relaxed a bit and took another drink, then grabbed the basket of onion rings. I was light-headed and euphoric like I'd been drinking beer all morning. "No ma'am, I don't reckon I am. Just call me Sam, Sam Barger." I bit an onion ring and grinned. I had made it.

The carhop parked her tray on her hip and looked me over. "I'm Karen. Me and Iris work together most days. She told me you were coming. Of course, I didn't believe her. I think I called you a lying dirt-bag. And here you are doing your Gary Cooper bit. I'll be damned."

After the second onion ring, I asked, "Iris. Is she OK? She didn't leave, did she?"

She put her hand on her hip and took a deep breath. "Well Sam, yesterday was a total mess."

"What happened?" The onion rings were forgotten.

Karen looked around to see if anyone was close enough to hear then said, "Well, her dad came, and you know what a jerk he can be. And he was yelling at Iris in the parking lot about something, and the manager came out. You know, to see what was going on." She stopped and took a breath. "Shit I've got to get back." She looked at the cars lined up in the parking stalls and then turned to go back to the kitchen.

I grabbed her arm. "Wait. What happened?"

"OK," she said, "quick version, the manager found out Iris was pregnant and fired her. Well, let her go or something. Her dad practically threw her in the car and drove off. Sorry," she said over her shoulder, and she trotted off to the brick building painted red and decorated like a barn.

I stared after her and absent-mindedly ate the rest of the onion rings without tasting them. I slumped against a post and drank my root beer the same way, looking at the cars coming and going in the lot that smelled of grilling burgers and frying potatoes. I was suddenly woozy with exhaustion. Beaten and tired, I had made it, but I was too late. I felt like Sherlock Holmes, always one step behind Professor Moriarity. I pressed the button on the little intercom.

"Welcome to the Round-Up. Can I take your order?"

"Yeah, I want a double cheeseburger."

"Sam? You're still here? It's Karen."

For some reason, I laughed. "Of course I'm still here. And bring me some water, too, please."

"OK, sugar, I'll be right out when your burger's ready."

She couldn't see me nodding at her as I understood her need to be businesslike. I didn't feel businesslike. I felt a crazy anger rising in me, and it was hard not to rush in through that glass door, find Karen, and shake the rest of the story out of her. Instead, I sat and looked around the dusty desert town I'd traveled all these miles to get to. It was similar to places in Alaska with its haphazard sprawl of businesses and houses along the highway, but there weren't many trees and a lot more mud-colored adobe structures, so I felt like Clint Eastwood should be riding down the street in his serape and flat-brimmed hat.

How nice it would be to just have a shootout with old man Davis and get it over with. I could almost hear the whistling and the plucking of guitar strings in the background as we faced off on the dusty street. Oh, if it could be that easy, but it wasn't. I had to figure out where Iris was living and find a way to be alone with her long enough to talk to her. Shit, was that too much to ask?

"Here you go cowboy," Karen was standing in front of me, holding a tray with a burger wrapped in bandana-print wax paper and a tall paper cup with a straw sticking out of it.

"Oh, sorry, I was somewhere else for a minute."

"You are somewhere else, period, trust me." She laughed. "This is definitely somewhere else. So you want to find Iris, I bet."

I dug in my pocket for some cash. "Yeah, you know where she lives?" I gritted my teeth anxiously and held out some bills.

"Forget it, the burger's on me. Well, actually, it's on them." She nodded at the Round-Up Drive-In. "Didn't even ring it up."

I stuffed the bills in my pocket and the burger in my mouth. I would let Karen talk uninterrupted, and she did.

"So, Sam. Anyway, see Iris and me. We hit it off working together, and it didn't take me long to figure out what was going on. Been there myself, but I never had a guy try to stick up for me like you. Anyway, the plan was—her dad's plan anyway—was for Iris to stay with her uncle for a few weeks, then move to a maternity home when she's close to the end of her term."

I nodded and looked around nervously. "Don't you need to get back to work?"

Karen waved a dismissive hand. "I'm on break. Those homes for unwed mothers are mean places where they treat you like nasty little sinners until you give birth, then they take the baby away. Wham bam, thank you, ma'am." She looked away blinking like she might start crying. "Then you never see her again." She took a breath and reset herself. "Anyway, her dad must have heard you were coming because he was steaming when he showed up here and started in on her. She was in tears when they left. And she doesn't cry easily."

"So you think it's all my fault," I said, wadding my burger wrapper and stuffing it into the paper cup. I stomped off to the garbage can.

"Well at least half of this is, don't you think? Things were peaceful here until they found out Sam Barger was coming, but it ain't your fault that her dad's an asshole."

I took a deep breath and said, "OK, I get it. So you probably know where Iris is living and how to get there."

Karen crossed her arms and gave me a challenging look. "What do you have in mind? You came all this way, but what are you going to do now? Elope? Beat up her dad? Come on, cowboy. What's the plan?"

Karen reminded me of my sister, Mary, the way she put me on the spot and made me verbalize what I was doing or planning to do. "I came here to talk to Iris and do the right thing. As you said, I didn't want to be one of those guys that did nothing."

"I'm off in about an hour. You come back then, and I'll show you where she lives. There's a laundromat down the road about a mile where you can get a shower." She raised her eyebrows and tilted her head in a way that made me think I ought to do just that. I left the Round-Up feeling hopeful but still frustrated, a feeling that was so common after the last few weeks that it was like putting on a well-worn shirt.

Two hours later, I followed Karen's blue Ford Falcon down a dusty road a mile from town. The dry grass desert rolled away on each side of the road with a few cows grazing in the distance. We drove in a straight line toward a mountain range fringed in forest. Karen drove fast, and her car was invisible in the cloud of dust boiling up behind her. I hadn't ridden much off the pavement, so I was cautious again like the first hours on the highway, and after being pelted by the rocks kicking up I kept well back of her dust cloud. Suddenly, the dust cloud decreased, I spied her car pulled off by a driveway, and a quarter mile away a double-wide trailer house squatted on a rise surrounded by junipers.

Karen rolled down the window when I came alongside. "There's your castle to storm, Galahad." I took a deep breath and tried to calm the ripple in my stomach. This was it, finally. Maybe. "Her daddy was driving a white rental sedan when I saw him. I don't see it there. You might have a shot if he's not home."

"All right then," I said. "Thanks for being a friend." It sounded corny, but this kinda dramatic crap was like that.

"Be good to her, and don't make me regret this." Karen shifted into drive and disappeared in a cloud of dust. I could see the cloud billow higher when she made a U-turn at the top of a rise a half mile away, then the contrail of dust came back toward me. She stopped hard and rolled the window again. "What the hell are you waiting for? Saddle up, cowboy, and tighten your cinch."

All I could do was nod at the Texas blonde shaking her head at me. She stuck a hand out with a slip of paper torn from a little spiral notebook. "My number. You might need a place to crash, alone or together, y'all are welcome." Then the engine roared and her dust cloud followed her away down the road toward town, leaving me with a gut full of nerves and a dry mouth.

A cow walked down to the fence line and pushed a dirty white face toward me. "What are you looking at?" I asked. "I'm going. Give me a minute." Then a minute passed, or more, and I started the bike and turned up the drive toward the doublewide. I had rehearsed several speeches for Iris and her relatives, but they were forgotten when I pulled in behind a Chevy pickup and spotted Iris sitting on a tiny lawn playing with a dog. She looked up, squinting into the sun.

I had imagined a dramatic moment when Iris would rush into my arms and hold me so tight I could feel her heartbeat. Her lips would be warm and full and her eyes wet, looking up at me with ardor and desperate passion. Instead, she stood up and sauntered across the lawn eying me across the fence like I was an encyclopedia salesman. "Well, it's about time you got here," she said. Yup, that was Iris.

I took off my helmet and parked the bike. Part of me wanted to jump that fence and grab her and not let go. The other side of me felt unsteady and weak. Yeah, I was scared. I put my hands on the chain link fence and leaned across. My eyes were binoculars focused only on Iris, and nothing around me was visible. Even the dog, which suddenly started barking, was out of my field of vision. Only Iris was in focus. "You look good. Real good in fact. Wow." I blushed with my honesty.

She walked toward me, still small and agile, but her breasts were larger, and the little bump was more obvious under her T-shirt. Her hair was thick and loose like the wind had filled it with air. "You just like my big boobs."

I blushed, "Why else would I come all this way?"

She laughed. "You a biker now?"

"You might say that."

"I might say anything."

"Some things don't change." I was breathing heavily, my heart thumping against my chest, and the desert heat was suddenly more intense.

"Took you long enough to find me."

"You didn't make it easy."

"I know." She laughed like she'd made a joke. She gripped the top of the fence and looked up at me. "You're taller than I remember."

"I lied about my height."

She smiled. "Good one."

"You're prettier than I remember."

"It's the tan and the boobs."

"Maybe. Wanna take a ride?"

She nodded heavily with pursed lips, then looked back at the house. "Give me a minute." She went and quickly came out of the house in a sweatshirt and canvas shoes and pushed through the gate without looking back. I untied the bedroll from the seat and leaned it against the fence, then started the bike and took it off the kickstand and handed her the helmet. "It'll be a little big." My hands shook as I adjusted the chin-strap.

I steadied the bike while she climbed on behind me and found the footrests.

"Ready?"

She wrapped her arms around me and leaned in. "Oh yes. I'm ready."

I walked the bike forward and gave it a little gas. The added weight reminded me that I really didn't know much about riding, and I had never ridden anyone on the bike with me. It didn't help that I was distracted by the feel of Iris hugging my back, pregnant Iris,—were we a family?—but we made it down to the road, weaving back and forth from ditch to ditch as I got a feel for balancing the bike again. I turned right and followed the brown dirt road toward the mountains. As I accelerated, Iris pulled herself tighter against me, and I imagined I felt her heartbeat. I just wanted to keep riding with the hot wind pounding my face and her chest pressed against me. It was the most right I had felt in forever.

After a couple miles she patted my shoulder and pointed to an old trace of a road on the left side, and I turned down it. The sagebrush was pushing in to hang over the ruts, slapping our legs as we went, and I downshifted to slow the bike. It was a short, bumpy ride to a broken windmill and rusty stock tank beside a wooden corral, chocolate brown with age.

I stopped, she dismounted, and I put down the kickstand. Her hair cascaded out of the helmet, and the wind caught it, so it swept away from her face. I bent and kissed her. She held me then, close like she was afraid. I felt her shiver. She stepped back and looked around in that way she had of creating space for herself.

"I wish I could draw," she said. "I'd sketch this place. Don't you feel like you're standing in a landscape painting?"

I turned and looked at the low brown grass and the narrow triangle of the windmill tower reaching up to blue, trying to see what she saw. I couldn't but said I did. "Yup."

"Nice bike. Where'd you steal it?"

"It's a long story with a happy ending."

"I got time."

"First, tell me how you're feeling."

"I'm good. I don't have morning sickness like some women, and look," she stuck out her chest. "My boobs are getting bigger—as if you didn't notice."

I blushed and grinned, "I noticed."

"I bet you did, you hound." She hugged me while I told her about Walla Walla and Aunt Sally and the bus ride to get there. I told her how I called home and got Mom to read her postcards. I told her how I met Harold and Betsy and how they loaned me the Honda because they wanted me to be here. "Why did you make it so hard to find you? You could have just told me."

"I did, I told my stepsister because I knew you would find her and make her tell you. If you wanted it bad enough, I knew you would find me." She walked away, pacing around the circular stock tank with her hand on the rusty rim.

"If I wanted to bad enough? What's that mean?"

"I knew if I asked you, you'd come 'cause you're a good guy. But I didn't want it that way. I needed you to want to come. I needed you to be willing to work at it."

"Work at it. Christ, I sure did work at it. You could have gotten word to Aunt Sally, but you sent your clever little postcards instead."

"I'm glad you're here. I wasn't sure you'd come all this way, that you'd want to. And now, look at all the places you've been thanks to me."

I kept looking at the windmill with the broken rusty vanes hanging loose like broken wing feathers on some iron bird. "I could have been here sooner."

"Yeah, but this way, I know why you're here because it's something you wanted." I waited as she circled the tank, tracing the rim with her hand. She circled it and then walked up close and put her arms around me. "And you're here, and I'm glad, but—" She laid her head against my chest, and the wind blew her hair up into my face.

"But what?" I wrapped an arm around her shoulders and stroked her hair.

"But it's a long way to come to say goodbye."

TWENTY-FOUR

"What do you mean, goodbye? I didn't come here just to try the onion rings, you know." I was leaning toward her, suddenly frustrated.

Iris leaned back against the old stock tank and stared at the sky, "I know, Sam, but it's complicated and all crazy now. I didn't think it would be this way, but it is."

"What way? You mean being pregnant? It's all new to me too."

She grabbed my forearm and squeezed it hard. "No, Sam. I'm talking about you and me and right now and my parents. I was supposed to be here for a while, and Dad was going back to Anchorage. Shit, Sam. I had a job and everything."

"Wait a minute. I feel like I walked into the second reel of the movie here. So what happened? What's changed?"

Iris kept squeezing my arm and I could feel her nails. She wouldn't look at me and that was scary as if there was bad news coming. She bit her lip and shook her head, then she said, "It's you, Sam. You should never have come. You should never have gotten involved at all. You just pushed your way in and now—now it's just a big—"

I jumped to my feet. "A big mess. I get it. It's all a big mess that I made because I decided to give a shit. Is that it?"

"There's more. But yes." She was on her feet now, too, and the desert wind was blowing our hair, and the old wind vanes tried to turn but only creaked sadly. I walked away, and Iris followed. "OK, here it is from the beginning. I was supposed to quit school and stay home and do correspondence first semester while we figured things out. Then you showed up at our door, and Dad gets the idea that you and I are going to elope or something. Wham! Iris gets shipped off to Aunt Sally, but Aunt Sally and Dad fight. Bam! Send Iris to Uncle Bob's house in New Mexico. Not perfect, but things are going well. I've got a job, and Uncle Bob and Aunt Edna are real chill."

I stopped walking and turned around, "So what happened?"

"You happened, stupid. Daddy finds out that good ol' Sam Barger, who never gives up, is hot on our trail. And Daddy doesn't want you anywhere near his precious little slut, Iris."

"I did this? This is all on me?" It felt like a punch in the gut. All the hope and pride that had carried me this far suddenly fell away. She saw it and grabbed my shirt. I pulled away, but she followed and grabbed me.

"I'm the one who encouraged you, Sam. It's my fault too."

"But you wanted me to come, didn't you?" I said.

She leaned against me, and I smelled the desert in her hair, the sagebrush and sunlight and mesquite. "I did. I wanted you to care, to want to come, but you shouldn't have. You should have stayed in Alaska and written me long letters that I wouldn't answer."

I had to chuckle at that one. "Yeah, you'd send your silly postcards. They led me here, you know. And now I'm sorry, I guess. But not really. I mean I'm sorry I messed things up for you, but I'm here now. So let's just be here. We can't do a damn thing about what's passed, but maybe there's a new plan."

"So it's time for plan B?"

"I think we're well past plan B, Iris."

"Well, Daddy's got a plan that's happening first thing tomorrow. I'm going to some maternity home, Brentwood Home for Wayward Girls or whatever it's called, which sounds like a reform school without the prison uniforms," she said. "And then they'll take my baby when it comes, and I'll never see it again." She leaned back against the old stock tank and closed her eyes. "I don't know what I want," she said, "but I want to decide, Sam, I want to hold my baby, Sam, but none of that is going to happen. Daddy's got this locked up, and that's that."

"We can go," I said. "We can go right now. We can get on that motorcycle and ride away. I mean it. You want me to marry you, I will. We'd be poor and we'd probably fight a lot, but we could do it."

She laughed then, "Oh Sam, you are so romantic, *You'll marry me if I want to?* I don't think that's how a proposal is supposed to sound. And what? Are we going to ride that borrowed motorcycle all the way to Alaska? I don't think so."

"I do want to marry you. I'm crazy about you," I said, "and we don't have to go to Alaska. We can go to your Aunt Sally. She'll put you up. I know it. Or back to my friends in Oregon where I have a job."

"Dad will find us and drag me off again. And probably shoot you in the process, and at the very least get you thrown in jail." She leaned against me, and I could feel her heartbeat, and I imagined I felt another heart beating as well.

"Then we'll go to Harold's place. He's got a trailer we can stay in. No one will find us there. Then we'll work things out. Your dad will calm down, and we'll convince him that we can do this." I kissed her then, and we kissed long and gently until the heat of it was too much. "See," I said, "we should be together."

"Shut up, Barger," she said. "I'm tired of talking about it." And she kissed me. That's all we did until almost dark. We just held on for dear life and kissed like it was the end of the world. She let me touch her belly, and even hours later, I could still feel that warmth in my palm, warmth from the life we made together. She called it *the bubble.* Then I said, "We better get back." I knew she wouldn't come north with me, and I didn't feel right asking again. I wanted to. I wanted to beg her, but I wouldn't. I knew she wasn't sure what she wanted.

"You came to see me, Sam, and that means so much to me. I can't believe you did. I feel like a real turd now that you did though." She strapped on the helmet and tucked her loose hair up in it. Her eyes twinkled when she looked up at me, "All this way, and you didn't even get laid."

"How do you know?" I said.

She punched my arm and we laughed. "You are such a brat."

We rode back to the house with her wrapped tight around me and her head lying against my back. When I pulled up to the house, she hopped off the bike and patted me on the back before we walked up to the porch together. The man on the porch was obviously Iris's uncle, so I stepped up and extended a hand and said, "How do you do, sir. I'm Sam Barger. Thanks for taking care of Iris."

"How do you do." He looked like Iris's dad, but he was sun-tanned and dressed in a plaid western-cut shirt and a hat that didn't look like it ever came off his head. "She's a nice kid. We like havin' her around."

Then he turned to Iris. "Your Dad's on the way back from town. He wants to leave first thing in the morning. Better make sure you're packed."

I stood restless on the porch thinking I should go but not ready to. Part of me wanted to be far away when Jack Davis came back, but the bolder, angrier me remained there, ready to punch him in the face.

"You best come in. We got what's left of dinner warming in the oven. Didn't know when you kids would be back." Iris's aunt was in the kitchen and tried to act like it was just another day with a pair of hungry teenagers to put a casserole in front of. We ate and made small talk in the tense way people do when waiting for something to happen, and Jack Davis didn't make us wait long.

He slammed in the door with a cigarette hanging out of his scowling mouth. "What the hell is that long-haired piece of shit doing here? Bob, I told you to run his ass off."

I stood up, and we stared across the table at each other. "Hello, Mr. Davis."

His brother crossed the room from the couch and put a hand on Jack's shoulder. "Take it easy, Jack. I told you he showed up. Let him alone. He just came to see Iris."

"Bullshit. He's seen enough of her." He was swaying and grabbed a chair to steady himself. Iris left the table and took our dishes to the sink. "Daddy, you want some supper? It's hot."

He put his hands on his hips and looked around the room. "Hell no. I don't want no damn supper. You need to get yourself packed, girl. That's what you need to worry about."

Iris left the kitchen with her head down and moved to the couch where she cowered and chewed her lip. I'd never seen her like that, and I knew my options were fading. Iris's aunt kept wiping the counter and scrubbing dishes.

"Now, Jack, you need to calm down," Bob said. "Getting worked up again ain't going to help matters one bit. This kid came all this way to make sure Iris was OK, and from what I can tell he don't want to cause trouble."

Jack pushed his brother away and turned like he was coming for me. "That long-haired punk has caused enough trouble already, and you know as well as I do why he's here. But if you think I'm going to let these two get married and ruin all our fuckin' lives, you're thinking wrong."

I was still standing and ready for whatever he brought even though the last thing I wanted was to get in a fistfight with him right there in front of Iris. "Nobody said anything about us getting married, Mr. Davis. I'm just here because I figured this is where I ought to be. I'm a part of this too. This ought to be between me and Iris, and I won't be left out, sir. And what the hell? Why shouldn't we get married? Wouldn't that fix everything? Family reputation intact!"

"A part of this? You ain't no part of this. Hell boy, you don't even know if it's yours. You have no idea who my daughter's been whorin' around with. And you two getting married, good God almighty wouldn't that be a mess. A know-nothing hippie, and my worthless, snot-nosed daughter."

"Daddy! Would you just stop?" Iris looked small and desperate. It was like some demon had possessed her and taken her spirit. I couldn't help but worry that I was to blame for that too. Maybe I was that demon.

Then Jack Davis showed me the truth. He took a step toward me and pointed a finger at Iris. "You think she spent all summer pining away for your worthless ass? I wouldn't count on it."

"Iris," I said, "tell him. Tell him we're in this together. Tell him we're leaving together. Shit! Tell him something." I had never seen her like this, small and afraid, unwilling to face someone down, and I wanted her riled up, mad, and shaking her finger in her dad's face.

Jack took a lurching move toward me, but Bob took his arm, "That'll be enough, Jack." Jack pushed him away. "What makes you think you're the daddy anyway?"

Iris's aunt stood in her kitchen with eyes shooting daggers. "Jack Davis," she said, "you shut your mouth or get out. We've all heard enough. This isn't your house, remember."

Jack glared around the room. Swaying unsteadily, he was like a wounded bear, but he was drunk on liquor and anger. He seemed not to hear the woman speaking from the kitchen. "I'm going to the head and take a shit, and when I get back," he pointed at me, "you better be gone." He started down the hall and then turned and spoke to Bob. "And if she tries to leave with that hippie son of a bitch, knock her on her ass if you have to. I don't care if she is pregnant."

He staggered down the hall and banged the bathroom door shut. Bob looked at his wife and shook his head. "Maybe you better go, son. There's no good to be done here tonight."

I looked across at Iris, but she sat staring at the floor, hugging herself. The color had gone out of her, and her hands were clenched into tight fists. "You know this isn't right," I said. "This is so damn wrong."

"You better go." Bob moved to the door, and I looked again at Iris, hoping she'd jump up and come with me, hoping she'd say something, hoping that something would happen to keep me from walking out the door that Bob Davis was holding open. Instead, the room was thick with silence, and none of us moved. I went to her and knelt down with my hands on her knees. "Talk to me, Iris. Tell your dad what you want. Make him listen."

She didn't look up. She just shook her head, and tears streamed down her face. She looked so frail and young at that moment that it was hard to imagine that she was pregnant or that she was even the girl I had known. I stood up and walked toward the door, and if I had kept going, things might have been different, but I didn't. I stood in that open door and turned to Iris, and it all came bubbling out of me. "I guess leaving is all I have left to do if you're going to sit there and be Daddy's little baby. Is that what you want? And to hell with me, huh? To hell with the guy who came all this way."

Bob stepped up cautiously and put a hand on my back. "Best keep moving, son."

I brushed his hand away and leaned into the room. "You come with me now or just forget I even came. Forget I cared enough to come all this way, and you won't come ten feet because your drunk-ass father thinks he knows best. Forget that one guy wanted to do right by you. Forget that you wanted to have this baby and decide what happens to it. Forget all that, Iris. Your daddy thinks he has all the answers. Well, maybe he does! Maybe everything he said is dead on."

Bob pushed me out the door then, and I picked up my pack by the fence and threw it down the driveway, and yelled into the night. Then I picked it up and rode to the end of the driveway, where I sat astride the motorcycle beside the mailbox and stared into the darkness of the desert night. A fever ran up my back, and I wanted to scream and cry and kick something. Then I realized what I had said and done. Had I really been that final?

My mom had been seriously pissed at me before and had sometimes said mean things, but I'd never heard anyone talk about their child the way old man Davis did that night. I felt pretty sick that I didn't knock him down for it, but instead, I just stood in that doorway and made things worse. And worse yet, left her there with him. I couldn't bring myself to ride away completely though. I didn't know where to go anyway, so I sat there by that mailbox looking at the moon rising over the shadowed desert.

It wasn't long before a pair of headlights showed on the road, and a sheriff's Impala pulled up and stopped. A tall, lean man in a wide-brimmed hat got out with a flashlight that he used to look me over. Then he walked close and stopped with one hand on his gun belt. "Everything OK?"

"No. I think I'm a hell of a long way from OK." Luckily the fight had burned out of me by then.

"What's the problem?"

"Just overall a bad day that was supposed to be a really good one."

"Yeah? It goes that way sometimes. Let's see some ID."

I dug my wallet from my jeans and handed him my driver's license.

"Alaska, huh? You're a long way from home."

"That's an understatement. Away from home and in over my head."

"What are you doing out here?"

"Just sitting, I guess."

"He nodded up the drive toward the house. You know these folks?"

"Yeah. I was here to see a girl."

He stood straighter like he'd gone to another level of cop alert, ready for action. "The Davis's don't have a girl." He waited.

"No. You're right. She's a niece. Did they call you? Is that what this is? You've got to be kidding me."

"Somebody called. I got sent here to make sure everything was OK. They want you escorted off the property."

"They really called the cops on me? No shit? This family likes callin' the cops."

"It happens. People get nervous. At least nobody pulled a gun on you did they?"

"No."

"What about you? Are you armed?"

"A Boy Scout knife. No wait. That got stolen back in Oregon. I got nothing but my wits. And that doesn't seem to be nearly sharp enough right now."

He hesitated like he was thinking of another question. "Well, you can't stay here. There's nothing for you out here but trouble. Have you got somewhere to go? If not, you better find somewhere. I don't want to ruin your night and mine."

The whole time we talked I never saw the man's face, and I didn't answer him. I just started my bike and pulled out on the road. I cussed all the way to that old broken windmill and sat down with my back against the stock tank where Iris and I had talked only a while and forever ago.

The night was chilly, and I didn't last long sitting in the wind. I got up and rolled out my sleeping bag on the lee side of the tank. I got in fully dressed, removing only my boots and jacket. I rolled the jacket for a pillow and lay back to look at the stars. The rusty old windmill creaked and growled above me, casting a dark and eerie shadow when the moon rose. I was suddenly tired and quickly fell asleep.

I dreamed of trying to cross a shallow creek on the motorcycle, but it was swept away by the current, and I heard ravens screaming at me as I waded slowly and helplessly against the water, even though the water was only barely over my ankles. Then the dreams that I thought were gone came back: the dream of me and the forest and the rain and shooting into the dark. Suddenly, I woke up, confused, forgetting where I was, and then I recognized the screeching, groaning windmill and heard the howl of a coyote coming to me from somewhere in the darkness. It was a call I remembered from home, and I was made lonesome by it, and I couldn't see the path I would take in the morning.

Another time I would have been caught up in the romantic imagery of a lone, lovesick outlaw camped on the desert, sleeping on the hard ground with coyotes howling in the dark. Another time the smell of sagebrush and the black sky full of endless stars like I'd never seen before would have had me awestruck. But not this night. The thought of living a cliché gave me no cheer, and I would have traded it all for my bed back home and one of Mom's wool quilts. "But you're not home, Sam," I said. "You're here in New Mexico, and your girl is down the road pregnant, scared, and all alone. What the hell are you going to do about it?"

TWENTY-FIVE

The woman stepping out of the pickup truck with a thermos in one hand looked familiar. She wore jeans and cowboy boots and a denim jacket that made her look lean and tall. "Morning, Sam. Want some coffee?"

"Sure." I was spooked, disoriented, and bushwhacked. I looked around for my boots and scrambled out of my sleeping bag. Who was this? The sun was shining in my eyes, and when she stepped out of its glare, I recognized Iris's aunt. "Oh, Mrs. Davis. How'd you find me?"

"I figured you'd be close, and then I saw your tracks where you turned in here. Not a lot of motorcycles riding around out here."

I nodded and accepted the thermos cup of coffee. The sun was just coming up over the hill and hadn't begun to warm the sagebrush-covered valley. I took a sip, then sat down and put on my boots and jacket. Edna Davis squatted and watched me, then reached into her jacket pocket and pulled out a paper bag. "Doughnut?"

I reached into the bag and took one. She seemed relaxed squatting there. Her face was brown and rough like the desert, so she seemed to blend into the background as if she was becoming part of it. "They're a couple days old and probably stale as hell."

"Beggars can't be choosers. Better than the cold canned beans I was going to have."

"If I knew you were living that high off the hog, I would have kept them for myself."

I ate two cake doughnuts and drank the coffee while I waited for her to speak. She stood up and walked around the stock tank and looked up at the windmill. "You know, Sam, New Mexico is a lot like Alaska. The country's wild, and people tend to stay out of each other's business."

"You've been there, to Alaska?"

"Yeah, I spent a few years there, but it's too cold and wet for me. I'm a prickly pear. I like the desert. Had to come back to it."

"I could see that," I said, but I really couldn't. The desert felt like heat and dry and dirt.

She stood with her hands in her back pockets and looked at the mountains when she talked. "My brother-in-law was a drunken asshole last night, and what he did and said stuck in my craw. You done good coming here, and that little niece of mine thinks a lot of you."

"Thanks. But I kinda made an ass of myself too."

She turned to face me. Yeah, yah did. Kind of blew the cork out of the bottle before you left. Sam, your hair's too long and you probably don't have a pot to piss in, but it showed me something you coming all this way. I'm betting your mama didn't think much of it."

I squatted and started rolling up my sleeping bag. "She wasn't too happy, but she'll get over it. I hope."

Edna smiled a crooked smile. "Don't count on it. You'll learn that about women. We have long memories and don't get over things easily. You did good last night. I'm sure you wanted to punch ol' Jack in the mouth, but you didn't. Just remember, never argue with a drunk, and don't make a girl choose between you and her daddy. Those are both losing bets. You kinda did that last night, that bait never fishes. He may be a narrow-minded son of a bitch, but he's her daddy."

I nodded and started to realize she was here to help me. "Have they left yet?"

"Ah, hell no. Jack kept drinking, and we'll be lucky to see him by noon."

My mind raced. I still had time. And I had an ally. But Edna kept talking, so I couldn't make a plan, and it turned out she already had one.

"They won't get on the road until tomorrow. If you want to see Iris and say your goodbyes, I'll be taking her to the drive-in to say so long to the gals there. If you show up at about two o'clock, you might get a little visit with her."

"That's good news. Thank you." I just kept smiling and nodding like a bobblehead doll.

"Now don't you get the idea that I'm helping you run off together. She's still going to Salt Lake with her daddy."

"Salt Lake? I thought—"

"Yeah, Salt Lake City. Jack's got a connection with a Mormon place up there that takes in girls and adopts out their babies. I'll give you the address so you can write to her, and I'll give you my address, too, but you gotta promise not to turn this into a damn melodrama. Iris is only seventeen, and if you run off together, Jack will bring in the law and there'll be hell to pay."

"Okay," I said, "I'll behave."

"Good. Now her delivery date is a long way off. You go home or back to Oregon and let this cool off. Hell, you and Iris might decide this is for the best, and you can go your separate ways or move on together, just the two of you. A lot can happened in the next few months."

She handed me a note card with addresses on it and looked around at the windmill and fallen fence rails. "Me and Bob used to come here and watch the sunset and listen to coyotes. It's a good place." She scooped up her thermos and walked to the truck.

"You are one fortunate fellow, Sam Barger," I said as I watched her back the truck around and drive away.

That's how I got to say goodbye to Iris before she went off to the Brentwood Maternity Home. I told her Cathy called it Prego

Prison, and she laughed though I think it might have scared her a bit.

The next day I passed through Salt Lake City, and I just had to check the maternity home. It was a large stone building in the center of an acre of grass on a quiet street and looked more like a library or a museum than a home for unwed mothers. To me it was a castle to be stormed, and my imagination ran wild. I cruised slowly around the block and noted all the entrances. An arched entryway with double doors was centered in the front, and there were smaller doors on each of the other three sides with fire escapes on the two ends of the second floor. The place had plenty of doors, but something told me that going in and out wouldn't be as easy as it looked.

In true Sam Barger fashion, I dreamed up a great rescue plan that involved scaling the fire escape in the dead of night. I would visit her the day before and pass a note telling her to be ready. I would stash the motorcycle behind a service station a block and a half away with a jacket for Iris to wear against the cold and a helmet that fit. I would be in, and we would be out in a couple of minutes. The details flashed through my mind like scenes from *The Avengers,* and I wished I had the steel nerves to go with them.

Of course, I hadn't figured out how to get through locked doors without waking anyone, and I didn't know for sure that Iris would go for my plan, but I couldn't stop thinking that it could happen. I kept remembering her, pale and silent, on her uncle Bob's couch with all the fight gone out of her and no way to stand up against her parents, and I knew I was the only chance she had. At least I could give her a choice and maybe more than one.

The goodbye visit arranged by her aunt Edna didn't give me much hope of Iris changing her mind. She was bright and cheerful with her waitress friends, but I could see the tension in her eyes, swollen from lack of sleep and crying. I sat on my bike waiting and sipping a root beer while the women did their hugging, weeping, going away thing before they broke up and went back to work. Iris turned and saw me then and actually ran and threw herself into my arms Hollywood style. I gave her the cool guy, "Oh hey, little lady," but inside I was bouncing like a popcorn popper.

"What the hell are you doing here, biker man?" she asked before she stood on tiptoe and kissed me.

"I just came for more onion rings. Had no idea you were within twenty miles of this place."

She smacked my chest and chuckled. "Liar. You came to check out the hot chicks."

I nodded toward the pickup truck where her aunt Edna waited. "Nah. Your aunt told me you'd be here and said I might get to say good-bye without getting shot. And so far so good."

"Yeah, last night was pretty heavy. I'm sorry you had to endure that, but we know now. It is how it is, Sam." Her face fell, and she leaned against me with her arms at her side like they were too heavy to lift. "I thought I'd never see you again. After, after what you said."

"You know I was just mad, don't you?" I said, bringing my hands up to hold her. "It's just so damn frustrating."

"No shit, it's frustrating, but I'll have lots of nights to cry about it and feel sorry for myself where I'm going. It is what it is, Sam." And with that she stepped back and started walking away.

"It is until it becomes something else."

"What?" She stopped and turned back to me. "What did you say?"

"It is what it is until it becomes something else."

We were past talking. We hugged and touched each other, then I leaned on the motorcycle, and she leaned on me, and she sipped root beer from my straw. Then Edna gave her a wave and said, "Let's go, girl."

Iris kissed me quickly and softly and then stepped away. "I never told you," she said with a long pause as she stepped away, "I never really liked root beer."

"Good. I hate sharing."

"That figures." She turned to go, and the wind caught her hair and tossed it in her face, and I couldn't see her eyes. Then the wind caught her white blouse as she moved away from me so that she seemed to be carried on the wind like the tumbleweeds that blew across the highway and piled against the fences. And as I rode out of New Mexico, I couldn't find her face in my memory, just her tossed hair and the blouse filling with wind like a bedsheet on a clothesline.

TWENTY-SIX

Cathy was filling salt shakers and listening to the country music top-forty when I walked into the café with my pack on my shoulder. "Well look who's back from his vacation! Did you get a little action down New Mexico way?"

"Gosh, hello to you too. And the answer is no. She is pregnant, you know." I plopped my backpack by the door.

"Sheesh! The girl's pregnant, not sick. Some of my best were when I was prego."

I waved a hand and blushed beneath my windburned face. Betsy was in the kitchen, and she looked up without smiling. Her face was pale and her scarf sweat-soaked. "Boy, am I glad to see you," she said. "This is too much like work. How are you, kiddo?"

"I'm good, Betsy. Let me stow this gear, and I'll help you clean up."

"If you got it in ya, I won't say no. I'm not quite up to speed yet, and I'm tired as a one-legged man at an ass-kicking contest." She leaned on the counter and downed a glass of iced tea.

"Sorry to leave you shorthanded, and I really appreciate Harold loaning me the bike." I moved my gear to the back of the kitchen and stripped down to my T-shirt. "You get off your feet. I'll get this cleaned up."

"Not until you tell me how it went. Did you see your girl? What's her name again?"

"Yeah I did. Iris is doing good." Cathy stopped her work and leaned on the lunch counter to listen. It was midafternoon and the last customers were fed and gone.

"Well, where is she? I was thinking you'd bring her back here and tie the knot. There's room for two in that trailer, you know."

I blushed again. "Well, it's not that simple, I guess. I don't think she was quite ready. Maybe both of us aren't."

Cathy said, "Well, if her folks weren't for it, you don't want to bring her across state lines if she's underage. Her daddy will have the law on you, and then you'll see how things can go from hugs and kisses to blood and tears in the blink of an eye."

"I'm not that stupid," I lied. I didn't know a damn thing about marriage laws and transporting minors across state lines.

Betsy waved a dismissive hand, "Oh, Cathy, quit being so melodramatic. Sam doesn't need a truck stop lawyer getting him all worked up. How old is this girl, Sam?"

"Seventeen."

"That's when I married Harold. Two weeks after graduation and not a moment too soon." She laughed and her hand covered her face.

"You're in good company, momma," said Cathy.

This was an embarrassing topic for me, but the gals seemed completely at ease. "So if it's so common . . . you know. Why is it such a big deal."

Betsy patted me on the shoulder. "It is a big deal, Sam. You're a parent your whole life after this. It never stops. But for some folks, it's a religious thing, and then other folks don't want to look bad because their daughter is a tramp. But the bad part is you boys get away scot-free." She punched my arm this time like Iris would. "Most of you anyway."

I stood there nodding my head like a bobblehead again. "Well, Iris's folks want me to disappear. They don't want me to help Iris raise the baby, and they sure don't want us to get hitched, so they're taking her to some home in Salt Lake City, and there's nothing I can do about it. Or so they think."

"I thought you said you weren't stupid."

"That doesn't mean I don't do stupid things."

Harold wandered in from the garage about then. "You got no corner on that market," he said. "How are you, kid? I saw you ride in, but I was wrestling a stubborn muffler on a Buick." He asked about the bike, and I told him it ran smoothly and got me there and back without a hitch.

He poured himself a coffee and tried to drape a dirty arm around his wife, but she skittered away. "Are you going to stick around?"

"If you'll have me. I figure I still owe you some time."

"Well, if he won't I will," said Betsy. "I was enjoying being a lady of leisure. With you here, I can supervise Harold more."

"Just what I need." Harold smiled. "You owe me five bucks, woman. Sam, Betsy bet me that you'd be bringing that girl back with you, and I said there weren't no way. Cathy said you weren't coming back at all."

"I did not!" Cathy flounced off to finish putting the dining room in order with Harold laughing behind her.

"She did say I was a fool to trust you with that motorcycle. But shoot, it's not the first time I've been a fool."

And so I moved back into the little trailer behind the café, working with this kind of adopted family surrounding me with something warm and supportive. The first night felt like coming home, and I slept like a dog in the sun for a couple of hours and then woke up and couldn't sleep.

I sat under a weak reading lamp at the settee table and wrote a letter to Iris.

Dear Iris,

I promised I'd write to you, so here I go. I'm back at the café, and the people here made me feel at home. I think they were a little disappointed you didn't come with me. Betsy said, "That trailer has room for two you know."

I had a good drive back. The weather stayed nice during the day, but the nights are getting cold. I stopped at Mesa Verde to visit the amazing cliff dwellings. It's so cool to see places like this. I've seen pictures in National Geographic and encyclopedias all my life, but there's nothing like the real thing. Glad I didn't have to grow up on the edge of a cliff like that.

Of course, I kind of feel like I'm living on the edge of a cliff now, haha. How is your new residence? I hope they are being kind to you. It was pretty hard to say goodbye, but I'm not going back to Alaska until we work out what we want to do. If I go home now, I'll just be fighting with Mom and trying to figure out what to do about the draft. Things are really getting real now, aren't they?

I look forward to an Iris postcard,

Sam

The next day I was back in the kitchen shaping hamburger patties, cooking soup, and making potato salad. Betsy was an early riser and kept cooking breakfast, and I came in later to back her up and cook lunch. During the slow afternoons, I would pump gas, sweep walks, and chop weeds. I got to enjoy the cool nights and warm days of fall, which were nothing like the cold, damp, and growing darkness we experienced in Alaska this time of year. I received a letter from Mom with fifteen dollars in it, and one from Joe with a picture of his new girlfriend posing like a pinup model by his Mustang along the highway with mountains in the background. I wrote back giving them enough detail to keep them from worrying about me doing something crazy.

I made myself take a week to let things settle down, and once my hands got busy in the kitchen, my brain calmed down, and I quit being mad and flustered when I thought about Iris in that maternity home. Thankfully, I didn't think about it all the time. In fact, I spent some time reading again and riding the Honda around eastern Oregon and into Idaho.

During slack times at the café, Cathy was tutoring me on the law, and she considered herself quite an expert. "You're eighteen, aren't you?"

she asked one day when she was telling me about a guy she knew who took his underage girlfriend to Boise for a concert and ended up in jail for taking her across the state line.

"Yeah, I am. Why?"

"Why? Because if you and Irene go running across the Utah border, they can throw your Alaskan ass in jail."

"Oh, come on. Now you're making stuff up. And her name's Iris."

"That may be the only thing you got right so far." Cathy shook her head then lit a cigarette. "Oh you are one sad case, Sam. You ask Harold this evening when you two do your man time out under the apple tree. And don't even think about getting married. That ain't going to happen until her folks sign on the line or she turns eighteen too."

"What about Nevada? Anything goes in Nevada, right?" I started wiping the counter with a cleaning rag. "I mean if that's what I wanted to do. We could just go to Nevada, and once we're married, that's it."

Harold walked in then and grabbed a coffee cup and filled it from the pot behind the counter. "What the hell are you two talking about?"

"Shit-for-brains here thinks he and his little prego gal can elope to Nevada and get married." She handed Harold the cream out of the cooler.

"Are you kidding me? Nevada's no better than anywhere else for kids getting married," Harold said, "You got one chance if you really want to marry that girl. One chance."

Cathy interrupted. "See, I told you."

Harold took a sip of coffee and leaned on the counter, "Sam, if you don't buddy up to her old man and convince him that you are Prince Charming, forget it. He holds the cards, and right now, you aren't even in the game. That's all I got to say."

"The best medicine tastes the worst. And the truth is the best medicine," Cathy said. "And we got customers." Two vehicles pulled in to park in front of the café, and a pickup truck pulled up at the gas pumps ringing the bell in the garage.

"I'll get the gas," I said, and without waiting I burst out the door and headed to the pumps. Suddenly my heart was revving again, and all the calm I had developed over those two weeks melted. I filled the pickup with gas, checked the oil, and cleaned the windshield like I was in the pits at Indianapolis. I took the man's money and brought him his change. I stood panting in front of the garage until Cathy stuck her head out the door and yelled, "Hey! Are you going to cook these burgers or what?"

I recognized that panicky, scared feeling I was having. I'd been there before with Joe in the woods last year, standing in the rain with Joe's blood spilling out. I was feeling it all again. Scared, alone, and helpless.

Harold and Cathy were right. I'd probably known it for a while but wouldn't face it. My harebrained plan to break into the maternity home and rescue Iris, my images of riding into the night with Iris on the back of Harold's motorcycle, and even the idea that she would go willingly were all just part of another Sam Barger fantasy. One thing was for sure. If I was counting on winning over Iris's dad, I was screwed.

TWENTY-SEVEN

Two days later I was back on the road heading for Salt Lake City. I wasn't going to scale the tower and rescue the fair maiden. I'd put that plan aside, but I could go and visit. I arrived about midday, found a department store, and bought a pair of cheap slacks and a white button-down shirt. I was following Harold's lead on this mission. "No faded jeans and flannel shirts," he said. "If you want to get past the front door, you have to clean yourself up. Buy some decent go-to-church clothes. I'll loan you a tie."

"Really? All that to just visit this place?"

"Trust me. You go in looking like some motorcycle bum, and they won't give you the time of day. And shave that scruffy beard while you're at it. The more you look like an innocent Mormon boy, the better."

"Okay."

"A haircut wouldn't hurt either, but I know that ain't going to happen. Remember this is Mormon country you're heading into. Act like a nice kid who wouldn't say shit if he had a mouthful."

I walked into the lobby of the Brentwood Maternity House with clean boots, new slacks, and a white shirt and tie. My hair was combed and tucked behind my ears. When I saw my reflection in the glass doors, I thought Joe would say I looked like a guy either going to court or to a funeral. I thought I looked pretty good.

By the time I had passed through the entryway and stepped into the lobby, a tall blonde woman about Mom's age was striding across the tile floor to greet me. Her hair was pulled back in one of those french rolls, and she was made up so that her black eyebrows and red lips dominated her face. Her dress was plain and business-like; it matched her manner.

"Good morning. What can I do for you?" She had gauged her walk across the lobby to block my advance, and we stood face to face. I realized her three-inch heels made her as tall as me. She tilted her head to the side to emphasize her question.

I extended a hand, which she ignored. "Good morning, ma'am. I'm Sam Barger, ma'am. I'm here to see Iris Davis." I looked around the lobby and tried to act calm and confident. The lobby was painted a pale green with beige trim. A couple of long couches and a coffee table sat over to the left, and to the right was a windowed counter that looked like the front desk of a hotel. Directly ahead of me was a windowed room that appeared to be set up for private meetings. It was occupied by a man and woman and a teenage girl. I didn't have to wonder about their story.

"OK, Mr. Barger," she said, "if you wait right here, I'll see if that is possible." She turned with a smile that didn't extend past her lips. The click of her heels echoed off the high ceiling and emphasized the silence. I paced back and forth across the space between the two couches and studied the bland landscape art hung on the walls.

The click of high heels on tile told me she was back. "Mr. Barger, thank you for waiting." Behind her, I saw the face of a young woman staring at me from the windowed counter.

"Sure. So we're set?"

"No. A visit is not possible today." She gestured toward the door with an open hand.

"Not possible? What's the problem?" I felt my temperature rise, and I ignored her invitation to leave.

"Well first, young man. You are not on our visitor list, so we can't allow you to visit any of our guests."

"Visitor list? There's a visitors list? You mean I have to be signed in or something?" I suddenly knew where the saying hot under the collar came from. I was feeling it.

Her face didn't change and her voice stayed even. "No, you have to be approved to visit by the family of the person you're visiting. If not, I'm sorry, we can't let you in."

I took a deep breath and looked around the lobby as if Iris might magically appear. She was somewhere here in this building, somewhere close. Maybe she could even hear my voice echoing against the walls of the lobby. "Listen," I said, "we both know why I'm here."

"Do we?" She said it like I should believe her innocence, which really pissed me off.

"Come on. Don't do that. Just let me see Iris. She's here, isn't she?"

The woman's iron face showed some emotion then. But the emotion was impatience. She took a deep breath and crossed her arms. "Mr., Mr. Barger is it? I don't think you understand that our guests are here for privacy and discretion. I can't even tell you if this *Iris* is a guest here."

"So what am I supposed to do? Huh? I am the father, you know."

She dropped her arms and turned like she wanted to walk away. She said, "No, I don't know anything about that. But I do know what you need to do. I do know that. You need to walk out that door and don't come back until you speak to the parents of the someone here you want to visit. It's their choice, not mine. Now, if you don't mind." She swept her arm toward the door dramatically and tilted her head with her lips pursed. I knew impossible when I saw it. The visit was over.

TWENTY-EIGHT

A few days later, Cathy put in an order for a hot roast beef sandwich and said, "Fella out here to see you. At the table by the window."

I wondered who knew I was in Ontario, Oregon. It didn't take long to figure that it had to be Joe on a rescue mission launched by Mom. I made up the plate and took it out to one of the tables along the window to meet Joe. But it wasn't Joe. Jack Davis sat at the table with coffee in his hand looking sober. I was taken completely by surprise. I set the plate in front of him and stepped back resisting the temptation to dump the plate in his lap. "What are you doing here?"

"Hello, Sam. I'm here to talk."

I looked around. There was no one else in the diner, and Cathy was a respectful distance away behind the counter pretending not to eavesdrop. "I didn't think you wanted to ever see me again."

Davis took a bite of meat and gravy, then a taste of potatoes, looking out the window while he chewed. "I know, I've been a real prick," he said. "But the first time I was mad, and the second time I was drunk. And both times I was wrong. I'm sorry."

"Thanks for nothin'." I turned my back and started to leave.

"Wait, there's more." I stopped and turned back to watch as he ate a couple bites. "I guess I ought to be eating crow here instead of roast beef. This is so good by the way. You made it?"

"I grabbed a chair and sat down with my arms crossed and my brain spinning. "Yeah, everything but the green beans. They're out of a can. What do you want to say?"

He laid the fork on his plate and wiped his mouth with a napkin. "I want to talk about Iris and this whole mess we're in. Maybe I can square this up for you. My brother was right, you came a long way and that's something. Most guys wouldn't."

Three truckers slammed in the front door and took a table behind me. "Okay, but I gotta work." I jerked a thumb at the men settling in at the table.

"Fine. That's fine. When are you done?"

"Come by about three-thirty."

The next two hours were too slow in the café to distract me from thinking about Davis and what on earth he came to talk about. I had to figure he'd heard about my visit to Iris, but he didn't seem pissed or ready to get tough. In fact, he seemed to be trying to mend fences, but some fences are barbed wire, and they can be dangerous—I knew that much. I'd have to keep my guard up and see what he had on his mind that brought him this far. His apology seemed like all syrup and no pancake.

Cathy bounced in the kitchen after he left and gave me the third degree. "Is that *him*? You know, her dad? I thought you said he was a jerk. He seemed nice enough to me."

"Everybody's nice until they aren't."

"What's that? Confucius?"

"No, Sam Barger. Confucius said, 'To be wronged is nothing unless you continue to remember it.'"

"How'd you pull that out of your ass?" she asked.

"My mom is into famous quotes like that. 'The road to hell is paved with good intentions.' Stuff like that."

Cathy turned heel and left the left kitchen looking over her shoulder. "You are so full of it. I think you're just making shit up as you go along."

I laughed for the first time that day. Then I looked at the clock and waited.

Cathy hung around after closing just long enough to say, "Hi there," when Jack Davis returned, and she let him in the locked door. "You boys be good now," she added as she left.

"How's Iris?" I poured us both coffee, and we sat across from each other by the window.

"She's good. She saw the doctor yesterday and everything is where it's supposed to be. Her health is excellent."

"I'm glad." There was a long pause while we sipped our coffee and tried not to look at each other. I let the air fill with tension, feeling like I had the upper hand here on my own turf. Then I leaned back in my chair and hooked my thumbs in my belt. "Okay. I'm here. What do you want to tell me that you haven't said already."

Jack put both hands on the table and took a deep breath. "First off, I was way off base back there in New Mexico. I don't remember all I said to you and Iris, but that was just drunken, stupid shit I ain't proud of."

I remembered every word he said. "Well, you called Iris a slut for starters and what you called me doesn't matter. She's the one you need to apologize to, not me. She's a nice girl, Mr. Davis, and all this is as much my fault as hers." Suddenly, I wanted to punch him for sitting there trying to get forgiveness.

"I know. I know she is, but people don't know that. I don't want people talkin' about my daughter behind her back. I know the way boys will talk in the locker room. And I didn't want—I don't want her making another mistake, and that's easy to do at a time like this. Shit, look at me."

I crossed my arms and set my jaw. "I'm not that guy. And Iris isn't that girl. People like her. Even people that don't know her like Iris. She's just really independent, and now you've locked her up. That place is like a jail."

"I know it looks that way, but it's for the best, the best for her, the baby, and for you. You'll see. And next time, you want to see Iris up at the home, I told them you're OK to visit. Really. I'm on my way back to Alaska and well overdue. Go and see her before you head back. I think she'd like that." He reached a trembling hand into his jacket pocket and laid an envelope on the table. "And this is for you."

I reached for it then pulled my hand back. "What is it?"

"Traveling money. To get you home or wherever you want to go after this." He pushed the envelope toward me.

"Really? You buying me off? Paying me to go away?" My chest went tight, and I leaned back sucking air while I tried not to swear.

"Come on, Sam. It's not like that. You came a long way and gave up a lot. And . . . oh hell. I guess now is as good a time as any. Iris is only four months along. We found out yesterday. I got to tell you the truth."

"What?" I flushed red. I could feel the heat rising in me, and there wasn't any air in the room. "What are you saying?"

"Do the math, son. You're off the hook."

"Don't call me son!" I was on my feet with the chair falling away behind me.

"Dammit, Sam. Four months ago you were sitting on the beach in Ninilchik picking fish. This isn't your problem anymore. Just take the money."

"What do you mean?" I stepped back and kicked the chair aside. Jack's hand came up like I was going to hit him, but I wasn't. I just needed to move. So I stomped up and down the dining room three or four times. Calendars and dates, letters, and postcards all spun around my head. Iris with another guy, Iris with me, and I could smell her, and I could smell the beach site, the smell of salt and fish. "Shit. No!"

"I don't know what she told you, son. If she told you anything."

"I can't believe this. Goddamnit!"

"Yes, Sam. Hell, I just found out too. There was another guy, one of the young guides at another camp downriver. And God knows who else."

Then I did hit him. He fell back in the chair and put his hands up but didn't hit back. "I guess you owe me that one."

"No shit! And I ain't done. I owe you plenty, goddamnit." I stepped forward, but strong hands grabbed me and pulled me back.

"Jesus, Sam! Easy, son." I was dragged to the far end of the dining room. I could smell the greasy garage odor on the hands that crushed my biceps. "Stop it!" Harold growled. "Stop it!"

The fight was out of me as fast as it came, and the three of us stood like overheated dogs, panting in the clumsy silence with the afternoon sun coming through the venetian blinds into our eyes.

"You okay, buddy?" Harold gave Jack a hard look over but didn't let go of me.

"Yeah." Jack waved his arms and leaned on a chair. "I just had to give Sam some bad news. This is my fault really."

Harold hadn't released his grip, and he gave me an extra squeeze. "You cool now?"

"I'm okay. Fine." He let me shake off his hands then.

"Mister, if you said what you need to, you best go. I don't think Sam wants to talk anymore."

Jack Davis walked out, and Harold and I sat down and drank a six-pack. I told him the whole sad story and while I did, I realized that what Jack Davis had said really could be true. Iris and I might have been just having a fling, a few hot days in the first sweet week of summer vacation. What did we have after that or before even? Letters from me and mysterious postcards from her? By the time I was finished drinking three beers and telling my story, I was mad at Iris, not Jack. And I was really pissed at my own stupid self. Between the half-empty coffee cups on the table, the white envelope glared in the afternoon sun.

I only remember one thing Harold said to me that day. He patted my knee and looked me in the eye, "Better a bruise than a break, son, and believe me, there is a big difference. This is just a bruise." I didn't believe him at the time because in those moments, I couldn't imagine anything hurting worse than that moment. And I'd seen hurt before, losing my dad and shooting my brother. I knew that knot-in-my-gut, heat-on-my-neck, electric-shock feeling, and this was another one.

TWENTY-NINE

After punching Jack Davis, I spent the night counting weeks, days, and months in my head over and over. I remembered that night in May when Iris and I did it the first time, and I counted forward. Then I did the same with every other time we had sex—yeah, we didn't always use a condom. Maybe when a guy is married a few years he doesn't remember every time he has sex, but each time Iris and I made love was a clear and distinct moment as clear as yesterday. When I worked the numbers and counted and counted again, I always proved Davis right. I wasn't the baby's father, not if Davis was telling the truth about how far along she was.

I didn't sleep much that night, and by dawn, I was ready to move. I told Harold I was leaving and used the money Davis left on the table to buy a ten-year-old Rambler station wagon he had sitting out back of the garage. I went to town and bought a pair of new boots from the ranch store, an ice chest, and a camp stove along with a cook kit and some groceries.

Harold and Betsy said their door was always open, and in some ways, it would have been easy to stay, but I wanted to go. Betsy said, "You don't have to run off like this, Sam. I know you're upset. Harold filled me in. But you can mope around here as well as anywhere else."

"Let the boy go, woman," Harold said. "He's gotta put some road behind him. I can see that."

Harold was right, at least so I thought. I was running away from all the mess of my foolishness, but it traveled with me like the smell of dog crap after you step in it, and I had really stepped in it. I had been suckered and played for a fool and jumped when I should have stayed put. No way I was fast enough to run from that.

Harold followed me to the Rambler with a box of canned food and sandwiches that Betsy thought I needed. "Maybe you ought to pay her a visit?" Harold said. "Get her side of the story?" He parked the box in the backseat.

I was restless to leave and loaded myself in the driver's seat and nervously adjusted the rearview mirror. "I figure I've listened to her stories long enough. That's how I ended up here in the first place, not that this is a bad place to end up. Thanks to her, I've been robbed, lied to, yelled at, punched, and rousted by the cops."

"I think you had some good times here," Harold chuckled and leaned heavily on the open door. "Shoot son, someday you're going to look back on this as a great adventure. What doesn't kill ya makes you stronger. Ain't that what they say?"

"What do *they* know? And besides, this is today, not someday, and today it feels like life is a shit sandwich and this is just one more bite." I slammed the car door and pulled out on the highway heading east, my foot heavy on the gas. The map on the seat beside me showed a route across southern Idaho and then north through Montana to the Canadian border. I was homesick as hell, and yeah, I could catch a plane home, but even though I was running with my tail between my legs, I wasn't ready to face the music. It was time to go home, but I needed time, and driving the highway across Canada would give me that.

Somewhere east of Boise, the chip fell off my shoulder, and I found a pay phone. I called the café, and Cathy answered. Before I could apologize to Harold, I had to wade through the mud with Cathy about how I left without saying goodbye, and how I was doing her wrong by doing so. She was right. By the time she let me talk to Harold, I was a mess again. "Harold, it's Sam. Hey, I'm sorry how I left," I said. "You've been good to me. You all have. I was an ass to storm off like that."

Harold hung a silent curtain for a full minute, then said, "You gotta watch burning bridges, Sam. Sometimes you need them when you retreat. Remember that. Take care." He hung up then, leaving me feeling like I'd scorched the gravy, and I guess I had.

Sometimes feeling guilty is well deserved, and I nursed that wound for another couple of hours driving through a crisp fall day in the rolling hills of southern Idaho. This was empty high desert country with not much between towns but miles of brown brush and the occasional herd of pronghorns. When I stopped at a rest stop to pee and stretch my legs, I discovered I was on the historic Oregon Trail. I forgot about myself for a time and let my mind wander back in time to crossing this empty dry country on a Conestoga wagon at the grueling pace of fifteen miles per day. Maybe I didn't have it so bad.

I drove on, squinting into the sun and watching imaginary strings of wagons lumbering across the dry Snake River plain. I could see the ruts of the original trail in a couple of places, and suddenly all the history in the place moved closer to me and felt real. Then I came to a fork in the road with a bold green-and-white sign pointing south for Salt Lake City. That jolted me into the present, for Salt Lake City meant Brentwood Maternity Home, meant Iris Davis, meant one last chance to look her in the face and let my pride get crushed one more time. I turned right.

The matron at Brentwood Maternity Home showed no more warmth this time than she had during my first visit, but this time she didn't give me the bum's rush. She did make me wait thirty minutes in the lobby while she went to fetch Iris. Down the hall, five girls in various stages of pregnancy were dancing to the Rolling Stones, and the music echoed off the walls and polished floors. Iris came out of a room between me and the dancers, so their twirling skirts and sweeping arms framed her entrance as she walked toward me in her corduroy jumper with a baby belly just starting to show. Her hair was braided, and her freckles stood out against her pale skin. She was full of life and energy, but the scene was a knife in my heart.

"Sam, you're here." She reached for me and stopped when she saw the look in my eye.

"Yup, I'm here. I'm not sure why." I put my hands on my hips and tried not to shuffle my restless feet. The room turned cold, and Mick Jagger shouted "Satisfaction" down the hall. She crossed her arms as if hugging herself.

The stone-faced matron guided us to the glassed-in room and closed the door behind her when she left.

"You talked to Dad, didn't you?"

"Yup. He came to see me. I think I gave him a black eye." I stuffed my hands in my pockets and stood braced in the center of the room.

"I'm sorry." She stepped forward again, then decided to sit on the sofa. "He told you, and you came anyway? To tell me off, I guess. I get it."

"I needed to hear it from you. Now I guess I have. But I don't understand. How do you know? How do you know—you know, that I'm not the dad?" The room floated around the two of us like we were on a giant turntable.

"Sit, Sam. Please." She looked at the floor and rubbed her hands up and down the corduroy on her thighs. "Believe me, I know. I've known all along. I wanted to tell you."

"All along? How do you know? I mean how do you really know? It could be me, right?"

"No, Sam." She looked around like someone might be listening, but the lobby was empty, and the girls down the hall were busy laughing and dancing to their music. "I am positive, Sam. I had my period after we—you know, after we were together. I started the day you left to go fishing. You know how all this works don't you?"

"Yeah, I know how it works." I stopped shaking, but the heat was building inside me. I sat on the coffee table across from her with my fists clenched. "So why all of this? What the hell am I doing here? Why me and not the other guy—or guys?"

"Oh come on. Don't hate me, Sam. I couldn't stand it if you hate me. I know I deserve it, but please don't."

"So why play me for the sucker? Shit! Iris! What the hell? Who is the father, or do you even know?"

She buried her face in her hands and then ran her fingers up into her hair and pulled at it. When she looked up, her face was blank and pale. "At first, back home, I hoped maybe it was you, that it was your baby, and somehow the period was just some silly weird thing that happened. And then you were there and being so *you*, all positive and interested." She paused to cry and dab her eyes. "And then I realized I was just lying to myself, and then I told Dad and Mom, and suddenly I was scared and trapped in this big ugly lie."

I leaned my forehead on my hands and let the words grind into me like sand in my eyes. "You basically ask me to come here. What was I supposed to think?"

"I know. It was a big lie. But you were the only one I could turn to. If anyone could get me out of this, it was you, Sam. You're the guy who stood up for me against the principal back at school, you're the guy who shot his brother and then carried him out of the woods on your back. You always think of a way out to make things happen. You're my hero, Sam. Oh god, I'm so stupid and selfish."

"Some hero. More like a lapdog that came when you called." I stood up. "Anytime, you could have told me. You coulda wrote me a letter about it. Maybe more than ten words on a damn postcard." The girls down the hall stopped dancing and stared at us through the music.

"I know. I just wanted you to rescue me. I thought you could." She was looking down then, and wouldn't look at me.

"I thought I could too. I tried, but now—But now, I'm done. The system wins again, Iris." I had to leave, but my boots were glued to the floor. I had to leave then or I never would.

She wiped her eyes and stiffened her back. "Yes. Okay. I know now. I can do this. This is where I should be." She stood and used her hands to smooth her dress. "What will you do?"

"I'm going home. Going up the ALCAN. Then I don't know. Maybe join the marines and make Joe proud. I'm eighteen now."

"Oh, Sam. No! Do that, and I know you hate me, but nothing would hurt me like that would. After all, we've done too much together. At least join the coast guard where you can do some good. Don't go fight that stupid war."

I was so full of air and pain and heat that I could barely speak by then. "I don't want to hurt you, Iris." I broke my feet loose and moved toward the door and opened it. The music from down the hall had changed to Bobby Goldsboro's "Honey," so the girls had stopped dancing and were staring down the hall at us whispering.

"I'll be home after the first of the year, Sam."

I nodded and kept my feet moving, afraid to look back.

The walk out to the Rambler parked at the curb in the late afternoon sun was as long a walk as I ever took. Twice I stopped and almost turned back, but something restarted me each time.

I guess I looked like a jerk, walking off the way I did. It didn't feel right, either, but I couldn't get past the deception, and until I could, there was no way I could completely forgive her. Yeah, we might have made it work, we might still have talked her dad into letting us get married and raise that baby. But *might* is an iffy word, and in reality, I couldn't get past the lie and my own selfish jealousy.

Iris was stuck in that baby factory and probably only going to see her child for a quick goodbye. She'd be lonely then, a lot lonelier than now. I guess we were both going to be pretty lonely, me on that dusty highway pointed north to the Canadian border and home, and Iris alone in that two-story stone maternity home, feeling a life growing inside her that she could never get to know. I don't figure she'll ever be quite the same, and me going back and holding her hand would help a little maybe, but the outcome was the same either way. I told myself all those things as I walked, but I still felt like a heel.

Out in front of me, college and Mom were waiting. I had to do something and who knows what that could be. I wasn't joining the marines, that's for sure, and telling that to Iris was one of the things I'd regret when I got over being an asshole. I didn't regret punching her dad, and I didn't even regret coming all this way on a fool's errand, as Mom would call it, but telling Iris I was joining up was salt in a fresh wound.

I was going home, and in a few months, Iris was going home, and, who knows, there might—there's that word again—be another chance for us. Whether I did the right thing or not, I'd have three thousand miles of highway to think about it.

THIRTY

I had the engine running and was shifting the Rambler into gear when the passenger door opened. Iris leaned in, panting. She had chased me across the lawn and stood wide-eyed and flushed in the afternoon sun.

"Dammit, Sam!" she said. "She put her hands on her hips and pumped air through her mouth. "Gosh. I'm out of shape."

"I thought we were done." I turned off the ignition.

"You thought we were done? I thought we were having a discussion. I thought we were going to rap about this. Maybe listen to each other for a change. Please, Sam. I have to tell somebody." She turned her back then, and over her shoulder, I could see the tall lady in the long skirt that had turned me away the first time I came. The scene was from some old movie, and I thought that at any second that matron would send a couple of no-neck orderlies in white uniforms to beat me up and drag Iris back to the home. All she did, though, was raise her hand as if calling Iris back.

I remembered the way that woman had looked at me and the cluster of girls in the hallway staring at us, and I knew then Iris was right. We weren't done.

"Get in, Iris. Let's get the hell out of here."

"Sam?" She looked down at me, and I reached out a hand across the seat to the open door. She looked over her shoulder at the women on the steps with her hand raised. She was calling now, "Iris? Iris!"

"Come on! We gotta go!" I hit the key and revved the engine for emphasis. Then she did it. She turned and sat on the seat and rotated her feet into the car. As soon as her butt hit the seat, I dumped the clutch and launched the Rambler down the street.

It might have been the craziest thing I ever did, telling Iris to hop in my car like that when I was so mad and hurt. The last thing I wanted was to be with her, but I did it, and I raced down the street like I was Steve McQueen. Iris reached out and grabbed my thigh, and I could hear her breathing, and she spoke, but I couldn't understand her over the roar between my ears and the growl of the engine that I had wide open. I ran one stop sign, but there was traffic at the next intersection, and I had to stop.

"My god, Sam! What are you doing? We can't do this," she yelled into my ear. "Pull over, dammit." She slapped my shoulder. "Jesus, Sam!"

I pulled to the curb beside a park with shade trees and a playground in the center. I turned off the engine. "I thought we were done," I said. "But obviously you want to talk. Go figure, Iris wants to talk. Well, this is as good a place as any. Talk."

"Yeah, I want to talk. I didn't say I wanted to run away with you." She threw her hands in the air. "Damn, Sam! What the hell!"

She was the fiery Iris again, the Iris that I first got to know back when we were protesting the war together, and she was taking on anyone who wanted to argue. It made me laugh. "You got in the car, though, didn't you. You could have turned around and walked away, but you didn't. You got in the car with me, and here we are. We did it, Iris. You're free. Isn't that what you wanted."

"What I wanted? Hell, I don't know what I want at this point except to talk to you. I couldn't let you bail like, just walking away."

"Go ahead and talk. But make it the truth this time. I deserve that much."

She took a deep breath, crossed her legs, and pulled her skirt down to cover her knees. "Yes, you deserve that much. That's why I got in your stupid car. Not to run away with you. I just want to tell you everything. Do you want to hear it or not?"

No, I didn't want to hear it. Who wants to hear about the other guy—or guys—that your girl has been with. Who wants to hear that he's not the only one who has kissed her and touched her breasts and felt the soft skin of her thighs? I wanted to be the only one that had done everything I had done with her. No, I wanted it all to go out of my mind, to be washed from my brain forever, but I didn't say that. I said, "I'm listening," and I clenched my teeth and tightened my gut like I was about to take a beating.

She bit her lip and closed her eyes for a moment and then started talking. "It's not like you think, Sam. It's not what you're thinking at all."

I leaned back and looked out the window. "Don't tell me what I'm thinking, Iris. Just say to me what you have to say."

"Sorry. It's just that I know you. . . You probably thought I was just some tramp screwing all the guys at the fish camp this summer. That's probably what Dad told you. His little girl, his little tomboy daughter that did all things with him like the son he never had turned out to be a little slut. Well, it's not like that, Sam. Yeah, I was with a guy—one of the guides from another outfit on the river, an older college guy. But I didn't want it to happen, Sam. Not like that, I didn't." Then she started crying, but she kept talking through the tears.

"We'd all hang out together in the evening just talking around the fire and stuff. One night—" I handed her my handkerchief, and she wiped her eyes and blew her nose. "One night we had some beers and some weed, and yeah I started making out with him. I don't know why, I just did it. Anyway, then he started getting all heavy, trying to get in my pants, so I left. I did, Sam. I just got up and went to bed."

I felt really uncomfortable by then, not wanting to hear any of this, and not being able to not hear it. I was tempted to leave again. I wanted to jump out of the car and run across the park, but I was rooted there with her in the front seat.

"I went back to my tent, Sam—alone—got undressed and crawled in my sleeping bag. I was embarrassed that people saw me acting that way with him. I had just fallen asleep when he came into my tent. He just came in, sat down, and started talking. I said I wanted to sleep, and we could talk in the morning. And he said—" She started crying again. "He said, 'I'm tired of talking, too,' and then he unzipped my sleeping bag and just climbed on top of me. I tried to tell him no, but I was afraid and scared. I should have screamed or something."

Iris was sobbing by then and couldn't talk. I had to move, and I got out of the car and walked up and down—I'd never seen her cry like that. Then she was out of the car, not letting me run away, grabbing my arm. "You don't have to tell me, Iris, OK." God, I wanted her to stop. I wanted to scream at her. "Enough, Iris! Enough!" but I didn't.

"I have to tell someone. You're the only one, Sam. Who else am I going to tell? I told him, 'No! Go away!' I did Sam, but he didn't listen. He just kept saying he was crazy about me, and I was special, and he didn't stop. And I was scared and finally, I just let him."

I held her then. I took her in my arms, and she tried to push me away, but I just held her and let her cry. Then she stopped suddenly and took a deep breath. "Damn, I cry all the time now," she said. "I hate crying." She took a deep breath. She still didn't look at me. She hadn't looked at me the whole time. "I have to pee."

I pointed to the toilets by the playground, and she walked there with my handkerchief over her face. I worked at washing the images from my mind, but I could see her so clearly in that canvas wall tent with this faceless guy all over her, and the sound of the river running by the camp and the silence of the sleepers in the shadowed tents of the darkless night of summer. I could hear the murmur of conversation of people sitting late around the campfire just yards away, unaware that this night was different from any other. I cried then too.

Iris came back walking erect and tried to act composed. "Do you have some change? I should call the home, and there's a pay phone by the bathroom." I dug out a quarter and a couple of dimes and handed them to her. "I'm sorry, Sam. I'm such a pain. Christ! They probably have the cops after us."

I walked with her to the phone. "Tell them we're going to have some lunch. You could eat, I bet." I wasn't sure I could, but I didn't know what else to do. "There's a café across the park it looks like."

The phone call was quick, just Iris telling someone on the other end that she was OK and would be back after lunch. We walked across the park and when her hand brushed mine, I took it, not remembering how small her hands were. "Your hands are cold," I said.

"Cold hands, warm heart," she said and leaned her head against my arm.

We ordered burgers and sat in a corner booth across from each other. We ate without talking much, at first, picking at our food, then finding solace in the flavor, and once we got started, we ate like it was our first meal in weeks. Iris sucked a milkshake through a straw and said, "What will you do now, Sam? You and your station wagon? Is that yours?" The light was back in her eyes, and she snickered when she stole the last of my fries.

"Yeah, I bought it. Going to drive the highway. What the hell, right? After that, I don't know. If I don't go to college, Mom will kill me. But don't worry, I'm not joining the marines or even the army. I wouldn't do that."

She dropped a fry halfway to her mouth. "Oh, Sam. I meant what I said. If you do that I'd know it's 'cause you hate me. Don't hate me. Even if I deserve it. And even if you do. Don't do that. Don't go over to them. I know you're not like that."

I just looked out the window, unable to look her in the eye.

"I thought you wanted college."

"Maybe. I can't think right now. I can't see down the road at all," I said. "Crap, they could draft me anyway."

"You talked about the coast guard, remember. You told me that. You could serve and not be caught in all that other shit. I'd be cool with that.

You love the water. You said that was the part you liked about fishing this summer, being out in the boat. Oh Sam. Don't give up just because of me."

"I know, but I can't see all that now. I went all in on you, Iris. All in. What else is there now?"

She bit her lip, and I thought she would start crying again. I didn't want that. I held up my hands. "But that was my choice," I said. "My choice. And now—" I looked her in the eye finally. "Now, I'm going to get in my wagon and drive to Alaska. That would be cool, huh. Do the Alaska Highway on my own. Then I'll decide. I'll have all those miles to think. And hell, Mom might kill me anyway."

Iris laughed then. "I'm jealous."

"Jealous that my mom is going to kill me?"

"No, silly, jealous of you driving off like that, totally on your own."

Then the waitress brought the check. "Anything else?" she asked. I waved her off.

I looked at the pregnant woman across from me with the little girl freckles and the grownup eyes and said, "I've got room for a passenger." We looked at each other through the indelible silence of the moment.

Iris looked away, and I thought then maybe that was the cruelest thing I'd said to Iris over this whole time, so I changed the station.

"What about you, Iris? What are you going to do after?" She knew what I meant. And I realized then that I couldn't say it because I was still feeling like the baby was ours not just hers, and that hurt as much as the lies and wasted effort. I couldn't undo the idea that it had been mine for this long for this far.

"I'll go home, I guess, but it won't feel like home anymore. I don't know if I can live with them, not after this. I only need like half a dozen credits plus government class to graduate. Then I'll get a job and try to go to college maybe. I'm not going back to that house. I know that much."

I nodded and paid the check, realizing suddenly that we had nothing more to say to each other right then. We sat and stared across at the park for a few minutes, then walked together out to the street.

I left her off in front of the long paved walk to the front door and watched her walk up that gray ribbon of concrete with the wind catching her hair and lifting it off her shoulders. She stopped on the steps and gave a little sad wave. Even from that distance, I could tell she was crying again. Then the matron opened the door, took her by the arm, and led her away.

"Damn it, Barger," I said. "You had her, and you let her go." But Sam didn't answer. He just put on his sunglasses and rode off into the sunset at two in the afternoon.

THIRTY-ONE

I drove like a demon into the afternoon sun then north on Interstate 15 toward the Idaho border. I drove through Idaho, only stopping for gas and toilets. I was too empty to eat, too worn out to rest, and too mad to care. In Montana, I lived on gas station coffee and Betsy's sandwiches until they spoiled in the heat because I forgot to put them in the cooler. The brown plains of Montana didn't impress me, and I drove without seeing the towns and mountains and river valleys I passed through. I was heading north without thinking about home or Iris or Mom or any of it. I just hurt, the sort of hurt that was so selfish that there is no room for anyone but me and a feeling like a cancer eating at my brain. For me there was only movement. And though I drove north, I wasn't going home. I was just going.

Sitting with Iris in the café I had been able to keep up my facade and put on the show, but once I was gone and the finality of it all hit me, my imagination brought it all to life. I could see Iris flirting with other guys. I could see the scene in the tent with her and that guy. I could see it, and I could watch it from every angle like one of those fancy movie shots with the camera moving in a circle around the actors. As I rode the empty evening highway, I tortured myself with those film loops, and when night was done, and morning brought the glare of daylight to shine on the reality of what was, I knew that things really weren't any different.

At the Canadian border a uniform asked me my destination and I said, "Home."

"Where's home?"

"Good question." That led to an hour of searching my car—for drugs and guns I guess—a sharp scrutiny of my driver's license, and endless questions. Luckily, I could show I had cash to buy food and gas on my way through Canada, so the uniform let me reload my car and depart. Before I could leave, though, the uniform became a human and said, "You look beat, kid. Better find a campground and get some sleep. About ten klicks up the road there is a caravan park. Don't keep drivin'."

Maybe it was bright lights and the officer's list of questions or maybe it was the kind words of the border patrolman as I left, but something jolted me awake enough to realize I was tired. I was tired, hungry, and alone. I suddenly wanted to be home like nothing else in the world, and home seemed to be far, far away. I thought of Iris then, pregnant and locked in that maternity jail to atone for her sins. She was a hell of a lot farther from home than I was.

I found a rest stop and slept in the back of the car for twelve hours. I woke up hungry and confused, not sure if the past two days were real or just last night's dreaming. At a roadside café, I ate a bowl of bland stew and a roll. At the cash register, I bought a postcard with a map of Canada on the front and a stamp.

I sat on the ground beside the Rambler with my boots stuck out before me and stared at the blank back of the card. I took Iris's address out of my wallet and copied it onto the card. Then I wrote.

Don't know where I'm going, but I'm making good time.—Sam I Am

On the front I estimated where I was on the map and made a star. Beside it I wrote,

You are NOT here, I am.

I smiled for the first time since lunch with Iris, and I smiled again when I dropped it in the mailbox. After that, I stopped each day and mailed a postcard with a wisecrack like Iris did for me last summer.

I burned through the miles constructing clever puns and observations about my trip, first through the endless blacktop of flat farmland, then over the steep mountain passes. I wrote about the weather, wildlife, and countless lakes and rivers. I wrote stupid stuff like: *It rained so hard I had to jump in a lake to get dry.* And *Today I saw three bears, two moose, a mountain sheep, and some bison, but I haven't seen one fox since I left Salt Lake City.* Some days I mailed two postcards because it felt good doing it, and I pictured Iris looking forward each day to getting some mail.

Mailing those postcards was maybe the first correct thing I had done, and it felt like I was on the right track. It wasn't like I had anything else to do but drive and talk to myself. For long stretches the radio wouldn't pick up any stations, so I sang and recited old poems. And I soon learned that traveling alone can make you hate your travel partner.

When I was loading the car back at Harold and Betsy's place, I had thought the drive would be a great adventure, camping and seeing the sights, but I was so restless, so forward moving that I mostly pushed on toward that bungalow back home where Mom waited to chew my ass off. Some days I fought the melancholy and moped my way through the hours, sore from the constant sitting and sleeping in the back of the car. On other days I was recounting my missteps and foibles in trying to help Iris. On good days, I was looking forward and thinking beyond my impulses and actually making a plan. Looking forward always buoyed my spirits, and I started anticipating my next steps. I started clicking off the miles to the next gas stop and beyond to the border and then to Anchorage.

When I reached the town of Dawson Creek, where the Alaska-Canada Highway starts, I had driven in the rain all day, so the car was splattered with mud, and I was dirty from changing a flat tire on the shoulder of a muddy road. I found a laundromat and washed my clothes and sleeping bag and changed into fresh clothes when they were still hot from the dryer. I bought a card with a picture of a black bear crossing the highway and wrote,

Dear Iris,
The road to hell is paved with good intentions,
but the road to Alaska is hardly paved at all.
　—Your friend, Peter Fonda

I wrote on the photo next to the bear: *It's BARELY a highway at all!*

Not far out of Dawson Creek the highway turned to a meandering ribbon of mud and gravel called the Alaska-Canada Highway. The ALCAN, as most people called it, was probably the roughest highway on the continent. I spent three days winding through soggy forests, splashing through mud holes, and bouncing over washboard gravel. By the time I reached the Alaska border, I had changed three flat tires, developed a powerful longing to be home, and came up with a plan that didn't sound harebrained. In all fairness, this was a plan put together by a guy with a lousy record for big plans during a week of being totally alone driving through Canada.

The wounds made by Iris's lies had scabbed over by then, and I was able to admit I missed her like never before. Even when I wanted to hate her and forget her, I could do neither, so I kept writing my cards and telling myself that I had done the right thing by leaving her. No way Iris could keep that baby, and maybe she didn't want to by now. Even when I thought it was mine, I didn't know if I wanted to keep it either. I was finally honest with myself about that.

I tried to picture how Iris was spending her days as the baby grew inside her, wondering what it was like to have another being developing in your body, another heartbeat sharing your life, a heartbeat that she would have to give away and never feel again. All I could do was write her another postcard, so she knew there was someone out there thinking of her every day.

By the time I drove down the Glenn Highway and to the outskirts of Anchorage, I knew that Iris and I weren't done. We had too many unfinished conversations and too much history now to just say so long and go our separate ways. I had left Salt Lake thinking it was over, and I would probably never see her again. Even when I started sending the postcards, I told myself they were about supporting her so she didn't feel alone and not about me needing to stay connected. But with all those miles to think, I realized I didn't want to be done with her, and I turned into the driveway and parked behind Mom's car with only the worry that the opposite might be true. Iris might be done with me.

THIRTY-TWO

"Did you drive that piece-of-shit Rambler all the way up the ALCAN?" Joe was standing in the parking lot behind his apartment staring at the grill of my station wagon.

"That's what it says on the grill, Rambler," I said, blushing a bit.

Joe laughed. "I can't believe you made it. Did you get towed part of the way? What's the world coming to? My little brother is driving a damn Rambler."

"Nice see you, too, brother. You know me: the price was right. And it's surprisingly comfortable." I opened the backdoor and grabbed the six-pack of Oly I'd just bought. "Too proud to drink with me maybe?" I asked, reaching a bottle out to him.

"You're not so bad after all." He took the beer and leaned on a fender while he used the church key off my keyring.

The day was cloudy and wisps of snow filtered down on the two of us as we drank our beers and stared at the mountains without mentioning the anniversary of our hunting misadventure. Joe looked fit and robust, and I felt a tremor of regret that I had brought beer to him. In the past, one beer led to another, and then god knows what. But it seemed right, so I did it.

"Have you seen Mom yet?" Joe swallowed half the beer and turned to read the label. "You know, this is the first beer you ever bought me."

"Cheers. Nope. Isn't it obvious I haven't seen Mom, I'm still alive."

"God hates a coward, Sam." I'm glad he chuckled after he said it.

I nodded and swallowed more beer.

"Really, though. You'll be fine. You stayed away long enough that she's more worried than pissed." Joe shook a Lucky Strike out of a pack and lit it with the same hand, waiting for me to talk.

"I started off with good intentions, stopping at home first before I came here, but I pulled into her driveway and Jake's Cadillac was there, so I thought I'd drop by and check on you."

"I think Jake's pretty much living there. Can you believe that? Four-square, Bible-totin' Mom shackin' up with some guy? The world is going to hell, Sam. No wonder her youngest son drives a Rambler. And speaking of Ramblers, I don't see anyone in the passenger seat, so I take it you didn't pull the trigger. The marriage trigger, I mean. I guess you pulled the other trigger pretty regularly."

I buttoned my jacket against the cold, took a long pull on my beer, and tried to act like I was cool with Joe's tone. "So Mom and Jake are getting serious, huh. I guess that's good. Maybe I better crash here then."

"Fine with me, but you better see Mom first. I mean, like, today! I don't want to catch hell from her just 'cause yer being a chickenshit. But let's get to the point you're avoiding. Where's your little gal, Iris was it? I thought you were going to rescue her and elope or some other stupid Sam brainfart?"

I could tell he was only half joking with his jabs. I remember how he thought I was crazy chasing off to find her and telling me I was basically burning a get-out-of-jail-free card. "It's a long story, Joe, with a sad ending."

"Well, little brother, I wouldn't expect anything less from you. Let's go inside where it's warm, and you can tell me all about it while I make us some chow."

That's how I landed back home. I skipped Mom's place and went right to Joe's. With Joe there was less judgment and fewer questions but more sarcasm and big-brother putdowns. Things felt even between us now, and

I stood toe to toe with my big brother like maybe he thought I was a legitimate person worthy of regard. Could I be that lucky with Mom?

After dinner, I took Joe's advice and went to see Mom. I was glad Jake's Cadillac was gone from the driveway even though I had pretty much resigned myself to the fact that Mom could still have men in her life and maybe even have the big S-E-X if she wanted to. None of that would make Dad any smaller in any of our memories or lives. But just the same, I didn't feel like dealing with it right then, and I certainly didn't want some stranger in the middle of this conversation.

It turned out that Mom wasn't home either, so I sorted through the pile of mail she left on my dresser. There wasn't much, a few offers from Columbia Records and two letters from the Selective Service. It's like the US Army and Columbia Records were the only people who really wanted me. Iris hadn't written so much as a Dear John letter.

I packed a duffel of clothes I'd left in the dresser and then sprawled on my old familiar bed. I woke to the smell of Mom's fried chicken and wandered into the kitchen and leaned on the counter.

"Well look what the cat dragged in. You gave me such a start when I saw that car in the driveway. I had no idea."

I grabbed a coffee mug from the hooks along the window and poured a cup from the stainless steel percolator. "Sorry about that. Yeah, it's mine. I know, *it's a Rambler.*"

"You must have seen your brother and gotten an earful about your choice of cars. On a hunch, I looked in your room and recognized the young man asleep on your bed." Then she came to me for a hug and just leaned into me and breathed into my shirt like I was a balloon needing air.

"Looking pretty hep in those bell-bottoms, Mom," I said. Her slacks were dark blue and she wore a pinstripe top cut like a man's shirt.

"Oh shush. What have you got to say for yourself now that you've had your beauty sleep?" Then after a pause. "I see you are alone."

"It's a long story, Mom. And like the ALCAN, it's full of mud and potholes." I was waiting for my real mom to appear with her critical eye and cynical questions, but she hugged me again and kissed my cheek.

"Sit down, son. Let me finish this chicken, and we'll have a bite while you tell me all about it." She lifted the lid on an avocado green electric skillet and turned the brown pieces of chicken within.

"Wow, Mom. No cast iron skillet for you?"

She tapped the skillet with her fork. "I'll have you know some people around here remember my birthday. Jake thought I needed it, and I don't know how I did without it all these years."

"Sorry about that. Guess I missed it, didn't I?"

"Not by much, and you did come home in one piece." She paused to work the milk into the browning flour to make gravy in the birthday skillet. "And alone. You are alone, aren't you?"

"Yeah, Mom, I came home alone." And then I told her everything. I just spilled my guts out on the kitchen table and told her the whole story from day one.

Wait! No, I didn't. I wasn't a little kid anymore running with a skinned knee from a bike crash or a bloody nose from some bully. I told Mom just enough so that she knew I wasn't married or running from the law. I ate fried chicken and told her about Harold's place and how I ran the kitchen there and how I got to see Iris and everything was alright. And then I ate a second helping of mashed potatoes and gravy and let Mom talk about Jake and work and sister Mary's baby and Joe's good job that left him time to take his mother to lunch once a week. And just like that, the Earth was back on its axis, and no one was worried that Sam was going to mess things up for himself and the people around him. It was a little slippery when I told Mom I was going to move in with Joe, but by the time I finished my cobbler and watched *Star Trek* with her, Mom was at peace.

I settled into Joe's spare room and tried to act like the world around me hadn't changed even though it had. Iris was far away and out of touch, the great allure of fishing on the beach like Dad had faded, and I had no place I absolutely had to be, no school, no job, no supervision. One thing that hadn't changed was the future. The future still lay behind a dark curtain that I couldn't see through and certainly wasn't ready to open.

I spent a couple weeks moping around Joe's place, cooking dinner for the two of us, catching up on the news, and doing tons of penance chores for Mom. I wrote postcards to Iris every couple of days, not letters just postcards but sometimes with paragraphs of life at the Barger house and early winter in Anchorage. I found a job washing dishes in a café down the street—they didn't buy that I had real cooking experience, so I was back to pearl diving. I stopped by the community college for application materials for the spring semester.

The cold of winter settled in around us, and even the sunny days had no heat, just light and very little of it. Snow was sparse, so we moved about on bare ground that was frozen hard like macadam, our feet crushing dead leaves that shattered like glass. I tried to get back to life as normal, but I had finally figured out that normal was a mirage that shifted like the aurora in a winter sky.

I stopped by one of the bookstores downtown to buy a variety of touristy postcards for my Iris campaign though her lack of response was wearing me down. My favorite postcard had a picture of a dilapidated outhouse with a thorny devil's club growing out of the hole. I posted that one first and labeled it *The All-New Paper-Free Outhouse.*

I had been home a month when a letter came from Iris, yes, a letter, well a note really, but I like to think of it as a letter. It was written in her tight cursive and folded into an envelope with cartoons of pregnant girls marching across the bottom.

Dear Sam,

Dear, Dear Sam. Can you believe I am actually writing a letter?

I didn't have any postcards, and anyway you stole that idea away from me, and I'm glad you did. When the first postcard arrived I took it as a peace offering, and I thought maybe you forgave me for all I did to you. And then they kept coming. Almost every day they come. Writing like you've been doing is the best thing you could do. My roommate calls you The One-Man Iris Davis Fan Club, and I think maybe she's right. And I will even forgive you for stealing my idea because it is the best thing ever. I can make it through this now, knowing you're out there thinking of me. You're the best friend a girl could ever have, and much more than I deserve.

XOXOXO The Browned-Eyed Girl

I finished reading, wishing there was more. So I reread the letter and decided there was enough. Then I folded it, returned it to the envelope, and put it in my pocket. That same mail delivery had a thick envelope from the US Coast Guard Academy and one from the Selective Service that probably held my draft card. All in all, quite a haul for a guy who didn't write many letters.

Epilogue

I never went back to fish camp, and Iris never worked for her father again. I went off to the coast guard and went through their cooking school and spent my tour of duty feeding coasties on a cutter based in Florida. Iris finished her high school credits while she was at the maternity home and went right to college from there, so we never got together. The letters and postcards were few and far between until we totally lost track of each other.

I'm still an Iris Davis fan, but I am not alone. She had enough fans to get elected to the state legislature right out of college. She was too busy then to ever get married, trying single-handedly to fix the state government and attending law school. I get a warm glow every time I see her name in the paper or her face on the news. I guess some things you never get over.

I finally saw Iris again when I was carving prime rib at a buffet she was attending, and she ruined her fancy dress hugging me with beef drippings all over my apron. Seeing her as a beautiful, grown-up woman about melted me on the spot, and the buffet line was stalled while I pulled myself together and helped Iris clean her dress as best I could. Of course, we promised to get together and never did. Maybe someday, we will meet again, but for now, I'll just be content remembering a brown-eyed girl who took me on a ride that changed my life forever and hope that someday a young girl will find out about her real mother and what a wonder she was.

Dan L. Walker is the son of Alaska homesteaders and a longtime Alaskan educator. The Sam Barger novels, *Secondhand Summer*, *Back Home*, and now *The One-Man Iris Davis Fan Club* are based on his life experiences coming of age in the 1960s. His family memoir, *Letters from Happy Valley*, tells the story of his homestead family through letters written in the 1950s.